Savannah Martin has always
expected and fully expecting life to fall into place in its turn. But when her perfect husband turns out to be a lying, cheating slimeball - and bad in bed to boot - Savannah kicks the jerk to the curb and embarks on life on her own terms. With a new apartment, a new career, and a brand new outlook on life, she's all set to take the world by storm.

If only the world would stop throwing her curveballs...

Savannah's husband, TBI agent Rafe Collier, is back in disguise and undercover, getting into the middle of a gang war. And since he wants to keep his pregnant wife out of harm's way, Savannah agrees to spend a couple of days under her mother's roof in her quaint and quiet hometown of Sweetwater, Tennessee.

But out of harm's way doesn't necessarily mean out of trouble.

When her brother's receptionist asks Savannah's help in looking for her birth parents, Savannah is happy for the distraction, even when the search takes them to places she'd rather not go again. From Doctor Denise Seaver and the Tennessee Women's Prison, to St. Jerome's Hospital and then back to Sweetwater again, the hunt is on.

But when the final denouement reveals lifelong deception and betrayal much too close to home, Savannah wonders whether knowing the truth really is better than blissful ignorance.

OTHER BOOKS IN THIS SERIES

A Cutthroat Business

Hot Property

Contract Pending

Close to Home

A Done Deal

Change of Heart

Kickout Clause

Past Due

Dirty Deeds

Unfinished Business

Adverse Possession

UNCERTAIN TERMS

Jenna Bennett

UNCERTAIN TERMS

Savannah Martin Mystery #12

Interior design and formatting: B. Gallagher
Cover Design: Dar Albert, Wicked Smart Designs

Magpie Ink

One

My husband showed up to my mother's birthday party with dreadlocks halfway down his back, a big, fat gold hoop in his ear, gold chains around his neck, and two gold teeth that hadn't been part of his smile when I said goodbye to him the day before.

I had made the hour-and-a-little-more drive from Nashville to Sweetwater the previous afternoon, to have dinner with Mother and to be there in the morning to admit the caterers so she could go to the spa and get prettified for her party later on.

Rafe, meanwhile, had stayed in Nashville, and—it turned out—had taken the opportunity to get in character for his latest undercover mission.

My new-minted husband—we'd been married just a bit less than two months—had spent ten years undercover for the Tennessee Bureau of Investigations before we met. Or before we met again, I should say, since Rafe also grew up in Sweetwater, and we'd gone to high school together for a year before he graduated, went to prison, and then disappeared into the TBI's undercover program.

It's a long story. Suffice it to say that we'd met again a year ago, just before my mother's birthday last August, and he'd retired from undercover work the previous Christmas, after his cover was blown sky high. The only reason he was going back into it now, in a very limited capacity, was because one of the rookies he was training had gotten himself recruited by a street gang, and Rafe felt responsible enough for the young man to want to back him up as he set about infiltrating.

And since his ten years undercover had been spent trying to root out the biggest SATG—South American Theft Gang—in the Southeast, it was unlikely that anyone in the Crips or Bloods—or whichever street gang Jamal was affiliated with—would know Rafe from Adam. They'd traveled in very different circles up until now.

So I had driven to Sweetwater by myself yesterday, and Rafe had stayed behind in Nashville to work. He was supposed to come down for the birthday party, and as people started arriving, I kept my ears peeled for the sound of the big Harley-Davidson he rides. When I heard it rumble up to the front steps of my ancestral home, the Martin Mansion, I excused myself and went out to greet him.

Only to stop, with my jaw unbecomingly slack, on the top step. "What happened to you?"

He arched a brow. That ability hadn't changed, anyway.

"It's my mother's birthday," I added. "And you look like some sort of combination between Captain Jack Sparrow and Bob Marley."

That got me a grin, and a flash of gold.

I moved a step closer and squinted. "Oh, my God! What did they do to your teeth?"

He chuckled. "It's just decoration. It'll come off."

"Can you take it off now?"

He shook his head. "Sorry, darlin'. The dentist's gonna have to do that. It's stuck till then. But it's just for a couple days. Until we get this business with Jamal sorted."

Sure.

"No big deal."

Easy for him to say.

"It's my mother's birthday!" I said. Or perhaps 'wailed' would be a better word. "Everyone's here. My brother and sister. The sheriff." My mother's boyfriend. "Todd." The sheriff's son, and the man my mother had intended for me to marry before I chose Rafe instead. The man who had intended to marry me, before I said no. "Half the town. And you look like the worst stereotype of what they've accused you of being all these years!"

He didn't say anything for a moment, just stood there at the bottom of the steps next to the Harley and looked up at me.

"This is terrible!" I insisted.

"I can leave."

His voice had all the calmness mine lacked. In fact, it was devoid of emotion. So was his face.

I took a breath. And another one. "No. I'm sorry. I didn't mean..."

But I couldn't finish the sentence, because—yes—I had meant exactly what I said.

"I don't want you to leave," I added. "I just..."

"Don't wanna walk in there with me looking like this."

Right. And yet not exactly right.

"I love you," I said. "I don't care what you look like." Not for my own sake. "If you want to keep the teeth and the dreadlocks after this is over, you can." Although I hoped he wouldn't. I might not stop loving him if he sported dreads and two gold teeth, but I wasn't particularly turned on by the new look, either. "It's just that this is Sweetwater. These are the people who didn't have a good word to say about you your whole life. Mother has just started liking you. I don't want that to change."

"Here's the thing," Rafe told me. "There ain't much I can do about it. The gold veneers are stuck until the dentist takes'em off again. The hair is stuck until the hair dresser cuts it off. I can take out the earring and pull up my pants—"

I think I may have neglected to mention that he was wearing baggy jeans of the sort that were belted under his butt, exposing a pair of plaid boxers, with the crotch hanging somewhere in the vicinity of his knees. He looked like his legs were a foot-and-a-half long. I had no idea how he'd even managed to straddle the bike on the way here.

"That would help," I said. "You couldn't have waited until tomorrow to do this?"

"Wendell didn't know it was your mama's birthday when he scheduled it, darlin'."

Wendell Craig is Rafe's superior in the TBI. While Rafe was undercover, Wendell was his handler. And while I have all the respect in the world for Wendell, at the moment, I wanted to kill him.

"Couldn't you have told him about the party? And put the makeover off for a day?"

"Not really," Rafe said. "This stuff takes time. I bet I spent more time getting worked on today than your mama did."

My mother had spent several hours at the spa, having her hair tinted and her face and nails polished. And yet, given the transformation, it wouldn't surprise me if Rafe had spent more.

At least now I understood why he hadn't buzzed his hair the way he usually does for the past couple of weeks. It was so the extensions could have something to hang onto.

"That's a lot of hair," I said, eyeing it.

"Gives me a headache."

I didn't doubt it. He was used to being almost bald, his hair so short it felt like fuzz against my palms. This had to be close to ten pounds of dreadlocks weighing down his head.

I hated to think what would happen when they got wet. He might fall on his butt from the weight.

And having a constant headache didn't bode well for our sex life. I was struggling with baby hormones—another way of saying I was frisky a lot of the time, now that the morning sickness had passed—and so far, Rafe had been more than happy to satisfy my needs, whenever and wherever I wanted. But if he was going to be coming home with headaches every night, I might be in for a lonely few days or weeks.

A car turned into the driveway, and we kept quiet while we watched it come to a stop behind all the others. Mother's lived in Sweetwater most of her adult life—my father was born here—and she has a fair few friends and acquaintances. There were a lot of cars.

This last one, a Honda, went silent, and after a moment, the driver's side door opened and a woman came out. Tall and dark-haired, a few years older than Rafe—around thirty-four or -five, at a guess—in a nice, but not flashy, black dress. Darcy, my brother Dix's and brother-in-law Jonathan's paralegal and Jill of all trades down at the law office my great-grandfather started on the square in Sweetwater back when the country was young.

We watched as she came closer. The dismay crossing her face when she saw Rafe was unmistakable. "Nobody told me this was supposed to be a costume party."

I giggled. Rafe rolled his eyes.

"It isn't," I said. "You look lovely, Darcy. And very appropriate."

"OK." Although she didn't sound sure. "What's with the... um... ghetto outfit?" She looked him up and down.

"It's what I wear to work," Rafe said.

"Oh."

"He works for the TBI," I explained. "The Tennessee Bureau of Investigations. Organized crime. This week, he's dealing with street gangs."

"Oh." Darcy hesitated. "Has your mother seen him?"

I shook my head.

"You got here just in time," Rafe told her. "'Scuse me."

He brushed past us both and headed up the stairs. I scrambled after, and Darcy brought up the rear, obviously determined not to miss anything.

Rafe's legs are a lot longer than mine, even in saggy pants. And I was wearing heels, to go with my fancy party dress.

Mother's birthday parties are always semi-formal. The sheriff and his son, as well as my brother Dix and brother-in-law Jonathan, were all wearing tasteful suits with ties. And the women, like Darcy and me, were in cocktail dresses and heels. Diamonds sparkled and pearls glowed dully in ears and around necks.

I caught up just as Rafe stopped in the doorway to the parlor, where Mother sat on Great-Aunt Ida's uncomfortable turn-of-the-(last)-century loveseat upholstered in peach velvet, accepting her accolades and well-wishes.

And I was in time to see the reaction his appearance caused. Mother looked up, and her face went from welcoming to shocked. Her eyes rounded, until I was worried her eyeballs would fall out of her skull and into her lap, and for a moment her jaw dropped, just as mine had. Until she hiked it up.

By then, everyone else had turned toward the door as well, and now everyone sported the same wide eyes and open mouths. I thought I saw a flicker of amused malice in Todd's eyes, but it could have been my imagination.

Mother cleared her throat. "Rafael," she managed.

"Sorry, Miz Martin." His voice was calm. "I can't stay long. I gotta get back to work. I just wanted to stop by and say happy birthday and give you this."

He hauled a little box out of his pants pocket—somewhere down around his knees—and made his way over to the sofa where she was sitting. There, he leaned down to give her a peck on the cheek—she didn't even flinch, but that could have been because she was still in shock—and dropped the box in her lap.

And then he withdrew. First from the sofa, then from the room. He glanced at me as he brushed past, but didn't say anything. I heard his footsteps cross the foyer, and then the sound of the front door opening and closing. It wasn't until I heard the roar of the Harley's engine, that I realized he was actually planning to leave.

I turned and ran, but I was too slow. By the time I had the front door open and made it onto the steps, he was halfway down the driveway. The tires screeched as he made the turn from the driveway onto the Columbia Road, and for a second I was afraid he'd slide and end up in the ditch on the other side. But then he straightened the bike and gunned the engine. The Harley took off up the road with a roar and a screech of tires. I have no idea whether he'd even noticed me standing there.

By the time I got back inside to the parlor, the shock had worn off and people were talking again. I could hear the buzz of voices as I crossed the foyer. Three guesses as to what they were buzzing about.

Mother was watching the doorway, and when I came back into the opening, her brows pulled together.

She straightened them out immediately—there's a reason she's fifty-nine and looks ten years younger—but not before I had read distress on her face.

"I'm sorry," I said. "I had no idea he'd show up looking like that."

Mother didn't answer, although everyone else stopped talking and turned to look at me.

"He has a new undercover assignment he's been getting ready for."

The wrinkle came back. "I thought he was through with undercover assignments."

"He is," I assured her, "for the most part. This is sort of a special case."

She looked politely inquiring.

"One of the boys—Jamal, do you remember him from back in June?"

Mother had met Jamal, Clayton, and José on what should have been my wedding day, when Rafe didn't show up at the courthouse to get married, and the police as well as the TBI had joined forces to try to find him.

"He's been recruited by a street gang. They're taking action against another gang, the one that killed Jamal's brother, so they asked Jamal to go in with them. And he said yes, because he thought he'd be able to feed the TBI some information they could use to take some of these guys down."

"And Rafael?"

My mother is one of only two people I know who use Rafe's full name. The other is my boss, Tim.

"He's backing up Jamal. And since he's somewhat well known in certain circles, he needed to change the way he looks. But I'm sorry he showed up here looking like that. I didn't know he was going to do it."

"Darling," Mother said, "he's your husband. He's always welcome here, no matter what he looks like."

My jaw dropped again.

This was disconcerting, to say the least. Somehow, when I hadn't been looking, I had turned into my mother, and she had turned into me.

How was it that *I* was the one worried about the way Rafe looked, and she wasn't?

She tapped the underside of her own chin—a silent reminder to hike my jaw up—and added, "Did he leave?"

I nodded.

"Don't you think you should go after him?"

"He's gone," I said. "The way he took off, he's probably halfway to Nashville by now."

"He's your husband," Mother said.

Well, yes. He was. But... "I don't want to miss your birthday."

"You were here last night, darling," Mother told me. "And this morning. Thank you for handling things while I was at the spa."

"Of course." It was the least I could do. I'd done it last year, too.

She didn't say anything else, just looked at me. Expectantly.

"He's upset," I said. And I wasn't looking forward to having to deal with it. At least not until he'd had a little time to cool down.

"All the more reason to go and talk to him, darling."

I suppose. I just never thought I'd see the day when my mother would encourage me—push me—to go after Rafe rather than stick around for her birthday celebration.

"What was in the box?" I asked. As a distraction and maybe to get a little time to think. And honestly, because I was curious what my husband had found to buy for my mother, a woman who pretty much had everything.

She lifted her hand. A slim gold chain dangled from one of her fingers. Necklace. At the end of it hung something that looked a little like a four-leaf clover, or maybe a four-petaled flower, with a stone in the middle.

"Pretty," I said. Elegant, and very tasteful. A lot more tasteful than any of the clunky chains Rafe had sported this evening.

"Looks like a tabono," Darcy said, craning her neck.

"A what?"

She glanced at me. "Tabono. African strength symbol. The loops symbolize oars or paddles. It stands for strength and perseverance."

Probably because that's what it takes to row a boat. Strength and perseverance.

Not that rowing a boat was why Rafe had given my mother a strength symbol. Mother wouldn't be caught dead rowing. But two months ago, she'd run afoul a serial killer bent on taking out Rafe and anyone else he had to, to get to him. Including Rafe's son David, who had made his way to Sweetwater and my mother's house.

It's a long story. I had gotten there in time to save Mother and David, and Rafe had gotten there in time to save me, so it was all good. But Mother was still feeling a bit rocky about the whole experience—as was I—and I imagined the charm for strength and perseverance had come out of that.

Very thoughtful of him, too. And it was elegant enough that Mother might actually wear it.

She looked at me. "Savannah, dear..."

I rolled my eyes and got to my feet. "I'm going."

"Thank you, darling."

There was no reason at all for her to thank me. And very weird that she did, considering her feelings for Rafe up until that meeting with the serial killer back in June. Before that, she would have applauded any sign of friction between us, and done whatever she could to add to it.

Now she was pushing me to go after him and make up.

I headed out of the parlor with the feeling that I'd fallen down a rabbit hole and my world was upside down, and I wasn't sure I liked it.

By the time I got back downstairs, overnight bag in hand, things had returned to normal in the parlor. I heard laughter and the murmur of voices, and best as I could figure out, they weren't murmuring about, or laughing at, my husband.

Mother saw me step off the stairs and start to cross the foyer, but she didn't come out to wave me off, just gave me a nod. I nodded back and kept going.

I had closed the front door behind me and was on my way down the wide steps to the driveway and my car when the door to the house opened again.

"Savannah."

I had been a little concerned that Todd might come after me. A year ago, he would have.

This time he didn't. It was Darcy coming down the steps

behind me. "Going home?"

I nodded. "Mother seemed to think it was best." I opened the door to the blue Volvo I drive—the only thing left from my first marriage to Bradley Ferguson—and tossed the overnight bag into the back seat before straightening to face her.

She looked worried, sort of wringing her hands as she stood there, twisting a gold ring around and around on her finger. "I hope it wasn't something I said."

"Not at all," I told her. "It was all me. All of it. I put my foot in my mouth all on my own."

"Is he all right?"

"I'm sure he is." At least I hoped so. He's used to it, after all. Just not from me. Or not anymore. There was a time when I'd look at Rafe like he'd crawled out from under a flat rock, just like everyone else, but that was a long time ago. I'd thought I was over it. So, I'm sure, had he.

Please let him be all right. Please don't let him hate me.

"I'll have to grovel," I added.

Darcy nodded. "Good luck. Do you know when you'll be back?"

"In Sweetwater?" I'd planned to stay until tomorrow, but of course that was out now. "I'm sure I'll be back down in a week or two. It's just over an hour's drive. I'm down here all the time."

"Give me a call next time you're in town," Darcy said. "If you don't mind. There's something I'd like to talk to you about."

"We can talk now." I was here, after all. And while I knew I had to go after Rafe and set things straight, part of me wasn't looking forward to it. Not to the groveling. He had every right to be angry with me, and probably was.

Darcy shook her head. "This is going to take some time. And I'd like some privacy. It's a personal matter."

Uh-oh.

I didn't say anything, though, just nodded. "I'll get in touch next time I'm in town. If you can wait that long. Or we can talk on the phone, if you want."

She shook her head again. "It isn't urgent. Next time you're in Sweetwater will be fine." She smiled. "Drive carefully."

"Sure," I said, and watched until she had gone back up the stairs and closed the door behind her before I got in the car and turned the key in the ignition.

Rafe and I live in a three-story brick Victorian in what can most kindly be called a 'transitional' neighborhood. It's full of old, decrepit houses nobody has the money to take care of, interspersed with a handful of recently renovated homes like ours, where someone with more optimism than sense has decided that the house is worth the inconvenience of dodging bullets and drug dealers. Mixed in amongst those is the occasional historic-looking infill, where an intrepid builder has scored a cheap lot and decided to see how far he can push the envelope on the price.

The first time I came here, a year earlier, I'd felt like I was taking my life in my hands. Now it was just home: a little rougher around the edges than I'd been brought up to expect, maybe, but not too bad for all that. The criminal element tended to give our house a wide berth, since word had gotten out that Rafe worked for the TBI in addition to being, not to put too fine a point on it, a bad-ass. The law-abiding neighbors were happy to have us, since the area around our house had become a little oasis, free from some of the crime that plagued the rest of the neighborhood. I knew most of them, liked them—the feeling seemed mutual—and felt reasonably safe.

That didn't mean my heart wasn't thudding a little extra hard in my chest when I turned off Potsdam Street and into the graveled driveway that led up to the front door. The house loomed in front of me, dark and a bit scary, like the house in *Psycho,* but with a round tower on one corner instead of a square tower in the middle. Rafe's Harley was parked at the foot of the stairs, so at least he was here. Part of me had been worried that he wouldn't be.

I cut the engine and opened the door, taking a moment to get used to the wall of moist, hot air outside the car before swinging my legs out. The gravel crunched under my feet as I hauled my overnight bag out of the backseat and made my way to the stairs. My heels clicked against the porch floor.

The house was dark, except for a single light in the kitchen, at the back of the house. The situation was eerily reminiscent of a night last fall. I'd had dinner with Todd Satterfield at the Wayside Inn in Sweetwater, and he had proposed marriage. I had expected him to propose. I had wanted him to propose. I had worn a special red dress and silver sandals, in an effort to get him to propose. And when he'd proposed, I hadn't been able to bring myself to say yes. I had hoped that doing the 'right' thing, and getting engaged to Todd, would take away the desire to throw myself at Rafe, but it hadn't worked that way. Instead, I'd said I needed time to think about it, and had driven through the night here. To Rafe's house.

And ended up in his bed.

And now I was back, standing on the porch in my party dress and heels, after driving here from Sweetwater.

Although this time I had my own key. My own way into the house. His ring on my finger and his baby inside me.

He loved me.

That wouldn't make it any easier to apologize, but would make it more likely that he'd forgive me.

I dropped the bag in the foyer and, after locking the door behind me, took a deep breath and headed down the hallway toward the light in the kitchen.

Two

He must have heard me coming, but he made no move to meet me halfway. When I got to the door, he was sitting at the kitchen table turning a bottle of beer around in his hands. It was mostly full, so unless he'd already polished off another, he hadn't had much to drink.

Not that he ever drinks much. He's too aware of the need to be alert to risk getting impaired.

The tangle of dreadlocks down his back gave me a jolt even though I knew they'd be there. And the look in his eyes, when he turned to face me, cut deep.

His eyes are black, or so deep a brown it can be hard to see where the iris ends and the pupil begins. They go hot and liquid when he's turned on, and flat as a cobra's when he's angry. In this instance, I should probably be grateful that he let me see what he was feeling at all, since it would have been an easy task for him not to.

"I'm sorry," I said, as I took a step into the kitchen, and then another. "I'm really sorry. I hurt your feelings."

He didn't say anything. Wouldn't admit it, but wasn't going to tell me I hadn't, either.

I stopped next to the table. And I wanted to reach out and touch him, but I didn't dare. "I feel awful. You drove all the way to Sweetwater for my mother's birthday, and you brought a gift, and you don't even like my mother—"

"I like your mother just fine."

His tone of voice said that at the moment, it was me he didn't like.

"I don't blame you," I said wretchedly. "She was nicer to you than I was. She's the one who told me I needed to go after you. I thought she'd want me to stay for the party, but she didn't. She wanted me to follow you. I can't believe my mother is nicer than me!"

That got a quirk at the corner of his mouth, if nothing else.

I twisted my fingers together on top of my stomach. "It's just... it was such a shock to see you looking like that. After all the time we've spent trying to convince everyone in Sweetwater that you aren't the way they've always imagined..."

"I never spent no time trying to convince nobody," Rafe said.

And shut me up.

Because he was right. He hadn't. He didn't care what anyone thought of him. That had been me, fretting over everyone's reaction to the fact that Margaret Anne Martin's perfect little girl was marrying the town black sheep.

God, would I never learn?

"I've told you before, darlin'. I am what I am. If you or your mama or anybody else has a problem with it..."

"I don't." It was the same thing I'd said back then. The other time he'd told me. I'd meant it then. I meant it now, too. "I love you. I have no problem with who you are."

"Except when I show up to your mama's birthday party looking like a gang banger."

He had me there.

"I love you," I said again. "I don't care what you look like."

Not entirely true. "I mean... I like the way you look. Usually. And I don't like this... costume as much as I like the way you look without it. But I still love you."

He quirked a brow.

"I just don't want everyone else to look at you and think...

things."

"Things?"

"You know what I mean. It's taken my family a while to get on board with us being together. My mother likes you now, but there's no telling how long that'll last, especially if you show up in Sweetwater looking like that. And I'm sure Todd was snickering."

There was a beat, just long enough for me to realize what I'd said. Much too late to take it back.

"You care what Satterfield thinks?"

"No," I said.

"Coulda fooled me."

Um. "I'm not sure what to say," I told him, wringing my hands. "I'm sorry. I hurt your feelings, and I know it. I wish I hadn't. I don't want to care what people think, but I can't seem to stop."

He was watching me impassively.

"I want them to look at you and see what I see. Past all that." I waved a hand over the dreadlocks, the saggy pants, and the gold teeth. And for that matter over the six feet, three inches of smooth skin and hard muscles that could bring a woman to her knees—and had, frequently. Because while he was nice to look at, he was a lot more than that. "You're incredible. Amazing. A hero. But when you show up looking like their worst nightmare, then that's all they see. And that makes me feel bad."

"I don't care what people think."

I knew that. He did the job he had to do, played the part he had to play, took the insults and the lumps he had to take because of what people thought they knew about him based on the way he looked and acted... and if it bothered him, he never let on. All the times I had thought the worst, he'd never bothered to set me straight. He might have given me a little help in reasoning out that he wasn't the criminal I thought he was, but he hadn't told me outright. He hadn't admitted it until I'd figured it out mostly on my own.

"I'm sorry," I said, for the... fourth? fifth? ...time. "I don't know what else to say. I'd take it back if I could. Do you want to go back to Sweetwater for the rest of the party?"

His lips quirked. "No."

"It would probably be over by the time we got there, anyway. Maybe we could go somewhere else. Together. And I could prove that I'm not ashamed of being seen with you."

He didn't answer.

"Maybe the FinBar? Or Beckett's?" Two rather nice local sports bars, frequented by a lot of upwardly mobile young executives and artist types. I'd never seen anyone who looked like Rafe did at the moment in either establishment. "Or how about Fidelio's?" A very upscale restaurant we'd been to a couple of times. My ex-husband Bradley had taken me there, and so had Todd. Rafe had, too—I guess in an effort to prove that he could give me the same things Bradley and Todd could. Until—unlike both of them—he realized that I didn't actually like going to Fidelio's. It had been eight months or more since either of us had set foot there. But I was willing to go back if it would help.

He shook his head. "That ain't necessary."

"Are you sure? I'd be happy to do it."

"They prob'ly wouldn't gimme a table anyway, looking like this." He glanced at me. "You hungry?"

I wasn't. I had nibbled on food at Mother's party, before he got there. And while I'm almost six months pregnant and can pretty much always eat, I wouldn't say I was hungry. My stomach felt too twisted for that.

"Tired?"

"I could lie down," I said, since I'm pretty much always happy to get off my feet. Especially right now, since I had put on high heels with my fancy party dress, and my feet were screaming bloody murder.

"You could show me how sorry you are."

I blinked. "I could do that." If he wanted. And it seemed he did. "I thought you'd be angry." And wouldn't want anything to do with me. Not until I'd groveled considerably more than this.

He shrugged. "I expected to get some blowback, showing up looking like that."

Yes, but surely he had expected better from his wife?

He shrugged again when I said so. And didn't respond. So maybe he hadn't expected better from me.

I wasn't entirely sure how that made me feel. Happy, I guess, that he wasn't as upset with me as I'd been afraid he was. But disappointed that he didn't think more of me than that. Even if he'd been right not to expect more.

My bottom lip started quivering.

He got to his feet. "C'mon, darlin'. Let's go upstairs."

"I feel bad," I said, eyeing the hand he was holding out to me. "I don't understand why you're being nice to me."

The hand didn't waver. "'Cause I love you."

"I was horrible to you." My eyes filled with tears. Pregnancy hormones mixed with guilt.

His voice didn't change. "I love you anyway."

"I don't deserve you," I told him, as the tears spilled over and rolled down my cheeks.

"That's OK." He reached out and put an arm around my shoulders. "C'mere."

He pulled me in, where I could rub my cheek against his shoulder and leak onto his shirt. His arms were warm and comforting around my body, and the scent of him was familiar, even if he looked different than I was used to. The beat of his heart was steady in my ear.

"I'm a terrible wife," I sniffed.

"You can make it up to me upstairs."

"It's not that simple."

"Sure it is." He moved toward the stairs. Perforce, I moved

too, out of the kitchen and down the hallway.

We'd done this once before, and by the time we got to the foyer, someone shot out the front window and we'd had to hit the floorboards. Our trip upstairs had been postponed until the police had arrived and taken statements, and until I had swept up the broken glass and Rafe had pasted a piece of cardboard over the shattered window.

That didn't happen this time. We made it through the foyer and up the stairs to the second floor with no interruptions, across the landing and into the bedroom.

I hadn't been home for over twenty-four hours, and Rafe obviously hadn't bothered to make the bed when he rolled out of it this morning. That was a case of déjà vu, as well. When he'd brought me up here after the window incident last fall, the bed had been invitingly rumpled then too. And it hadn't taken him long to get me into it.

It didn't this time, either.

He pulled me into his arms and kissed me, and about thirty seconds later, my back hit the mattress.

"Careful," I managed when he followed me down.

"I know." He twisted, and ended up next to me instead of on top. "Don't worry." His hand smoothed over the roundness of my stomach before skimming south, over my hip toward the hem of the dress.

Neither of us said a lot after that, or at least nothing very coherent. One thing led to another, as the saying goes, and when it was all said and done, I don't think he was in any doubt that I still found him as attractive as ever, dreadlocks and gold teeth notwithstanding.

I guess he'd needed that, maybe more than the verbal apology.

Sometimes I can be really stupid.

"Huh?"

I glanced at him. "Nothing." No need to spell out just how much of an idiot I am.

And anyway, I'm sure he knew.

He twisted the end of a strand of my hair around his finger. "I'm glad you came home tonight."

Me, too.

"But tomorrow you're gonna have to go back to Sweetwater."

"What? Why?"

"'Cause I don't want you staying here alone."

"Why would I be alone?"

"I gotta be somewhere else for a couple days, until this is done."

I opened my mouth to ask why again, but closed it before I said anything. The answer was obvious. He couldn't stay here because everyone in the neighborhood knew who he was and that he worked for the TBI. A few of them even knew he'd almost singlehandedly taken down the biggest South American Theft Gang in the Southeast last year. And that was something that probably shouldn't get back to Jamal's associates. If it did, they'd smell something off.

And apart from that, if he was involving himself even on the periphery of a gang war, he wouldn't want me anywhere near him. So he'd spend the next few days somewhere else, and he'd pack me off to Sweetwater, where I'd be safe.

I wanted to argue, but I really couldn't. It made sense.

And besides, I didn't really want to stay in the house by myself. It was just a month since someone had broken in and tried to kill me. I had handled it, and survived—one of the burglars hadn't been so lucky—but I wasn't looking for a repeat. I'd much rather be somewhere where there were other people.

"Where are you going to be?" I asked.

"The duplex."

I should have guessed. The duplex was located in South

Nashville, about halfway between the airport and Antioch, and it was where Rafe had stayed whenever he'd blown through town during the ten years he'd spent undercover. A rinky-dink house in a neighborhood where nobody paid much attention to what the neighbors were doing was just what he needed for the job at hand.

"I could stay with you," I said.

He shook his head. "Not a chance. I don't expect anything to go wrong, but if it does, I want you outta here, and safe."

I turned on my side and wrapped my arms around him. "You better make sure nothing goes wrong. I want you safe, too. If you get yourself killed, I'll never forgive you."

"I'll keep that in mind," Rafe said, and kissed me.

And one thing led to another one more time.

Usually, he just leaves me asleep when he goes off to work in the morning. Growing a baby is hard work, and I'm pretty much always tired. After all the emotional turmoil, not to mention the exercise last night, the next morning was no exception. However, he came into the bedroom just before he headed out.

"Darlin'."

"Mmmm?"

"I'm going."

Going. Right.

And then I remembered, and forced my gluey eyelids open. "Wait."

He was sitting on the edge of the bed, in the same oversized shirt and saggy pants he'd worn yesterday, with hair straggling halfway down his back.

"Going," I said.

He nodded. "Won't be back tonight. Jamal's gonna introduce me to some people. And tomorrow's the big night."

"When one gang is planning to kill a bunch of members of

another."

"I was thinking, when we make a clean sweep and slap'em all in jail," Rafe said, "but your way works, too."

"I like yours better." There was no killing in it.

I scooted up a little higher on the pillows. The blanket slipped, and he smiled appreciatively as I hiked it back up to cover my breasts. "Don't get used to them," I warned him, my cheeks still hot after all this time together. "They'll go away after the baby's born. And what's left will probably be saggy."

"Don't mean I can't enjoy them now," Rafe said, which I guess was true.

However, instead of making any attempt to enjoy them, he got to his feet. "I just wanted to let you know I was heading out."

"I appreciate it," I said. "I'll get ready and go, too. And make it to Sweetwater by dinnertime."

His brows drew together. "Why not by lunchtime?"

"Things are going on at the office today. Tim signed us up for this lead generation software, and someone's coming to do a workshop on it after lunch. It'll cost me a couple hundred dollars a month, but I'm hoping I'll actually get some business from it."

Even if I got just one sale a month, or for that matter every couple of months, it would pay for itself.

I'd had my real estate license a little over a year, and in that time, hadn't exactly set the world on fire. Granted, other things had happened to steal my focus—like Rafe and a long line of dead bodies—but I hadn't had the success I'd been hoping for in my new profession. It's hard to find clients, and harder when you're a well brought-up Southern Belle who has been taught not to put herself forward. I was hoping that this new software would generate some leads I could work, that would hopefully turn into buyers and sellers, and eventually, commissions.

"You know," Rafe told me, "you don't have to work. I make enough to take care of you."

We were living rent-free in his grandmother's house, and

while we had some expenses—like Mrs. Jenkins's care at the home where she lived—we were both used to living cheap. Rafe because he'd grown up that way, and me because I'd had to learn after Bradley dumped me.

"I know," I said. "But I like real estate. I just wish I was better at selling it."

"You're fine at selling it. Your clients love you."

All four of them.

"Anyway," I said, "I have to wait until the workshop is over to drive back to Sweetwater. So I won't get there until early evening. Can I call you tonight? Just to see how things are going?" And hear his voice.

He hesitated. "Prob'ly better if you wait 'till I call you."

"Will you?"

He hesitated again. "Might be late."

"I don't mind. Although I might not answer." Since I fall asleep early and sleep deeply.

He shook his head. "If I gotta call, you gotta answer."

"Fine." I resisted the urge to roll my eyes. "I'll keep the phone turned on, and next to my bed. Hopefully I'll wake up."

"How about I just call you in the morning instead?"

I thought about it. "That would work." If I was asleep, I wouldn't be worrying, anyway. "Just don't forget."

He promised he wouldn't, kissed me goodbye, and left. I went back to sleep.

Three

By the time I woke up again, it was later. A lot later. Rafe was long gone. I rolled out of bed slowly and took my time getting ready. I had a shower and a nice, healthy breakfast of raisin bran and milk, I threw in a load of laundry, and repacked my bag for another couple of nights away. That done, I got on the phone with my mother.

"I'm driving back to Sweetwater tonight."

There was a beat. "Oh, dear," Mother said.

"I'm sorry. Do you have a full house?" I hadn't realized that she might. All the people at the party yesterday had been local, save for Rafe and myself. Nobody should have needed to stay over; they all lived within a few miles. And my childhood home is a five thousand square foot antebellum mansion with rather a lot of bedrooms. You'd think she'd be able to find a spot for me somewhere. Even if it was in the old, restored slave cabin on the grounds.

On second thought—since the cabin was authentic and didn't have air conditioning, and the temperature was in the nineties—maybe not there. "I can stay with Dix, I guess. Or Catherine. Or Aunt Regina."

"Of course not, darling," Mother said. "You'll stay here, of course. There's no one else here."

Then why hadn't she wanted to put me up?

Or—my nose wrinkled involuntarily—maybe she'd been planning to get it on with the sheriff tonight. In the parlor.

She sighed. "I'm so sorry you and Rafael weren't able to work thing out."

What? "Of course we were able to work things out."

"Then why are you coming back to Sweetwater?" Mother demanded. "Why aren't you staying in Nashville with your husband?"

"Because Rafe's going undercover," I said. Surely that had been obvious? I'd even said so, hadn't I? "And he wants me out of the way so he can concentrate on his job."

"Oh." Mother sounded relieved. Never thought I'd see the day.

"It won't be for more than a day or two. The big night's tomorrow, so I'll probably be able to go home on Saturday."

"You can stay as long as you want, darling," Mother said.

"Do you have plans tonight? With the sheriff?"

She didn't. Bob was on duty, since he'd taken yesterday off for Mother's birthday. "We'll have dinner together," she told me. "There's a lot of food left. You can help me by eating some of it."

For the first time in my life, Mother wasn't on me to eat like a bird. If I could, I'd stay pregnant for the next ten years. It was the only way I didn't feel guilty about eating what I wanted when I wanted it. I even had chocolate ice cream at eleven o'clock at night—when I managed to stay up that late—and I didn't feel any guilt at all.

Hardly.

I promised I'd help her with the leftovers, and we hung up. And since I still had plenty of time before I had to be at the office, I called the Martin and McCall office on the square in Sweetwater next.

Martin and McCall is the family law firm. The Martin half is my brother, Dixon Calvert Martin, and our father and grandfather before him. The McCall half is my brother-in-law Jonathan, and for that matter my sister Catherine, who has a law degree even if she doesn't use it much anymore. They have three kids, Robert, Annie, and Cole, and Catherine stays home with them. Robert's in school, but she ferries the others to Mother's Day Out a couple of days a week so she can get some peace and quiet for a couple of hours, and since Sheila died last November, Catherine also pitches in with Abigail and Hannah, Dix's daughters. They and Annie have always been close, anyway. I'm sure, when they're all in school, she'll go back to work at least part time, but for now, she's enjoying being a mother.

I was becoming a mother soon, too. And I really did appreciate Rafe's offer to support me, so I didn't have to work.

Not that I was working all that hard. Or not that the work I was doing resulted in much money, more accurately. And not that he was making a ton of money, either, for that matter. Sure, he could support me. We lived cheap. But law enforcement is notoriously badly paid. It isn't a profession you go into for the monetary reward.

As I'd told him, I do like real estate, though. I like the houses. The run-down, decrepit ones, with so much potential, the renovated ones, and the ones people live in. It's fun to see how other people live. As a girl, I'd adored poking through my friends' houses when I came to visit.

What I don't like, is the business end of real estate. Having to rustle up clients. Convincing them to let me help them. It felt pushy. Wrong.

Maybe I should take Rafe up on the offer of support, and spend my time writing that steamy romance novel I'd been threatening to work on. The one where he inspired the tall, dark, and dangerous hero. I could work on it during the few moments a day when I wouldn't be sleeping or feeding and changing the baby.

"Good morning," a voice said on the other end of the line, and brought me back to myself. "Martin and McCall law office. How may I help you?"

"Darcy," I said. "It's Savannah."

"Oh." She sounded surprised, and it took her a second. "Who are you calling for? Your brother or Jonathan?"

"Actually, neither." Although Dix, at least, would probably be worried—or curious—about what had happened yesterday. Before I hung up, I should probably touch base with him. However— "I was calling to talk to you."

"Oh," Darcy said.

"I'm driving back to Sweetwater tonight. I thought maybe you'd want to have lunch tomorrow. And talk about whatever it was you wanted to talk about."

She blinked. I didn't see her, but I knew she did. Then— "That would work, I guess. Although I don't want to take you away from anything you're doing with your family."

"I'm killing time," I told her. "Rafe's getting involved in Jamal's gang war, and he doesn't want me around for it. So he's sending me back down to Sweetwater for a few days, until it's safe to come home. I'll just be sitting around doing a whole lot of nothing. I'd love to have lunch." And hear whatever it was she thought she wanted from me.

"If you're sure..."

"I'm positive. Where do you want to meet?"

I waited for her to suggest the Café on the Square—very convenient, just down the row from the law office, and with excellent salads and rolls—or the Wayside Inn, or even Beulah's Meat'n Three, up the Columbia Highway, but she didn't. "How about the Cracker Barrel at the interstate?"

"Oh," I said. "Um... sure."

Nothing wrong with that. The only reason I was surprised, was because it seemed like a long way to go when there were plenty of places closer by, and with more exciting—or at least more authentic—food. "Would you like me to come pick you up?"

"I'll meet you there."

OK, then. Was it my imagination—well-honed, I admit—or did it seem like maybe she was trying to sneak off somewhere where not so many people were likely to recognize us?

But if that was the case, why? It wasn't like we were doing anything wrong. Unless she thought it was weird to be having lunch with her boss's sister, or something. But if so, why suggest it in the first place?

Naturally I didn't say any of that. We settled on a time, and I told her I'd meet her at the Cracker Barrel, and that was that. I hung up and prepared to head to the office, but I admit I kept wondering what it was she wanted to talk about, and why she might want privacy to do it.

Every licensed real estate agent has to be affiliated with a real estate brokerage. We can't just hang out our own shingles and go to work. My affiliation is with a company called LB&A—Lamont, Briggs and Associates. Walker Lamont founded the company—it was called Walker Lamont Realty back then—but he's in prison now. Timothy Briggs is the replacement broker, and the one who suggested the name change. Partly to get his own moniker into the mix, I'm sure, but also partly to mitigate some of the fallout of having a business named after a man who murdered a couple of his employees and tried to murder a few more.

Walker hired me, and he and I always got along well, right up until the moment he tried to kill me. Tim and I have never really gotten along, and I'm not quite sure why. He's nice enough to me when he has to be—polite with a side of snide—but I can tell he doesn't like me. Or at least he likes to tweak me a lot.

Today was no different. I walked through the door into the conference room, and Tim looked up from his iPad to give me a bright and malicious smile. "Savannah. Glad you could join us."

I was early, as a matter of fact. It was more than ten minutes until the meeting started. But of course it was into the afternoon by now, and the first time I'd set foot in the office so far today, so maybe he was commenting on that.

Then again, there are days when Tim doesn't show up at all—times when he spends the entire day away from the office showing properties to people—so it wasn't like he had a lot of room to talk.

I thought about a few retorts I could make, none of them particularly clever, and before I could make my mind up, he added, "Hard to get out of bed this morning?"

I'm pregnant, so yes, it's pretty much always hard to get out of bed. Both because I'm always tired, and because I've got this basketball attached to my stomach that didn't used to be there, so literally hauling my bulk out of bed is difficult.

That's not what he meant, though. Tim developed a raging crush on Rafe almost as soon as he saw him a year ago, and he never lets an opportunity go by to refer, in some way, to my husband's charms.

"I hope Rafael is treating your right," he added, right on cue. What his expression said, was that he wished Rafael was treating *him* right. Like Mother, Tim also prefers to call Rafe by his full name, and the way he wraps his tongue around it is almost indecent.

"He's treating me just fine," I said, quellingly. The conversation was starting to make me uncomfortable, since—in spite of it being ten minutes until the workshop started—the room was full, and the instructor was among the people present. So was Tim's assistant Heidi, who smirked at me from the other side of the table. She doesn't like me either, and the feeling's mostly mutual. The instructor was busy setting up for the class, but I could see her ears vibrate.

There was an empty chair at the far end of the table, and I

went for it, hoping that would end the conversation.

Of course it didn't.

"You should bring him by," Tim said, "and show him off."

"No, thank you." Not the way he looked now. And anyway, it was disconcerting to watch my boss almost visibly drool over my husband. Not to mention my husband getting a kick out of it.

Although, if I presented Rafe the way he looked now, maybe Tim would stop drooling. I imagined he wasn't any fonder of dreadlocks and gold teeth than I was.

Then again, it was Rafe. It would take more than saggy pants and gold veneers to kill his appeal.

The workshop started right on time, and Tim kept his mouth shut, at least about Rafe. I soaked up as much information as I could about how to turn this lead generation opportunity into money in the bank for yours truly. It sounded good, at least on the surface. The leads would come in, they would get distributed among the agents who had signed up for the software (the dozen or so of us ranged around the table), and it would be our job to work the leads, meaning that we would have to build relationships with the people behind the email addresses or phone numbers, and then turn them from looky-loos to buyers. I imagined a lot would depend on my ability to be friendly and ingratiating, and to stay on top of staying in touch with them.

The class ended promptly at five. While the others gathered around the instructor to ask questions and express their thanks, I hightailed it out the door before Tim could waylay me with more insidious comments about Rafe. I would be sleeping alone for the next couple of nights, and I didn't need any reminders of just how hot my husband was. I wouldn't be getting any. The pregnancy hormones would have to wait.

By five-fifteen I was on my way out of town at a snail's pace. Rush hour had started—more than an hour ago, actually; we become more and more like Los Angeles every day—and the highways were clogged with commuter lemmings going home to the suburbs for dinner. They started peeling off as we made our way south, and by the time we passed Franklin, there were only a few of us left. I got off at the Columbia exit and made my way south and west, toward Sweetwater.

I reached the mansion before six-thirty, but not by much. Rush hour adds another thirty minutes to the drive, easily. Mother had dinner on the table—leftovers from yesterday—and we sat at the kitchen island and munched our way through the spread. By which I mean that I munched my way through, while Mother graced. She looks damned good for fifty-nine, and is a lot more slender than I am, at least at the moment.

Then again, she isn't eating for two.

While I concentrated on feeding myself and the baby, Mother made small-talk about the party yesterday and the local gossip I had missed by leaving early.

"Your aunt Regina has lost twelve pounds. I thought she looked thinner when she walked in, although she was wearing black, and it's always so slimming, so I couldn't be sure. It wasn't until after you left that she said she's been walking every day this summer. An old relative of your uncle's passed away, in some god-forsaken place—Wyoming or Montana or somewhere—and left him some money, and they're going on a cruise in October. And Regina, bless her heart, wants to get into a bathing suit for it. Audrey said she'd help her find something suitable."

"That was nice of Audrey," I said, between bites of caviar, while I tried desperately not to imagine my aunt—who, even after losing twelve pounds, still looks like a Martin: short, dark, and gently rounded, a lot like my sister Catherine—in a sexy little two-piece.

"Todd looked very handsome, I thought. But then he always does."

I muttered something non-committal. My mouth was

halfway full, and besides, I didn't want to encourage her. Not that she'd been throwing Todd at me lately. Not since I married Rafe. She kept at it right up until the last moment, but as soon as the knot was tied and the ring was on my finger, she stopped. I didn't want her to start again, though, and if I admitted that Todd was handsome—especially after what had happened with Rafe yesterday—she might.

"I told him he was welcome to bring a date, but he came alone."

"Maybe he's not dating," I said. I didn't think he was. Not as far as Todd was concerned. There was a woman in town he'd gotten close to in the months since I'd made the choice to shack up with Rafe, and I rather suspected she had feelings for him, but if he reciprocated, I wasn't sure he realized it yet. It was just two months since he'd sat outside the mansion on the occasion of my wedding to Rafe and hoped I'd have last minute jitters.

Although two months is long enough to change someone's life. Two months last fall had changed mine.

Anyway, I knew that Todd and Marley spent time together. He'd been with her—on her couch—the night his ex-wife was murdered. But I don't think he saw it as anything more than friendship. I hoped, for Marley's sake, that he'd come around. But I could understand that he might not want to bring a date to Mother's birthday party. She and everyone else in town would make something out of it. Aunt Regina would probably put it in the *Reporter*. And Marley's past—and Todd's part in it—would only make it worse.

"Darcy looked nice," Mother added.

I nodded. "We're having lunch tomorrow."

"You and Darcy? Why?"

"She asked me," I said. "Said she wanted to talk to me about something."

"Oh, dear." Mother clicked her tongue. "I hope she doesn't have her eye on Dixon."

Dix? "Isn't that her job? To keep an eye on him?"

"You know what I mean," Mother said.

It took me a second, but then I did. "Oh. No, I'm sure that isn't it." If Darcy was carrying a torch for my brother, I had seen no sign of it.

Mother looked unconvinced.

"She's too old for him," I said. "Dix is thirty. She must be thirty-four, at least. Maybe more."

"Four years is hardly a cause for concern, darling."

Well, no. Rafe was three years older than me. My dad had been at least a year or two older than Mother. But it would be very awkward if Darcy had a thing for Dix, since Dix had a thing with my friend, homicide detective Tamara Grimaldi in Nashville. The last thing any of us needed was to complicate the matter with another love interest.

"It would be terribly awkward to have to let her go," Mother added. "She's not from around here, so we'd essentially be kicking her out of town. And she's been doing a wonderful job at the law firm. But it's been less than a year since Sheila passed. Dixon isn't ready for another relationship. And if she forces the issue, we won't have much of a choice."

"I'm sure she won't," I said, while I crossed my fingers and hoped really hard that she wouldn't. And not just because firing her would be awkward, but because her coming on to Dix would be mortifying for him, and embarrassing for her when he turned her down.

"If you say so, darling. But if she says anything tomorrow that leads you to think she might..."

"I'll disabuse her," I said. Nicely, of course. "But I really don't think that's it."

"I hope you're right, dear." But she looked anything but convinced.

I went to bed early, as usual. And lay there for a few minutes before drifting off, hoping that maybe Rafe would call with an update on the situation in Nashville. He'd said he'd call tomorrow, so he probably wouldn't, but I could hope.

I missed him. It was strange to be sleeping alone again. After two and a half years of it between Bradley and Rafe you'd think I'd be used to it, but the last six months of living in sin had made me very comfortable with that warm, hard body next to mine. Now the bed felt empty and too big without it.

Aside from that I must admit to being a little worried. Bad things sometimes happen when Rafe goes undercover, and getting between two street gangs trying to exterminate each other didn't seem like a very smart move.

Not that he could have done anything else. When Jamal decided to go ahead and get involved in the gang war, Rafe's involvement was sealed. I would have thought less of him if he had abandoned Jamal to his own devices. Not that doing so would have crossed his mind. But there was no question that that level of chivalry and heroism could be inconvenient for those around him sometimes.

Eventually I drifted off, into weird dreams about my brother and Darcy and Todd and Marley Cartwright and Detective Tamara Grimaldi in some sort of weird musical chairs dating game. They'd go around and around four chairs set up back to back, and when the music stopped, four of them would sit and the fifth would be left standing. And when the music started they'd do it again, and ended up switching partners over and over. There was kissing, which was weird.

Eventually the music woke me. Sunlight slanted through the gap in the curtains, and the air conditioner hummed. My phone was vibrating on the bedside table, emitting the dulcet tones of Donna Summer's *Hot Stuff*, my new ringtone for Rafe.

I rolled over on my side and reached for it. "'lo?"

"Rise and shine, Goldilocks," my husband's voice said in my

ear, brightly.

I squinted at the clock. A little before eight. That meant I'd had a solid ten-plus hours of sleep. He probably hadn't. "Morning."

"Sleep OK?"

"I missed you," I said. "The bed's empty."

I could hear the smile in his voice. "Sorry, darlin'. We'll fix that in a couple days."

I told him I was looking forward to it. "Is everything all right where you are?"

"So far. I got settled into the duplex yesterday. Jamal introduced me to some of his friends last night."

"How did that go?"

"None of'em shot me," Rafe said.

"Nobody pointed to you and screamed 'traitor'?"

He chuckled. "No."

"That's good. So what are you doing today?"

"Just hanging out here. Jamal's cousin Ry'mone don't have no job."

"You're kidding," I said.

"Ry'mone's connected, darlin'. He don't need to work."

"That's not what I meant." I realized he couldn't go to work at the TBI office. Of course he couldn't. What if someone followed him? "Your name's Ry'mone?"

"It's always a good idea to stick close to your own name when you have to be someone else," my husband informed me, without a trace of the Southern drawl or for that matter the less-than-proper grammar he uses most of the time. He can put on pretty much any kind of speech he wants when he has to, but the ain'ts and gonnas fall trippingly off his tongue when he doesn't think about it. "Makes it easier to remember to answer when people talk to you."

"You didn't have any problems being Jorge Pena," I

reminded him. "That sounds nothing like Rafe Collier."

"Not like I could pick and choose that one, darlin'. You don't like Ry'mone?"

Not so much.

"Ain't that a shame?" His voice sounded amused. "I was thinking maybe I could talk you into naming the baby Ry'mone. Or Ry'mona, if it's a girl."

"No," I said.

"You sure?"

I was positive. My mother would have a conniption if I told her we would be naming her grandchild Ry'mo-anything.

"I could probably be talked into Ramona," I offered. "If you insist." Or Ramon, in a pinch. Although it might be a bit too Hispanic, when there was nothing Hispanic about either of us.

"I was mostly kidding," Rafe said. "How are things down there?"

"The same. My mother eats like a bird and talks about the neighbors. My aunt Regina is on a diet because she's going on a cruise in October. I'm having lunch with Darcy today. Mother is afraid she's setting her cap for Dix."

"Darcy? The woman who asked about the costume party? I don't see it."

Thank you. "I don't, either," I said. "And anyway, if she were, why would she involve me? It's not like we're particularly close. She'd be better off talking to Catherine. She's Dix's sister, too, and Darcy probably knows her better than me."

"Maybe that's why she wanna talk to you and not Catherine."

I suppose. "I just don't get that vibe from her. But I guess I'll find out in a couple of hours."

"Guess so."

There was a moment of silence.

"So you're just going to sit there all day?"

"Ry'mone don't need to work, darlin'."

"You're not Ry'mone," I said. "Aren't you going to be bored?"

"There's plenty to look at," Rafe told me. "I think the folks next door are cooking meth."

What? "Why? How do you know?"

"I listened to'em coming and going all night. And there's the usual signs."

"What are the usual signs of someone cooking meth?" And why didn't I know these things?

Oh, wait. Because, until I met Rafe, meth labs hadn't crossed my consciousness.

"Aside from the coming and going all night?" Rafe said. "Blacked out windows, burn pits in the yard—"

"They make methamphetamine outside? That can't be safe!"

I could hear from his voice that he was laughing at me. "No, darlin'. They cook the meth inside the house. But they dump the chemicals in the yard, and it kills the grass."

"Oh. So there are patches of grass missing."

"Like I said. Burn pits. And they've been leaving their trash in my can while this place has been empty."

"Getting the incriminating evidence off their own property?" I suggested.

"Something like that. Or maybe their can's full. Meth production makes for a lot of trash. I found a sack full of boxes of cold medicine and bottles of antifreeze and used coffee filters when I went out to dump the empty pizza box last night."

Cold medicine and antifreeze and used coffee filters sounded innocuous enough to me—I'm sure I've had any and all of them in my trash can at some point or another, maybe even at the same time—but what do I know? If he said they were signs of methamphetamine production, he was probably right.

"You're not in any danger," I asked warily, "are you?"

"From the folks next door? Not as long as they don't figure

out who I am. As long as they think I'm just another stupid gang banger, everything'll be fine. If they start thinking I'm here because of them, things could get ugly."

He sounded very calm about it. I wished I could be.

"I'm not sure I like that," I said.

"Don't worry, darlin'." There was a smile in his voice, and not because he was laughing at me this time. "I'll sit around and look degenerate today. When the gang bangers start coming and going, I'm sure that'll take care of any questions they might have."

"What are the gang bangers going to be doing? Eating pizza?"

"Buying weapons," Rafe said. "Jamal's cousin Ry'mone can get his hands on guns."

Yowch. "So you're providing the weapons they're planning to use to shoot their rivals tonight?"

"Something like that. And getting them on illegal weapons purchases at the same time."

"So will you arrest them when they show up at your house? Or wait until they ride out to kill the other gang? What's going to happen, exactly?"

"All out gang war," Rafe said grimly. "Jamal's posse has picked out eight or ten targets, and they're planning to strike all of them at the same time tonight. The word is to take out anyone else who gets in the way. Girlfriends, mothers, even kids. Jamal knows who a few of'em are, because they're the ones who killed his brother. But he don't know the rest. I have until tonight to figure it out, or we're gonna have a bloodbath on our hands."

Yikes. I could see why a meth operation next door was the least of his worries at the moment.

"I'll just leave you to it," I said. "I can tell you have your hands full. Just... be careful, OK? Don't take any stupid chances. And call or text me if you have a chance?"

He promised he would, and we hung up. He to sell guns and

sniff out gang members marked for execution, and me to shower and primp before my lunch with Darcy. Sometimes, the dichotomy of our lives together really hit home with a vengeance.

Four

The Cracker Barrel at the height of lunch hour was something of a madhouse. I got there, and had a hard time finding a parking space. All around me were RVs with Ontario plates having made a pit stop on their way down to the Florida panhandle, and cars with Florida plates escaping from the onslaught of Yankees.

At long last, a Minnesotan, surely on his way south for the winter, moved his RV, and I scooted into the vacated space and cut the engine.

Darcy had already gotten us a table. She waved at me from a chair by the window as I walked by, and I headed inside.

Every Cracker Barrel consists of a restaurant as well as a country store that sells garden gnomes, cutesy signs, and old-fashioned candy. I made my way through the maze without knocking anything off the shelves with the stomach, and reached the restaurant, where I had to maneuver carefully around the tables and the people sitting at them.

I arrived at the window safely, without anybody accidentally elbowing me in the baby—it happens—and sank down onto the (hard, wooden) chair with a sigh of relief. "This place is crazy."

"It's rush hour," Darcy said tolerantly. "And we're right next to the interstate."

Yes, we were. "Was there a particular reason you wanted to meet here? Instead of, say, the Café on the Square or Beulah's Meat'n Three?"

"Privacy," Darcy said. "And Beulah's is closed."

"It is?" I had driven past it coming and going for the past two or three days, but to be honest, I hadn't been paying attention. "And what do you mean, privacy?"

There must be more than a hundred people taking lunch in the dining room right now. The noise level was insane. We had to raise our voices to be heard, just across the table from one another, and the closest person to Darcy—closer than me—sat two feet behind her.

"Nobody here knows me. Or you."

That was true, anyway. I didn't see anyone I knew. "So what is it you wanted privacy to talk about?"

"Let's order first," Darcy said, opening her menu as the waitress approached the table. "I'll have sweet tea, please. And a Cobb salad."

"The same," I said, since I hadn't had time to look at the menu and I didn't want to hold things up while I did.

The waitress withdrew and I turned back to Darcy.

She sighed. "This is a little weird."

"Sorry. We can make small-talk first, if it'll make it easier."

She smiled. "That's not necessary." And then she launched into small-talk anyway. "How's your husband?"

"Fine," I said. And tacked on a silent, *'so far.'* "I spoke to him this morning. He thinks the people in the house next to the duplex he's staying in are cooking meth in their kitchen, but he can't bust them for it, because it would jeopardize the gang investigation and a bunch of people would die. So he just has to stay there until that's all taken care of. Although I'm not real happy about him living next door to a meth lab, even just for a couple of days. Those things blow up, don't they?"

Darcy stared at me for a few seconds, seemingly speechless. "I think so."

"That's what I thought. And there's also the worry that they'll figure out who he is—that the meth people will figure out that he works in law enforcement, I mean, although there's always the chance that the gang members will figure out the same thing—and if they think he's there because of them, they could hurt him." Either group.

"That would be bad," Darcy said.

I nodded. Yes, it would. "So I'm a little bit worried. I know he can take care of himself, but there's really no way to protect yourself from the house next door exploding, you know? If you're afraid it might, you just stay away from it. But he can't. He has to be there, at least until tomorrow."

Darcy nodded. She looked fascinated, in the way of someone who's just waiting for the other shoe to drop. "I'm glad everything worked out the other night."

"It was my fault," I said. "And I'm lucky he doesn't hold my upbringing against me."

Darcy nodded. "Speaking of upbringing..."

Oh, Lord. She wasn't from around here—hadn't been here more than a couple of years, as far as I knew—so she hadn't grown up with Rafe or the stories about LaDonna Collier and the fate that can befall a girl who isn't 'careful.'

"He grew up in the Bog," I said, since I assumed Darcy was fishing for information about Rafe and the fact that I had married the man everyone in Sweetwater had always thought of as LaDonna Collier's good-for-nothing colored boy. "The trailer park on the south side of town. It isn't there anymore—Ronnie Burke bought the land last summer and was going to put up affordable housing there, so it's called Mallard Meadows now, although the project is on ice for the next twenty-five to life—"

Just like Ronnie.

"I heard about that," Darcy nodded. "Your brother was quite upset about the fact that Todd Satterfield was a suspect."

"He had an alibi. And as soon as he coughed it up," and threw Marley Cartwright under the bus, "it was obvious that he couldn't have done it."

Maybe Mother was wrong and it wasn't Dix Darcy had her eye on. Maybe it was Todd.

I wasn't sure I liked that idea much better. If Marley wanted Todd, I wanted her to have him. She'd been through enough; she deserved some happiness with a guy who wanted her. Assuming Todd could be convinced he did.

"Anyway," I said, "that's where Rafe grew up. In a trailer in the Bog. With his mother and grandfather. And of course I grew up in the mansion."

Darcy nodded. "I grew up in Mobile."

"Alabama?"

She nodded, and waited while the waitress placed two glasses of iced tea on the table and withdrew, with the assurance that our food would be right out. "I haven't lived here long. I worked in Birmingham until a couple of years ago."

"How did you end up here?" Sweetwater is a nice enough place, but it isn't exactly the center of the world. I don't know many people who have moved here to work. A few to get married, like Mother—who's from Savannah originally, and one of the Georgia Calverts. But most of the population is here because they were born here.

"Your brother was advertising for a new receptionist," Darcy said, "and I applied."

"Was something going on in Birmingham you wanted to get away from? Or were you just looking for a change of pace?" Or had the ad perchance included a picture of my brother and she'd been struck by lust?

"My husband had left me," Darcy said, "so I was looking for something different. But I wasn't looking up here. I was thinking I'd go back to Mobile."

"What changed your mind?"

Something had. She was here, after all.

"This came in the mail."

She dug into her bag and came out with an envelope. From it, she pulled a folded-up piece of newspaper.

It was a bit like déjà vu. On our first date, Rafe had done the same thing. His newspaper clipping had been about the shooting death of a young man by the name of Tyrell Jenkins thirty-one years ago, before Rafe himself was born. Tyrell had been Rafe's father and LaDonna's boyfriend, and Old Jim Collier was the one who shot him. The clipping had come from LaDonna's possessions in the trailer in the Bog after she'd died.

Darcy's clipping wasn't as exciting. When she unfolded it, I saw it was part of a page from the classified section of the *Sweetwater Reporter*. The name of the newspaper was up in the corner. An ad halfway down the page was circled in black magic marker.

"Receptionist needed for Maury County law office. Two years experience necessary. Law background preferred. Send resumes to Martin and McCall..."

I handed it back. "Who sent it to you?"

"That's just it," Darcy said, folding the clipping and sliding it back into the envelope. "I have no idea. But I sent in my resume and was invited to come in for an interview. Then they offered me the job."

"And you never found out who sent you the ad?"

She shook her head. "I asked your brother if he knew—after he'd hired me—and he looked at me like I was crazy."

I could well imagine. "The most likely explanation is that it was one of your friends in Birmingham."

"Yes," Darcy said, "but how would one of my friends in Birmingham know about a job in a little town in Tennessee?"

"We're not that far from Birmingham." A couple hours. "And people from here do go there occasionally. I went to high school with a girl who lives there now. Darla. She teaches gym."

"I don't know her," Darcy said. "And anyway, I asked them. They said they hadn't."

That was a little weird, then. It wasn't like any of her friends would have a reason to lie. At least not on the surface of it.

"The envelope was mailed from here," Darcy added.

"Sweetwater?"

"That's why I asked your brother if he'd mailed it. I thought maybe he'd heard about me or something like that, and wanted to make sure I applied for the job."

"But he said no?"

Darcy nodded.

"When was this? A couple years ago, you said?"

"More like two and a half," Darcy said, which meant that Sheila had been alive and well at the time. She might have sent the clipping, if somehow she had known about Darcy. We'd never know now, since we couldn't ask her. But Dix certainly hadn't had any reason to do it, or to lie.

"That's interesting," I said politely, as the waitress approached with two salad bowls, "but I don't know anything about it. I wasn't even in Sweetwater two and a half years ago."

At that time, if memory served, I had just managed to ditch Bradley and was working at the makeup counter at the Green Hills Mall to make ends meet. "I didn't send the clipping," I added, "and I don't know who did."

The waitress deposited a Cobb salad in front of each of us, cast an experienced eye over the glasses of tea to determine the need for a refill, and took herself off.

"I didn't think you did," Darcy said, lifting her fork preparatory to digging in. "That's not what I wanted to ask you."

"What did you want to ask?" I armed myself with my own fork and plunged it into the lettuce while I waited for Darcy to search out the words she wanted. It took a few seconds.

"You've had to investigate some murders and things," she said eventually.

"I wouldn't say I had to," I answered, since I'd mostly

inserted myself where I had no business being, "but yes, I have."

"When your sister-in-law was killed, you were the one who figured out what happened."

With a little help from Marley Cartwright and a few other people, including Rafe. But yes, I had figured it out, and had had occasion to pepper-spray the murderer, too. It had felt good, even if I'd gotten shot for my trouble.

"And when Todd's ex-wife was killed, you were the one who figured out who did it."

With, again, a lot of help from a lot of people.

"That was personal," I said. "Sheila was family. And Jolynn died in my bed. It might have been me. We were concerned it was supposed to be me. I had to do something about it. But I'm not a PI or anything. I don't have a license to snoop."

"I'd like to hire you to look into something for me."

"I'm not sure I can do that," I said. "And not just legally. Rafe wants me to be careful. I'm pregnant. I can't go chasing murderers around."

Darcy shook her head. "There are no murderers. I just want some help figuring out where I came from. And how I ended up here."

I put my fork down. "You told me you grew up in Mobile. And you ended up here because someone sent you that newspaper clipping. And I can't think of any way we can possibly figure out who. Not more than two years later."

The staff at the post office wouldn't remember who came in to mail a letter that long ago. And that was if anyone had come in at all. It's easy to stick a stamp on an envelope and drop it in the mailbox. Unless you need postage, you never need set foot inside the post office.

Darcy nodded. "That's not what I want. I want you to figure out where I was born, and who my parents were."

I opened my mouth again, and she continued, before I could tell her that her parents were the people in Mobile who had brought her up, "I was adopted. My birth certificate says that my parents are my parents, so growing up, I never knew any different."

"So how do you know you're adopted?"

"My parents died," Darcy said. "Suddenly, in a car accident. Four years ago now."

"Both of them at once?"

She nodded. "I was the executrix for their estate. I found a letter in their effects, that they had left me. One of those 'to be opened after my death' things you read about."

You certainly do read about them. But to be honest, I had thought those appeared only in books.

"They hadn't wanted to tell me as long as they were alive," Darcy said. "They wrote that they were afraid it would make me feel different toward them. But when they were dead, they wanted me to know the truth."

I pushed my salad bowl away. The lettuce was wilted, and anyway, I had inhaled most of it. "I'm so sorry."

Darcy shrugged. "The letter said I was born at a hospital in Nashville, but they didn't tell me which one, and they said they weren't told who my real parents were. I guess that's common."

I'd come face to face with a lot of adoption practices, good and mostly bad, during the investigation into Sheila's murder, and yes, closed adoptions are common. Thirty-plus years ago, they would have been more common. Open adoptions, where the adoptive parents know the birth parents and vice versa, are a fairly new thing.

"It is," I said. "Rafe has a thirteen-year-old son named David, who was adopted away at birth. Rafe didn't know about him until last year, and anyway, he was in prison when David was born."

Darcy swallowed wrong, and went into a coughing fit. I pushed the glass of iced tea at her.

"He served two years for assault and battery. I'm sorry. I thought you knew."

Darcy shook her head, dashing tears away from her eyes with he knuckles.

"While Rafe was eighteen and in prison, this girl he'd knocked up the previous spring had a baby. It was taken away from her and given to someone else, and she was told the baby was stillborn. It took her years to track him down."

"That's terrible." Darcy had gotten the coughing under control and was wiping the last of the tears away with her napkin. "What happened?"

"She died," I said. "David's still with his adoptive parents. They're great. He and Rafe are getting to know one another. He was here for the wedding. Best man. You saw him, didn't you?"

Darcy nodded. "He looked like a miniature version of your husband. I thought maybe they were brothers. Or half-brothers."

I shook my head. "Father and son. Although I guess their relationship is really more fraternal. David already has a father. Sam's great. None of us want to change that. David's happy. And we all want him to stay that way."

Darcy nodded.

"At any rate, it wasn't just a closed adoption, it was a secretive and pretty much illegal one. The people responsible are either in prison or dead now. But closed adoptions are common. Your parents probably had no idea who your biological parents are."

"Thank you for that," Darcy said. "I don't want to resent them, you know? They were my mother and father. They brought me up. And I can understand that it would upset them to think that I'd want to know where I came from and who my other parents are. I understand why they chose to wait until after they died to tell me. But I have a right to know who I am, don't I?"

It was hard to argue with that. And at any rate, I didn't have a chance to, because my phone jingled.

"I'm sorry," I said, digging into my purse for it, "but I might have to take this." It wasn't Rafe's ring tone—just my generic incoming call—but it could still be important.

"No problem." Darcy pushed her chair back. "I'll go freshen up before heading back to the office."

That's code for hitting the bathroom, as I'm sure you know. I nodded and looked at the phone.

Alexandra Puckett, it said.

Alexandra was the sixteen-year-old daughter of my colleague Brenda Puckett when Brenda was murdered last fall. We'd struck up a kind of friendship in the aftermath of Brenda's demise, and Alexandra would call me once in a while, when she had a question or needed something, or just wanted to talk.

Usually about something she didn't feel comfortable talking to her dad about.

I put the phone to my ear. "Hi, Alexandra."

"Hi, Savannah," Alexandra said.

I waited a second, but when she didn't go on, I asked, "What's up?"

"Where are you?"

"A Cracker Barrel off the interstate in Sweetwater," I said, glancing out the window to where the RVs and trailers were parked.

"You're not in Nashville?"

Obviously not. "I'll be back in a couple of days. Rafe's working on something this weekend, and he wants me out of the way. Is something wrong?"

Once, a couple of days after her mother's murder, Alexandra had called me late at night and asked me to pick her up from a party that hadn't turned out the way she had wanted it to. As it happened, I'd been on my way home from having dinner with Rafe when she called, so I took him with me. It turned out to be a good move on my part, since the neighborhood where the party was, wasn't one I'd have been comfortable traversing on my own back then.

As it happened, it wasn't too far from where I'd ended up living. And I'd still think twice before venturing down that particular street.

"No," Alexandra said. And amended it to, "Maybe."

"Do you need help? Where are you?"

"At home," Alexandra said. "I was sick this morning, so I had to stay home from school. And I don't need help. Or not right now. But I'd like to talk to you about something."

She and everyone else.

I glanced around, at the full dining room, the waitresses milling back and forth, and Darcy, making her way back to the table. "This isn't a great time for me. Like I said, I'm at a Cracker Barrel. There are people everywhere. Can I call you back? Maybe in an hour or so, when I'm back at the house?"

"Your mother's house?"

"Yes," I said as Darcy took her seat across the table again. "I'll call you when I'm back at my mother's house."

"OK," Alexandra said, although she sounded a little forlorn.

"Are you sure you're all right?"

"I'm fine. I just want someone to talk to."

"Boyfriend trouble?" That had been the problem last year. At that party I'd had to rescue her from, she had seen a check her mother had written to her boyfriend the morning Brenda was murdered. I'm not sure whether it had upset Alexandra more that her boyfriend might have killed her mother, or that he had taken money to stop seeing Alexandra, but either way, she'd been distraught.

Now she made a sound that sounded a bit like a sob, but I think it was actually a laugh. At least she didn't sound like she was crying when she told me, "You could say that."

Darcy arched her brows on the other side of the table.

"I'll call you back," I told Alexandra. "Just hang on. I'll call you later, and then we'll figure it out. OK?" Whatever it was, it couldn't be that bad. She was only seventeen.

"OK," Alexandra said.

"I'll talk to you then." I disconnected and dropped the phone back in my bag. "Sorry about that."

"No problem," Darcy said. "Trouble?"

"A sort of friend of mine. She was down for the wedding, too, so you probably saw her. Tall girl, seventeen years old, with long, black hair. Her brother Austin goes to school with David Flannery."

"I think I may have noticed them. Is she all right?"

"She said she was. She just wants to talk. And she doesn't have a mother to talk to. Sometimes she talks to me instead." I guess I was a sort of an older sister substitute, or something. "I'll call her back later and find out what's going on."

Darcy nodded.

"To get back to where we left off when the phone rang, I agree that you have a right to know where you came from. But I'm not sure how to go about figuring it out. If your parents didn't know, and your birth certificate says that they're your biological parents..."

A bell rang faintly in the back of my head and I trailed off.

"What?" Darcy said, tilting her head. For a second, the expression on her face was familiar, and I wrinkled my brows. "What?" she said again.

I shook it off. "Nothing. David's birth certificate says that Ginny and Sam are his biological parents, too. And when Marley's baby was stolen and given to someone else, their birth certificate said that Oliver was theirs." Although they'd called him Owen, if memory served.

"So?" Darcy said.

"So that was something St. Jerome's Hospital did. That's

where David was born. St. Jerome's Hospital in Brentwood. It's about forty, forty-five minutes from here."

"We could go there," Darcy said.

We could. Although I didn't think it would do any good. "None of the doctors who were involved in the adoption ring are there anymore. And I think the police confiscated all the records for the adopted babies, so they aren't at the hospital anymore. I could call my friend Tamara Grimaldi and ask her about them..."

"Would you?" Darcy asked eagerly.

"Sure. Maybe, if she's available, we could run up to Nashville tomorrow and go through what they have. See if the records go back far enough that you might have been one of the babies born there."

"Do you think your friend will let us?"

Maybe, maybe not. Detective Grimaldi likes me, but at the same time, she can be a stickler for procedure. "I'll call her and ask. Just be prepared that it might be a big waste of time. We may not find anything."

Darcy nodded. "But we could get lucky."

We could. "It's worth taking a look. I'll call Grimaldi later." And Alexandra. If I was driving up to Nashville tomorrow, maybe I could squeeze in a visit with her, as well. "I'll let you know what she says."

"I appreciate it," Darcy said, and reached for the check when the waitress dropped it on the table. "Lunch is on me."

"Thank you." I reached for my bag. "I'll call you after I talk to Detective Grimaldi. And tomorrow, we'll go to Nashville."

"Works for me," Darcy said, and we headed for the door.

Five

I met Detective Tamara Grimaldi a year ago, on the occasion of Brenda Puckett's murder. Rafe and I found the body, and we both had to go into downtown to give statements to the police. Tamara Grimaldi was the detective who caught the case, and she intimidated me at first glance. Tall and severe, in a dark business suit, with short hair, a Mediterranean nose, and a no-nonsense attitude, she was everything I'm not. And I could tell she didn't think much of me, either.

Somehow, over the next few months, we became friends. And then Sheila was killed in November, and Grimaldi handled that case too, and met Dix. And now she's a friend to both of us, and maybe something more to Dix. Or maybe set to become something more, when he's ready to move on.

If he hasn't moved on already. It isn't something you can ask your widowed brother. But he has two daughters, not to mention Mother, and I can definitely understand why he's taking things slow.

At any rate, I dialed Grimaldi. Who greeted me with her usual, "Ms.... Savannah."

She's been calling me Ms. Martin for as long as we've known each other. I'm Mrs. Collier now, and I guess it's too hard to get used to, because she has finally, reluctantly, switched over to calling me by my first name. At least when she remembers to do it.

"Detective," I said. I'm not all that comfortable with calling her Tamara, either, although if she ends up in a relationship with my brother, I guess I'll have to.

"What can I do for you?"

"I need a favor," I said.

And that was all I got out. "The gang unit is working with the TBI on your husband's operation. And no, I can't tell you anything about it. Nor can I go down there myself to keep an eye on him. I have dead bodies here that need my attention."

Sheesh.

"I spoke to Rafe this morning," I said and tried my best to sound dignified. "He's fine, but he thinks there's a meth lab next door to the duplex. But there's nothing he can do about it right now. And that wasn't the reason I called."

"What's the reason you called?"

I explained about Darcy. "You guys confiscated all the records from St. Jerome's after Sheila died, right? Any chance we can get a look at them? Just in case Darcy was born there?"

Grimaldi hesitated. "I don't suppose it would hurt. Although I don't know how you'd know you had found her. Her name won't be on the original birth certificate, if it exists, and her biological parents' names won't be on the amended certificate."

"We know her birthday," I said. "Or she does."

"It might not be accurate, either. Her adoptive parents may have been celebrating the day they adopted her. And that could be days or even weeks after she was born."

Dammit. I mean... darn it. I hadn't thought of that.

"Can we still look?" No stone unturned, and so on.

"If you want to," Grimaldi said. "I'll have the records brought up into one of the conference rooms on this level. You can't take them out of the building."

I hadn't assumed we could. "Is there a copier, so we can make a copy of something, if we find anything?"

Grimaldi said there was, and we would be allowed to do that. Just not remove any original records.

"That's fine," I said. "When do you want us there?"

We settled on a time, one that would give Darcy and me time to make the trek from Sweetwater to downtown Nashville. And then, before saying goodbye, Grimaldi added, "How's your brother?"

"Dix?"

"Do you have another brother?"

I didn't. One sister and one brother, and that was all.

"I assume he's fine," I said. "I haven't seen him for a couple of days. He was at Mother's birthday party, of course, but I didn't have occasion to say much to him. He was talking to Todd Satterfield, and I tend to avoid Todd. And I didn't see him yesterday. Or this morning. But if something was wrong, I'm sure Darcy would have said so."

"She's the receptionist, isn't she?"

I said she was. "She's been working for them for a couple of years. And that's another interesting thing." I recounted the story of the newspaper clipping Darcy had received in the mail, for a job that nobody she knew claimed to have known about.

"And no one in Sweetwater has admitted to knowing Darcy before she came to work for your brother?" Grimaldi asked.

"Not that I know of," I said, "although she only told me that she'd asked Dix. If she asked anyone else, she didn't say anything about it. I'll find out."

"She probably didn't," Grimaldi said. "And whoever sent the letter isn't likely to admit it, anyway. Too obvious. But while you're at it, you could ask her if anyone in Sweetwater has shown a special interest in her. Anyone who might have had a reason to want to get her there."

"Like a man?"

"Or a woman. Or anyone at all."

"I don't think she's dating," I said. If she were, and wasn't keeping it a secret, surely Mother wouldn't have worried about

Darcy setting her cap for Dix. "So it probably wasn't a potential boyfriend. They'd be together now."

"Not necessarily," Grimaldi said. "It might have been someone who thought of himself as a potential boyfriend at the time, but then things didn't work out when she got there. She either wasn't what he expected, or she wasn't interested. You might ask if she's been involved with anyone in the time she's been living there. Or if anyone's been asking her out, but someone she hasn't gone out with. Or even someone that she has gone out with."

All good points.

"That's why I'm the detective," Grimaldi told me when I said so. "I know how to ask questions."

"Yeah, yeah." I made a face, one she couldn't see. "I'll see you tomorrow, OK? Thanks."

"Don't mention it," Grimaldi said, and hung up.

I called Darcy and set up a time to pick her up so we could make the drive to Nashville together. And I didn't mention any of the questions Grimaldi had brought up, about men and dates and whatnot. It would give us something to talk about in the car, I figured.

With that done, I dialed again. Alexandra Puckett's number this time.

She picked up on the first ring. Like she'd been sitting beside the phone waiting for it to ring. Or more likely, like she'd had her cell phone sitting right next to her, so she could be sure she wouldn't miss a call. Mine or someone else's.

"Savannah!"

"Hi, Alexandra," I said. "I'm sorry I couldn't talk earlier."

"That's all right. Are you alone now?"

I said I was. "I'm back at the house." Where it was nicely air conditioned and I could concentrate on talking instead of driving. "So what's up?"

"I'm in trouble," Alexandra said.

Not again. "What kind of trouble?"

I wasn't in Nashville to be able to rescue her from another bad boyfriend situation, and Rafe couldn't help right now, either. "If you need the police, I can give you the number for my friend Tamara Grimaldi. She's a homicide detective, but I'm sure she can figure out whatever you need." Drugs came to mind. Alexandra was seventeen. It's an age when things like that happen.

"Not that kind of trouble." Alexandra rolled her eyes. I could hear it. "I thought everybody your age knew that expression."

"What do you mean, 'my age?'" I wanted to know. "I'm twenty-eight. That's only eleven years older than you are."

Alexandra did another of those audible eyerolls.

"Fine," I said. "You're in trouble. You..." And then it clicked. "Oh, my God. You're not serious."

She squirmed. I could hear that, too. "I am, sort of. I mean, I think I am."

"You're pregnant?"

"I think so. I mean, my period isn't always... you know..."

"Regular," I said. "Yes, I know." It happens to a lot of us. And she'd already told me she was home from school today because she had vomited this morning. I should have caught on much sooner. Especially since it wasn't that long since I'd stopped throwing up every morning myself. "Have you done a pregnancy test?"

"No," Alexandra said. "I'm afraid to talk to the nurse at school. She'd have to call my dad. And if I go to another doctor, it's the same thing. Plus, it's my dad's health insurance. He'd know I'd gone to see someone, and he'd ask why. And I was afraid that if I went to the store to buy a pregnancy test, they'd have to call him then, too. Since I'm under eighteen."

"I don't think there are age limits on pregnancy tests," I said.

"It's not like cigarettes or alcohol."

Although I could understand why she'd been worried. Last year, when I'd accidentally found myself pregnant with Rafe's baby, out of wedlock, I hadn't wanted to tell my family, either. And I hadn't been seventeen and reliant on their goodwill. I'd been an adult, with my own apartment, car, and job.

But it's hard to admit something like that, even to people who love you. Maybe especially to people who love you.

"Tell you what," I said. "I'm actually making a trip up to Nashville tomorrow. My friend Darcy and I have to go through some files at the police station downtown. Maybe we could meet for lunch or something, and I can go out and buy a pregnancy test and give it to you, and you can use it and tell me what happens."

"That would be OK," Alexandra allowed cautiously.

"Great. We'll be in downtown. You still have a car, right?" Brenda had bought her a zippy, little red Mazda Miata just before she died—a Sweet Sixteen birthday gift—and I assumed Alexandra still had it. Unless her dad had confiscated it for some reason, or she was barred from driving.

"Why don't you meet us somewhere in East Nashville? It'll be convenient for all of us." Right across the bridge from the police headquarters in downtown, and down the road a couple of miles from where Alexandra lived in Brush Hill. "Do you have cravings yet? What about heartburn?"

"I'm not even sure I'm pregnant," Alexandra said.

"Why don't we make it simple and hit the barbeque place on Main. It's close to downtown, and Darcy might want to get back home quickly after we're finished at the police station."

I didn't have high hopes that we'd find anything at all in the files, let alone anything explosive, but just in case we did, and just in case it was bad news, we might have to make a quick getaway.

That was fine with Alexandra, and we made a date for a time

I figured would give Darcy and me enough time to dig through the confiscated hospital records before we headed out, but not so late that I would be starving by the time we got there. The baby gets quite annoyed if it doesn't get fed regularly. As it was, I'd probably have to pack a snack I could eat while we were going over adoption records.

"How's Rafe?" Alexandra wanted to know once the arrangements for tomorrow were in place. Like Tim, she developed a crush on him pretty much as soon as they met last fall. He has that effect on women. And girls. And gay men.

And me.

I told her he was fine.

"You said he's back undercover? I thought he wasn't going to do that anymore."

So had I. "It's just for a couple of days," I said. "One of the rookies he's training got himself into some trouble. Different trouble than the kind you've got. Rafe's trying to get him out."

"Who's that?"

"A kid named Jamal. Why?... Oh. You met them at the wedding, right?"

The boys had come down to Sweetwater for Rafe's and my wedding, and of course Alexandra had been here, too. I hadn't noticed any interaction between them, but then I'd had other things on my mind. And we hadn't stuck around all that long, anyway, since we had to drive to Florida that afternoon for the honeymoon Catherine and Dix had arranged.

Long story.

"What's wrong with Jamal?"

"Nothing, as far as I know. He's joined this gang—the same one his brother was a member of..."

"Gang?" Alexandra said faintly.

"He didn't really join. They asked him if he wanted to help avenge his brother. Members of another gang killed him. So

Jamal said yes, and now he's working to have them all arrested. And Rafe's helping him."

Alexandra didn't say anything.

"That's why I'm here and Rafe's there," I added. "He wanted me out of the way in case bullets started flying. And if you happen to see him in the next two days, try to remember that his name is Ry'mone. Although you might not recognize him. He has dreadlocks halfway down his back and two gold teeth."

"Rafe?!"

"He looks awful. Although it'll all go away again next week, so I guess it isn't too bad. And it's not like I have to look at him. He's in Nashville."

"Are you going to see him tomorrow?"

I hadn't planned to. I mean, he'd told me to stay away. If I showed up—especially if I showed up next door to a meth lab—he'd have every reason to be angry. And if I accidentally got in the way of bullets from a gang war, he'd be furious.

"Probably not. Although we'll see." I'd probably talk to him between now and then. Either tonight or tomorrow morning. He might be willing to risk a quick visit. If he missed me, too. And if he felt like the visit would be worth the potential risk.

Which he wouldn't. I knew that without having to ask. He'd put my safety first, and his own desire to see me—if he had one, and I had to trust he did—last.

"But I'm looking forward to seeing you," I added, brightly. "One o'clock, at the barbeque place. I'll bring the pregnancy test."

Alexandra said she'd be there, and we hung up. I headed out to the drugstore.

Thirty minutes later, after choosing a pregnancy test and spending a couple of minutes debating the relative benefits of a Snickers bar over 3 Musketeers or Kit-Kat, I reached the register, where I was greeted with a friendly, "Hi, princess."

I blinked. "Yvonne?"

Yvonne McCoy was... I hesitated to call her a friend, since we'd never had much to do with each other growing up, but we'd gone to school together and had some friends in common. Including my brother Dix, and Rafe.

Yvonne was two years older than me, and she and Dix had been in the same class in school. She'd always had a soft spot for him, or so she'd told me.

Rafe, meanwhile, had been a year older, but he and Yvonne had been part of the same clique. The troubled and the troublemakers. They hadn't been in the same class, but they had ended up in the same bed once. Yvonne had also told me she would have been happy to repeat the experience, but Rafe hadn't suggested it, so she hadn't either.

It didn't bother me much. A little, if I thought too hard about it, but there had been a lot of women in Rafe's life, many of them I didn't even know about. The fact that he'd slept with Yvonne once in high school hardly mattered. She didn't act weird about it, and anyway, he had married me.

"I didn't know you worked here," I added.

Last time I'd seen her—and several times before that—she'd been a waitress at Beulah's Meat'n Three. Although she'd had a close brush with death last fall—courtesy of another of Rafe's old flames—and I guess maybe she'd reassessed her life since then.

Not that there was anything at all wrong with being a waitress at Beulah's.

Her face darkened. "Beulah died. A couple of weeks ago."

"Oh, wow." Darcy had mentioned that Beulah's Meat'n Three was closed, but not that it was because the owner had died. And I guess Mother had thought I wouldn't be interested in something like that. "I'm so sorry. You worked there a long time, didn't you?"

Yvonne nodded. "She didn't have any kids, so she left the

place to me. It said so in her will. But her sister-in-law has a daughter, and the daughter wants it. So they're trying to say I exerted—" She used her fingers to draw quotes in the air, "—'undue influence' to get her to leave it to me. Hell, I'd worked there for twelve years! Ever since I finished high school. It was almost as much mine as it was hers. She'd been teaching me to run it."

"I'm so sorry," I said again, inadequately.

"And that bitch never set foot in the place for as long as I worked there. And now that Beulah's gone, suddenly she's all about saving the family business!"

"What are you doing about it?" If there was a will, duly witnessed and signed, giving the restaurant to Yvonne, she had at least a fighting chance of hanging on to it. "Have you hired a lawyer?"

"Lawyers cost money," Yvonne said. "*They've* hired a lawyer, to get the will overturned. I'm just waiting to see what happens. They shut the place down while they're figuring it out, so I'm out of a job. I'm working here while I wait." She sighed. "By the time they get Beulah's up and running again, there won't be any business left to worry about."

"I'm so sorry. But you really should be represented, too." Especially if the sister-in-law and niece were.

"I can't afford a lawyer," Yvonne said. "They pay minimum wage here. I made good money waiting tables, but I need every bit of what they're paying me now to make ends meet."

Understandable. I wasn't making much of a living myself, so I could definitely relate to counting pennies. I couldn't have afforded a lawyer when I divorced Bradley, either, if Catherine hadn't stepped in to help, *pro bono*.

"I did a couple of years of law school," I said. Before I dropped out to marry Bradley. "I can take a look at the will, if you want. If you have a copy of it. At least I'll be able to tell you whether there's anything hinky about it. Anything you have to worry about."

"Would you?"

"I'd be happy to," I said. "Just as long as you understand I'm not a lawyer. I can't give you legal advice, and I can't represent you. But I can look at it and tell you what I think."

"Thank you." Yvonne sniffed. "That's so nice of you."

"I'm happy to do it," I said. "Maybe I could come over to your house tonight, after you get off work, to take a look at it? Or we could go somewhere for dinner instead, if you want."

"Come to the house," Yvonne said. "I'll cook. I'm a good cook."

Fine with me. "Six o'clock?"

"I don't get off until five-thirty. Better make it seven."

I told her seven was fine, and then I nudged the pregnancy test and chocolate bar toward her. She looked down, and up again. "You don't need that."

"Excuse me?" I was pregnant. I had cravings. If I wanted chocolate, I got chocolate.

"I can tell by looking at you that you're pregnant," Yvonne said. "You're due in a couple of months, aren't you?"

"More like three." But yes. I was rather visibly expecting. "It isn't for me. It's for a friend."

Yvonne's eyebrows arched. "Darcy's pregnant?"

"No!" Or at least not as far as I knew. And that was a rumor I didn't want to be responsible for having started. "It's for a friend in Nashville. She's seventeen, and afraid the pharmacy will call her dad if she goes to buy a pregnancy test. So I told her I'd get one and give it to her. I'm driving up there tomorrow."

"Just to give her a pregnancy test? We don't have to report when someone buys a pregnancy test, you know. Even if that someone looks like a kid."

"I know," I said. "It's not just to give her the test. I have a couple other things to take care of, too, while I'm there." I mean,

I liked Alexandra, but not enough to drive more than an hour back to Nashville just to give her a pregnancy test. If I hadn't been going anyway, I would have talked her into getting it herself.

"What made you think of Darcy?" I added, while I watched Yvonne scan the barcode on the side of the box.

"Someone saw the two of you at Cracker Barrel for lunch." She scanned the Kit-Kat and dropped it into the bag on top of the pregnancy test. "I thought maybe she was afraid to buy it herself. You know how people talk."

Yes, indeed. There's no privacy in a small town.

And as if to prove it, Yvonne added, "How's Rafe? I heard you guys had a blow-up at your mother's party the other night."

"It wasn't a blow-up." Nobody blew up. "And he's fine. Working. That's why I'm here."

"Oh," Yvonne said, and managed to infuse the single syllable with a whole lot of doubt. "People are saying you're breaking up."

"People are wrong." I hauled the plastic bag off the counter.

"No trouble in paradise?"

"None at all," I said firmly. "The only reason I'm here, is because Rafe is working on something in Nashville that he doesn't want me to get involved with. But we talk every day. I spoke to him this morning. Everything's fine."

Yvonne nodded. "If you decide you don't want him anymore, I'd be happy to step in and take him off your hands."

I'm sure she would.

"I don't even mind the dreads." She grinned. "He had cornrows in high school, remember?"

I did remember. And tried hard not to imagine those cornrows in bed with Yvonne. "Mine," I told her.

"Sure. Tell him I said hi when you talk to him."

I told her I would. "I'll see you at seven."

"You know where to go?"

"As long as you haven't moved. The house in Damascus?"

Yvonne confirmed that she still lived in the house in Damascus—a little town a few miles up the road from Sweetwater—and I took my plastic bag and headed out. I ate the Kit-Kat in the car, and wished I'd bought another for later. One chocolate bar just isn't enough.

Six

Mother had plans to have dinner with the sheriff anyway, so she had no problem with me going out to meet a friend. Her nose wrinkled a little when I mentioned Yvonne's name—the McCoys aren't 'our kind' of people; we're much like the Hatfields that way—but she confirmed that yes, Beulah had gone on to the big buffet in the sky a couple of weeks back.

"Heart attack, I heard. All that rich food." She shuddered.

The meat'n three fare at Beulah's had been artery-clogging, no question. Chicken fried steak, mashed potatoes and gravy, green beans cooked in bacon fat, not to mention the pie crusts...

Then again, my father had also passed away from a heart attack, and he hadn't been eating bacon fat and chicken fried steak. Mother would never have allowed it.

"Yvonne said Beulah left her the restaurant," I said, and Mother's perfectly shaped eyebrows rose.

"You don't say?"

"I do say. Or at least Yvonne did. I'm going over there, to her house, to take a look at the will tonight. I may not have finished law school, but I'll be able to tell whether it's valid or not."

"Of course you will, darling," Mother said.

"And if I think she needs a lawyer, I'll talk to Dix. Maybe he can work something out with her."

Mother looked pained. She probably remembered Yvonne, and didn't want to contemplate what kind of something she and Dix might be able to work out.

"Apparently, Beulah's niece is also after the place," I added. "She and her mother—Beulah's sister-in-law—are contesting the will. Do you know anything about them?"

Mother shook her head. "Beulah was quite a few years older than me, you know. We weren't contemporaries. And I didn't grow up in Sweetwater. But I can ask Bob tonight, and see what he knows."

"I wouldn't mind if you did," I told her. "If the will is valid, and if Beulah was *compos mentis* when she wrote it, then I don't want the sister-in-law and niece to take what's rightfully Yvonne's."

Mother nodded.

"She's been working in that place since she was eighteen. Beulah was training her to take over. She'd do a much better job of running the place than two women who don't even live in town."

They couldn't possibly live here. If they did, Mother would know them. Or know of them, at any rate.

"I'm sure you're right, darling," Mother said. "I'll mention it to Bob and see what he might know."

I told her I appreciated it, and that I was going to go upstairs to lie down for a bit before I had to leave again. My ankles were swollen and the baby was sitting on my bladder. I wanted a break.

So I took one, and crawled onto the bed in my room for a while, just enjoying the coolness of the air conditioning and the sunshine coming in through the windows. I even took a quick nap for thirty minutes or so, until I was interrupted by the telephone.

Waitin' for some lover to call...

I dove for it. "Rafe!"

I hadn't expected to hear from him so soon, or at all tonight, so this was a nice surprise.

"Evening, darlin'."

It wasn't quite evening yet, but I guess he'd had a long day.

"What's going on?" I asked.

"Not much. I had a minute and figured I'd give you a call before I get too busy."

"I appreciate that," I said, making myself comfortable against the pillows with the phone to my ear. "Have you had a good day?"

"Eh." He didn't sound thrilled with it.

"Is the meth lab still up and running."

"So far. I've seen'em come outside to smoke a couple times."

Smoke? "Lots of people go outside to smoke because they don't want the smell to linger in the furniture."

"And folks who cook meth in their kitchens don't wanna blow up themselves and their whole operation if the chemicals catch fire, so they go outside to smoke, too."

That made sense. And he probably knew more about it than I did.

Correction: he definitely knew more about it than I did.

"Yvonne says hi," I told him. "She says, if we're not able to work things out after I insulted you the other day, she's ready and willing to console you."

Now he sounded amused. "You don't say?"

"I don't. She did. I'm having dinner with her tonight. At her house. You don't think she'll try to poison me to pave the way to you, do you?"

"No, darlin'. There ain't a mean bone in Yvonne's body."

"You'd know," I said, and then grimaced. Not jealous, huh? "I ran into her at the drugstore this afternoon. She works there now. Beulah died, and they had to shut down the restaurant while they figure out probate. She left the place to Yvonne, but her sister-in-law and niece are contesting the will."

"That can't be good," Rafe said.

"I don't imagine so. I'm going to take a look at the will, and see if there's anything about it that makes me think it isn't valid. If it is, Yvonne might need to hire a lawyer of her own." One who had actually finished law school. "I thought I might sic her on Dix. Or maybe Catherine would be better."

Yvonne would undoubtedly prefer to deal with Dix, but Dix might prefer that Catherine handle it. And Catherine can be ruthless. When Bradley and I divorced, she would have nailed his ears to the wall if I hadn't stopped her. My sister takes unfairness in a deeply personal way. If Yvonne needed legal representation, she could do a lot worse than Catherine.

"Have a good time," Rafe said.

"Thank you. So you think the food will be safe?"

"I'm sure it'll be fine. She don't really want me."

"She said she'd be happy to take you off my hands."

"She was joking," Rafe said.

"You slept with her once."

"When we were bored and had nothing better to do. It didn't mean nothing."

He'd said that before, perhaps in those exact words. I should probably believe him. "I'll tell her you said hi. And tomorrow Darcy and I are driving up to Nashville."

There was another beat. "Why?" The question was halfway between suspicious and what I'd call a tacit warning to me to be careful what I said.

"We're going to see Grimaldi," I said. "And look through the records they confiscated from St. Jerome's Hospital last year. It turns out Darcy is adopted. She's trying to figure out where she came from."

"And you think she came from St. Jerome's?"

"I think there's a good chance she did. Her parents said they got her from Nashville. And her birth certificate has her adoptive parents listed as her birth parents, the way St. Jerome's did. The way David's birth certificate looks."

"Other places mighta done the same thing."

I nodded, even though he couldn't see me. "I know. But we know St. Jerome's did. And I don't think the investigation turned up any other hospitals that were involved in the baby-selling ring. It was just St. Jerome's and Dr. Seaver in Columbia."

Rafe grunted something that might have been agreement or the opposite.

"Anyway," I added, "it's somewhere to start. And something to do. It's a little boring down here. I miss you."

His voice warmed. "I miss you, too, darlin'."

"Does that mean maybe I'll get to see you tomorrow? Since I'll be in Nashville anyway?"

He hesitated. "I guess that depends on what's going on. If we take care of business tonight, I might could be available tomorrow."

"We're having lunch with Alexandra Puckett," I offered. "At the barbeque place on Main Street. One o'clock, if you want to join us. I'm sure she'd be happy to see you."

It was probably best if I didn't mention anything about the pregnancy. Or the possible pregnancy. Alexandra might not be pregnant. If she tended toward having irregular periods, she might just be a bit late, and the worry was playing tricks with her body and making her think she was seeing signs of pregnancy when they weren't there.

No, much better to wait to say anything until I knew for sure. Especially since Alexandra's pregnancy had absolutely nothing to do with Rafe and he had other worries at the moment.

"Tell you what," he said. "I'll talk to you in the morning. I'll have a better idea of what's left of the cleanup and whether I can take an hour for lunch and a quickie with my wife."

The quickie hadn't really been on the table—no pun intended—since I'd have a teenager with me and Darcy to get back to Sweetwater in one piece, and I couldn't really ask her to make herself comfortable in the restaurant while Rafe and I went out to the car to make love. Not that the idea didn't have appeal.

But even so— "That'll work," I told him. "Do what you have to do tonight, and call me in the morning. If you can get away for lunch, that'll be great. If not, I'll just see you when I can."

"Sounds good. Have a good time tonight. Tell Yvonne I said hi."

I said I would. "You have a good time, too. If that isn't the wrong thing to say about a gang war sting operation."

"Oh," Rafe said grimly, "I'm gonna have a great time. The more people end up in prison and the less people die, the happier I'll be. I love you, darlin'."

"I love you, too," I told him, and let him go.

I'd been to Damascus a few times before. Elspeth Caulfield lived there—the woman who gave birth to Rafe's son David—and I had accompanied Dix to her house the day after she died to look for her will.

I'd even been to Yvonne's house before, and once Rafe and I had kept her from bleeding out on her living room floor.

That was almost a year ago now. The last time we'd stopped by had been on occasion of my high school reunion in May. People had been dying then, too—people were always dying, it seemed—and we'd thought that maybe Yvonne could shed some light on why.

I knew the place would look different from the first time I'd seen it. After Yvonne almost died, she had bought new furniture and rearranged the room. The sofa was up against the wall now, instead of in front of the window, and the carpet was shaggier than it used to be.

She met me at the front door. "C'mon in." She stepped aside to let me pass through into the house. "It's so hot I didn't go crazy on the food. But there's plenty of it. I figured, if you're pregnant, you probably eat a lot."

Not the most flattering way to put it—I much prefer to think that I'm eating for two—but OK.

"It looks great," I said.

She had set up the dining room table—small and round—with a big bowl of salad bristling with vegetables, a plate of grilled chicken, a big pitcher of iced tea brimming with ice cubes, and what looked like homemade rolls.

"Wow," I added. "It smells great, too."

It did. The air was redolent of baked bread and grilled chicken.

Yvonne flushed with pleasure. "Thanks. I don't entertain a lot. I wasn't sure if it was too much or not enough."

"It looks perfect to me." As if to concur, my stomach rumbled.

Yvonne giggled. "C'mon. Sit down."

I made my way over to the table and sat. It really did look great. And the Kit-Kat bar was a very long time ago.

"We should eat before the chicken gets cold," Yvonne said, "and then I'll show you the will later."

Sure. She didn't have to ask me twice.

So we ate and made small-talk. I told her about life with Rafe—without most of the titillating details. In justice to Yvonne, she didn't ask me for them, either. And she told me about life in Sweetwater, which hadn't changed much from when I grew up here.

"So are you dating anyone?" I asked between stuffing bites of chicken and salad into my mouth. "This is delicious."

"Thanks." She shook her head. "No. After what happened—" She gestured to her chest, where the scars from the knifing were still visible above the low-cut neckline of the T-shirt she was wearing, "I decided that life's too short to waste on losers. I'm gonna take over Beulah's and make it into the best damn meat'n three in the state, and the next guy I get involved with is either going to get behind me or get out of my way."

"That sounds like a good plan." I reached for another roll. I was eating in ways unbecoming a lady, but Mother wasn't here to see me, and I was starving. I may have felt a little frisson of guilt, but it wasn't enough to make me stop. "I'm sorry about Beulah. I didn't know her, other than to say hello when I saw her, but you'd worked with her a long time. You must have been close."

Especially if Beulah had willed Yvonne her business instead of leaving it to relatives.

"She was a little bit like a mother to me," Yvonne said. "Or a gramma, anyway. She was older, you know. But my own mama's never been much good, and ever since I started working for her, Miz Beulah took care of me."

I nodded.

"She wanted me to have her place. Because she knew I cared for it the same way she did. That she'd be leaving it in good hands."

We sat in silence a few moments.

"What happened?" I asked. "I mean... was she ill? Or in bad health? I know she wasn't young, and I guess it's been a while since I've seen her, but she didn't look like she was dying."

"It was sudden," Yvonne said with a sniff into her napkin. "Sorry. I just can't believe she's gone, you know? Every day when I got to work she was there, and now the place is locked up and I can't even get inside. And when I went to the funeral, you shoulda seen the looks those two gave me. Like I didn't have the right to be there. Like working for Miz Beulah for a dozen years didn't give me the right to go to her funeral."

"I'm sure they were just grieving," I said soothingly.

Yvonne snorted. "Didn't look like it to me."

Perhaps not. I hadn't been there, so I couldn't say. "I didn't even know Beulah had family," I said.

"Nobody did," Yvonne answered. "In all the time I worked

for Miz Beulah, I didn't see the two of them even once. Nor Miz Beulah's brother, neither. They never came to see her, and she never mentioned they invited her to visit them. She was alone for all the holidays and everything. And as far as I know, they never set foot in the restaurant. I never saw'em."

She shook her head. "I really hope there's nothing wrong with Miz Beulah's will and that I get the place. Not just because she wanted me to have it, and I want it, but because I don't want them to get it."

I could certainly understand that. "Let me take a look at the will and we'll see."

We finished eating, and then Yvonne handed me a manila envelope she said contained the will and told me to go sit in the living room while she cleaned up after dinner.

I wandered into the living room and sank onto the sofa with a muffled groan. I had eaten way too much, and my feet hurt. Pretty soon I'd have to stop wearing heels altogether, and then where would I be?

They don't call it barefoot and pregnant for nothing, do they?

I pulled the will out of the envelope and started reading.

It was pretty straight forward. Beulah must have bought a kit to help her put it together.

I, Beulah Marie Odom, residing at 405 Hackberry Lane in Sweetwater, Maury County, Tennessee, declare this to be my last will and testament, and I hereby revoke any and all wills and codicils I have previously made.

So far, so good. That part was legal, anyway, and removed any questions of previous wills and testaments.

Beulah then went on to the division of her assets. Yvonne got the restaurant, on the condition that she kept calling it Beulah's Meat'n Three, and didn't change the name to Yvonne's. The house Beulah had lived in, on Hackberry Lane, was to be sold and the proceeds—after debts, funeral expenses, and taxes were paid—were to go to the Diabetes Foundation.

The will was duly signed and witnessed by two people. I didn't know either name, and when Yvonne wandered back into the living room, I asked her, "Who are the witnesses?"

She didn't even glance at the will. "Two of the regulars at the restaurant. They've been coming in every morning for decades."

"So when they say that Beulah was of sound mind, memory, and understanding when she made this will, they'd know what they were talking about."

"Oh, sure." Yvonne nodded. "They've known her longer than I've been alive, probably."

And again, excellent. "It looks fine to me," I said, folding it up and putting it back into the envelope. "It's properly put together. It has all the necessary verbiage and components. It's witnessed, and the witnesses agree that Beulah was of sound mind when she asked them to sign. I don't see any reason at all why it wouldn't hold up."

"They're saying I pressured her," Yvonne said, taking a seat on the other side of the table, her lower lip jutting.

"Did you?"

She sniffed. "Of course not. I had no idea she would consider leaving the place to me. She liked me, sure, but she had family. That—" she gestured to the manila envelope and the will inside, "is huge."

Yes, it was. Simply handing off an on-the-face-of-it successful, long-running business with a clientele that had been eating there for three decades... that wasn't hay. The place was probably worth a fortune, or at least a pretty tidy sum. No wonder the sister-in-law and niece were loath to see it go to Yvonne.

"So she never mentioned it to you? That she was going to leave the place to you, I mean."

Yvonne shook her head. "Not a word."

"When did you find out?"

"She had the will in her bedroom," Yvonne said. "In a drawer in the bedside table. Sheriff Satterfield showed it to me."

So Bob was involved in this. I'd have to ask him some questions, unless Mother provided the answers after dinner tonight. Hard to guess whether she'd ask the same questions I'd ask, or not.

"How did she die?"

"Heart attack," Yvonne said. "Or that's what the sheriff said. It happened overnight. When she didn't come in to open the restaurant in the morning, one of the cooks drove up to Columbia to see if something had happened to her. He saw her through the window and called 911, but she was already dead."

"Any sign of foul play?"

"Not that I know about," Yvonne said with a shrug. "She was old."

She was. But not that old. Although people do die of natural causes sometimes. Most of the time. I'd just seen more than my share of unnatural deaths, and that was probably why I was overly suspicious.

"Had she been ill?"

Yvonne shook her head. "She had diabetes, but she took insulin for it. And her blood pressure was high, but she took pills for that, too. I don't think anything else was wrong."

"Do you know why she felt it necessary to write a will? Most people don't." Fifty to seventy percent of people who die, die without one.

"I guess she wanted to make sure the business was taken care of," Yvonne said. "That place was her life. She probably just wanted to make sure she left it in good hands. Didn't mean she expected to die, or anything."

No, it didn't. Or maybe something had been wrong, something we didn't know about—something she hadn't wanted to share with Yvonne—and she'd thought it best to put her affairs in order, just in case. Maybe she'd been scheduled for heart surgery, or something like that.

The sheriff might know. Yvonne obviously didn't. And this wasn't what she'd asked me here for, anyway.

I put the envelope with the will on the coffee table. "Best as I can see, there's nothing wrong with it. Who's the lawyer they hired to represent them?"

"Some hotshot from Columbia," Yvonne said, with a curl of her lip. "I think he got his law degree online."

Possibly. Although he'd have had to pass the bar in order to practice. Not just anyone can hang out a shingle and say they're a lawyer.

"Do you have any idea when a judge is going to rule on this? Or anything else about it?"

Yvonne shook her head. "It's only been a couple of weeks since Beulah died. They hired the lawyer last week. I'm sure it takes longer than that."

It does. Probate can take anywhere from a couple of months to years. This should have been a fairly simple one—Beulah hadn't died intestate, but had written a will laying out how she wanted her assets distributed, and her estate was fairly small, considering. The will was beyond simple. The wrench in the works was the sister-in-law and niece contesting it. With that wrinkle in the mix, the timeline for this was anyone's guess. But it wouldn't be quick.

"That's what I figured," Yvonne nodded, when I said so. "Do you think I need a lawyer?"

I hesitated. "Probably not. Not right now. But it wouldn't hurt to talk to one, just in case you need one later. I'll give you my sister Catherine's number."

Yvonne's lips turned down.

"You could call Dix," I added, since I assumed he was the reason for the pout, "but he's staying pretty busy. He might not have time to take on something like this. Catherine doesn't practice much anymore, so she has the time, and she's a real bulldog."

Yvonne didn't look convinced.

"Besides," I added, "you'd get to see Dix when you went to the office to talk to her."

Yvonne brightened. "That's true."

"It's been less than a year since Sheila died, you know. He's not ready to get married again."

Yvonne chuckled. Ripely. "I don't wanna marry him, Savannah. Just have some fun. I told you, I don't wanna get involved with anyone right now."

She had. Although she had indicated her desire to stay away from losers. My brother isn't a loser.

However, while I wasn't sure Dix was ready for Yvonne's definition of fun—correction: I was pretty sure he wasn't—he was a big boy. He could tell her that himself.

I gave her Catherine's phone number and decided to let the chips fall where they may. None of my business.

Seven

Rafe didn't call that night. I hadn't expected him to—I knew he had his hands full—but I was still sad I didn't hear from him. And I was out cold when Mother came home from her date with the sheriff, whenever that was. All I know was, she was there in the kitchen when I stumbled in just after eight the next morning.

"Food."

"Goodness," Mother said, looking me up and down as I reached into the cabinet for a bowl. "Rough night, darling?"

"No worse than usual." I pulled a box of raisin bran out of the cabinet, dumped some in the bowl, poured milk over the top, and dug in. "I have to hurry. I'm picking up Darcy in thirty minutes."

"Then you might not want to hear what Bob told me about Beulah Odom," Mother said, sitting there at the island sipping her tea, with every hair in place.

I did. "I do. Just talk fast."

Mother arched her brows, but spoke. No faster than usual, though. "She lived in Columbia. One morning a couple of weeks ago, she didn't show up to open the restaurant at five so the cook could get started on the biscuits and grits. He tried to call her, but couldn't get a response. So he made his way to Columbia to see whether something was wrong."

"And found her dead from a heart attack," I nodded. "Yvonne told me."

Mother ignored me. "The gentleman called 911. Because it

happened in Columbia, the police there got the call instead of Bob."

Bob Satterfield is the Maury County sheriff. Columbia is a town in Maury County, but it has its own police force. I'd had to deal with them briefly a couple of months ago, during that murder spree at my ten-year high school reunion.

"Makes sense." I spooned up more raisins, bran, and milk.

"Bob wasn't involved, but he stopped by the crime scene, since it happened in his jurisdiction. He said she was lying on the floor next to the bed, as if she'd woken up in the middle of the night because she felt bad, but had died before she made it to the phone to call for help."

I nodded.

"The M.E. ruled it a natural death. Her heart stopped. Bob said there's no reason to think it was anything but old age and diabetes."

"Except for the will."

"Having a will is not suspicious," Mother said. "I have one."

"Who gets the house?" I slurped up the rest of the raisin bran.

Mother looked at me down the length of her nose. "That's an inappropriate question, darling."

Of course it was. I rose and put my bowl in the sink. "Don't leave it to me. It would freak Rafe out to have to live here."

"But you would appreciate the history of it," Mother said. "And unlike your brother and sister, you don't have a career."

I had a career. I just wasn't very successful at it. And what that had to do with the house, I had no idea. Maybe she was intimating that I couldn't afford to buy my own?

A moot point anyway, since Rafe had a house.

"Darcy and I are driving to Nashville," I said. "We're meeting Detective Grimaldi at police headquarters at ten. We're looking at adoption records until we're done, or until about twelve forty-five—whichever comes first. Then we're meeting

Alexandra Puckett for lunch. After that, we'll either drive back to Sweetwater or go back to the police station to finish up the records. We should be back sometime this afternoon or early evening. If something changes, I'll let you know."

Mother nodded. "Don't forget your bag."

"Bag?"

She gestured to it. A plastic bag from the drugstore with an empty Kit-Kat wrapper and a pregnancy test inside.

"Oh," I said, flushing.

"I don't mean to pry, darling. But if Darcy is pregnant, your brother and Jonathan need to know, so they can make arrangements."

I scooped up the bag. "She's not." Or not as far as I knew. If she were, she hadn't confided in me. "This is for someone else."

Mother looked unconvinced.

"Alexandra Puckett," I said.

Mother blinked. "But she's just a girl!"

"She's three years older than LaDonna Collier was when she got pregnant with Rafe." And since that wasn't likely to be a point in anyone's favor, I added, "And she's not sure. That's why she needs the test."

"You better take it to her, then. And hope it's negative."

There was no need to tell me that. I already did.

Darcy lived in what she said was a rental house in a little 1960s subdivision on the south side of Columbia. I passed Beulah's Meat'n Three on the way there, the small cinderblock building sitting dark and the dusty parking lot empty of cars. The orange and white sign in the window said *Closed*.

It really was a shame. Beulah's had been a fixture in Sweetwater for as long as I could remember. So had Beulah herself.

I could understand why Yvonne wanted the place, and not

just because of the value. She wasn't afraid of hard work. She had worked hard every day of her life, and she'd probably looked on Beulah's Meat'n Three as partly her own for twelve years now. Not because she expected to inherit it—I thought she had told me the truth about that—but because the place was her job, and most of her life. She had no family that I knew of—an only child from a single mother—and although she probably had friends, I bet most of her waking hours was spent at Beulah's. Beulah was her family.

It would be a damn shame if Beulah's sister-in-law and niece managed to take it away from her.

At this point in my ruminations, I arrived at a sign saying Stonehenge, and had to focus on making my way through the winding roads of Darcy's subdivision over to her house.

It was low-slung and not much bigger than Yvonne's little 1940s tract house. Red brick, with a tiny porch and a big picture window in the front. The front door was painted a cheerful blue. The grass was neatly trimmed, and a few yellow flowers were still clinging to life in pots on the front steps. The temperature was approaching ninety, and it wasn't even nine yet. By three o'clock, it would be a hundred, and the flowers would be dead.

Darcy must have been watching for me, because as soon as I pulled into the driveway, the blue door opened, and she stepped out.

Unlike yesterday, when she'd been dressed in a proper skirt and blouse, with high heels, today she was wearing Capri pants and sandals, with a yellow T-shirt. Very summery and light. The sunny color set off her short black hair, brown eyes, and tan skin.

"You look great," I told her when she slid into the car next to me. "I don't think I've ever seen you in anything this casual before."

She smiled. "I don't think your brother or brother-in-law would appreciate it if I showed up to work looking like this. It's too hot to make much of an effort today, though."

Yes, it was. Although I'd made the effort anyway. I always make the effort. I've had effort ingrained in me from an early age.

"I've been meaning to ask you something," I said, as I put the car in gear and headed out of Stonehenge, toward the Columbia Road and the interstate, and beyond it, Nashville.

"Go ahead." Darcy stowed her big shoulder bag on the floor between her feet and got comfortable.

"It's kind of personal. I don't mean to pry. I'm asking because I think it might be important. Or have some bearing on... something."

"I don't care," Darcy said. "I've already told you some pretty personal things about myself. And if I think it's none of your business, I'll tell you so."

OK, then.

"Tamara Grimaldi wondered whether you'd been dating anyone since you got here. Or whether anyone has been trying to date you."

Darcy looked at me.

"I swear I'm not just nosy," I said. "Grimaldi suggested that maybe some guy wanted to date you, so he made sure you knew about the job opening, so he could get you up here."

"That'd be a lot of trouble to go to for a date," Darcy said. "I guess we should be looking for someone without a lot of social graces."

Maybe so.

"I did wonder if maybe my ex had sent the clipping. Or his new girlfriend. Or old girlfriend."

I arched my brows, and she added, "He cheated on me, and left me for his mistress."

I nodded. "Been there, done that." Or rather, been there, experienced that. Bradley was the one who had done it. "My ex left me for his mistress, too."

"Bastards," Darcy said.

Yes, indeed. Although Bradley was in prison and Shelby was dealing with a newborn on her own, so I'd had my revenge.

"Did you ask him about it? Or her?"

"Not her," Darcy said. "We're not on speaking terms. I asked him, though. He laughed at me." She shrugged.

"Do you think he was lying?"

She hesitated. "Not sure. He might have done it, if he wanted me out of the way. Not that he'd care himself, but if the new girlfriend was cutting up about me still being around, or something. But he didn't act like he'd done anything."

I nodded. "And her?"

"I asked Lew if maybe she'd done it, that she wanted the reminder of me gone, in case she was afraid he'd go back to me, and he said she didn't have to worry about that. Pissed me off."

It would have pissed me off, too. There's nothing quite like having your husband telling you that his new wife couldn't care less about you being around since you're absolutely no threat to her newfound happiness, and he wouldn't go back to you in a million years and can't understand what he ever saw in you in the first place.

As Darcy had said, bastard.

Filing away the possibility that her ex or his new wife in Birmingham might have sent the clipping, I asked, "So have you gone out with anyone since you moved here? Been asked on any dates? Turned anyone down?"

Darcy opened her mouth, probably to tell me she hadn't, and then seemed to think better of it. "I was going to say no," she told me. "I'd just gotten divorced when I moved here. I wasn't interested in getting involved with anyone again. But there was this guy who came into the law firm—a client of your brother's—and he asked me out. I said no, but he asked again when he came back the next week. And then he called and asked."

"That's a little creepy."

"He seemed nice enough," Darcy said. "But I told him that I'd just gotten divorced and wasn't ready to be in another relationship again so soon. He backed right off."

It probably hadn't been him, then. Although I'd keep him in reserve. "Anyone else?"

"Not until recently," Darcy said. "One of Sheriff Satterfield's deputies asked me out in the spring. Cletus Johnson."

"No kidding?" Cletus had been married to Marquita Johnson, until she left him with a couple of kids and moved up to Nashville to act as a live-in nurse for Rafe's grandmother. A couple of months after that, Marquita had been killed. Cletus had blamed Rafe, of course, and with cause, as it turned out. Rafe hadn't killed her, nor wanted her dead, but the fact that he was who he was, had contributed to her death.

"Did you go?" I asked curiously.

"I didn't see the harm in it. He seemed like a nice enough guy. Widower. Cop. Upstanding citizen."

Well, yes. I guess he ticked all those boxes. And I didn't really have anything against the man, other than that he didn't like Rafe much. But then, it was hard to blame him for that.

"Are you going to see him again?"

Darcy arched her brows, and I made a face. "I know, I know. None of my business." It had nothing to do with what she'd asked my help for. "It couldn't have been him sending you the clipping anyway. Two-and-a-half years ago, he was happily married to Marquita."

Or married to her, at any rate. How happily, only Cletus would be able to tell us. Just because I had disliked her—and the feeling had been mutual—didn't mean her husband hadn't loved her. When she died, interspersed with the anger toward Rafe, Cletus had certainly seemed to grieve.

"I'm not sure," Darcy answered my question. "I liked him well enough. But in this case, I'm not sure he's ready to move on.

Like your brother, he lost his wife last fall. And like your brother, he has two small children." She shrugged. "We had a nice time. At least I did. But he hasn't asked me out again."

A pretty sure sign that he either wasn't interested or wasn't ready. And since it wasn't any of my business anyway, I abandoned the subject of Cletus Johnson. "Who was the other guy? The one who kept asking you out? How did he take it when you told him you didn't want to get involved with him?"

"Fairly well," Darcy said. "I think he understood that it wasn't him. I didn't want to be involved with anyone."

"Have you seen him since?"

She shrugged. "On and off. He came into the office once or twice more, and was polite but distant. And I think he's involved with someone else now. I saw him at the Café on the Square sometime this spring, with a woman."

"Good for him. But at the time, he might have sent you the clipping, if he knew about you. Name?"

She gave it to me. It wasn't a name I recognized. "I'll have to ask Dix about him. Does my brother know the two of you went out?"

In most businesses, personal involvement with the client is frowned upon.

Darcy pressed her lips together as she nodded. "The first time he asked me out, I told him I couldn't go out with a client. He just nodded and left. And the next time he came in, he asked Dix if it was OK for him to ask me out. Dix said I could go out with anyone I wanted."

"And you went out once, and you told him you weren't ready to get involved with anyone since your divorce was too fresh."

Darcy nodded. "He left me alone after that. I haven't talked to him for two years."

So if he had been responsible for getting Darcy here, he'd been remarkably willing to stop pursuing her once she was here.

"And that's it? You haven't gone out with anyone else? Nobody's been weirdly insistent on having a relationship with you?"

She shook her head. "It was probably Lew. Or his new squeeze. Or one of my friends in Birmingham, who just didn't want to admit it."

Maybe so. We'd probably never know, anyway, so there was no sense in spending any more time talking about it. I accelerated and zoomed up the interstate in the direction of Nashville.

We arrived at police headquarters on James Robertson Parkway with a few minutes to spare. By the time we'd parked and made our way into the building and through security, Grimaldi was waiting. "Good to see you again," she told Darcy.

I arched my brows.

"We talked a bit at your wedding," Darcy said.

Of course. They'd both been there. Grimaldi as my maid of honor, and Darcy as one of the guests. I remembered her sitting on a folding chair next to Audrey, my mother's best friend, in the tent on the lawn beside the mansion during the ceremony. They must have compared notes during the reception.

At any rate, they knew one another and I didn't need to perform the introductions.

"We really appreciate your doing this," I told Grimaldi as she led us down the hall toward the elevators. "We realize that this is a long shot, but we may as well try. Just in case we get lucky."

Grimaldi nodded. "It never hurts to try. I've got you set up in the small conference room on the second floor." The elevator doors parted, and she stepped inside. We followed. "My office is just down the hall," she added. I guess for Darcy's benefit, since I already knew that. "If I get a call, I'll have to leave, but otherwise I'll be nearby, if you need anything."

The doors closed, and we headed up.

"I've done this before," I said. "I'm sure we can manage."

Grimaldi didn't respond to that, just stood with her hands in the pockets of her suit and watched the number 1 above the door become a number 2. The elevator stopped again, and the doors opened. We exited into the hallway.

"We've arranged to meet Alexandra Puckett for lunch at one," I told Grimaldi as we stopped in front of the door to the conference room and she unlocked it. "You're welcome to join us if you haven't caught a case by then."

"I might do that." She pushed the door open and gestured us in. "You should have plenty to keep yourselves busy here until then."

Yes, indeed. The table was piled high with record boxes. Ten, twelve, twenty of them, on the table top and stacked on the floor.

My jaw dropped. "That's a lot."

"They've been in operation a lot of years," Grimaldi said, waving us in and closing the door behind us. "There's been a lot of babies born at St. Jerome's Hospital in the past three or four decades."

Yes, indeed.

She added, "Since you know roughly the time frame you're looking for, it shouldn't be too onerous, though. Most of the records are grouped by year, and chances are you'll only need to go through a year, year-and-a-half at the most. Start with Darcy's birthday—the one you know about—and go forward and back from there."

Right.

I took a deep breath, rolled up my metaphorical sleeves—I was wearing a sleeveless sundress—and headed for the table. Grimaldi headed for the door. She was almost there when she did a Colombo and turned around.

"Have you heard from your husband today?"

Oh, God. "No," I said, fumbling for my phone to look for call or text I knew hadn't come in. "Should I have?"

Who was I kidding? Of course I should have. He'd called before eight yesterday morning. Now it was after ten.

Grimaldi watched me turn pale. "Relax," she told me. "I don't know that anything's happened to him."

It wasn't enough to make me relax, but it did take a little of the weight off. "Are you sure?"

"Someone would have let you know. Mr. Craig is involved in this operation on the TBI's side. He'd know to call you."

Wendell Craig had been Rafe's handler back in the undercover days, and Rafe's supervisor at the TBI since he started working there legitimately. And yes, Wendell would know to call me if something happened to Rafe, and he would know how to get in touch with me, too. A little more of that weight lifted. "So what are you saying?"

"I had a call in to one of the guys in the gang unit," Grimaldi said. "They were coordinating with the TBI. He told me things didn't go according to plan last night."

Uh-oh. Visions of everything from a bloodbath to the meth lab next door to the duplex blowing up and taking Rafe with it, danced through my head.

"I thought maybe you knew something more," Grimaldi said.

I shook my head. "He hasn't been in touch yet today. I figured that meant there was a lot of cleanup to do after the operation."

And suddenly the concept of cleanup had more sinister connotations than before. I'd pictured administrative loose ends. Now I imagined body parts needing identifying and crime scenes having to be fumigated.

"I'm sure it's fine," Grimaldi said. "He'll call when he's ready."

I hoped so. I really did. And although my fingers were

itching to call him, to assure myself he was alive and in one piece, I dropped the phone back into my purse and went to work on the adoption records.

Eight

"Did you always live in Mobile?" I asked Darcy after Grimaldi had left the room. "Did you move around at all?"

"I don't remember moving," Darcy said. "Why?"

Chances were, her parents couldn't have passed her off as more than a month or two younger or older than she was at first. Babies change so much during their first year, that for them to show up with a six-month-old, trying to pass it off as a newborn, would have been practically impossible.

That was if they'd adopted her as a newborn, of course. David had barely been out of his mother's womb before he'd been whisked off and given to the Flannerys, but Marley's son Oliver had been several months old, and stolen out of the baby carriage on her back deck.

"There are pictures of me as a baby," Darcy said. "With my mother and father. They had me when I was very little. And the letter said they adopted me when I was a newborn."

Good. At least we could be sure they hadn't shaved a year or more off her age—or added it—somewhere along the line. That wouldn't have been possible if she'd grown up with the same neighbors and friends her whole life. And if her parents had told the truth about adopting her shortly after birth, we had our baseline of the day and month listed on Darcy's birth certificate.

Even with that, there were a lot of records. St. Jerome's Hospital had been a place for young pregnant women without many options to go, and a lot of them had. A staggering number of birth certificates listed no father for the baby, just the mother's name.

"Were all these babies adopted?" Darcy wanted to know after a few minutes of looking through the records.

I shook my head. "I doubt it. Some of the girls probably kept their babies. And I'm sure not all of them were single, either. I'm sure there were plenty of married women with husbands who came to St. Jerome's, as well."

"Here's a baby born on what my birth certificate says is my birthday."

I leaned closer. "A girl?"

"Obviously," Darcy said. "Or I wouldn't have mentioned it. Are you sure you don't want to call your husband and make sure he's OK?"

"I'm positive. He'll call when he's ready. Let me see."

She passed over the file, and I looked at it. "Hmm. Yes. Maybe."

One Laurissa Carter had given birth to a baby girl. According to the records, Laurissa had been only seventeen.

Like Alexandra Puckett, my mind supplied. I shushed it. Alexandra had options. She wouldn't end up somewhere like St. Jerome's because she didn't know what else to do.

"The police did investigate these cases. I wonder if they traced Laurissa's baby." If they had, it should be in the file.

I flipped over a few pages. Yes, there it was. Adopted by a couple in Chattanooga. The girl—woman, now—was thirty-four, and working in social services. Laurissa, meanwhile, had passed on. Drug overdose at twenty-four. No way to know whether losing her baby had contributed to that, or whether she'd given up the baby willingly, since she was already headed down that road and didn't want to be saddled with a kid.

"Not you," I told Darcy. "Keep looking."

We kept looking. And kept eliminating.

"Here's one," Darcy said. "Born two days before my birth

certificate date. No record of placement. No record of the mother after she left the hospital."

"Let me see." We put our heads together over the file.

The mother's name was Ora Sweet. Twenty-six years old. Thirty-four years ago, she'd lived on Water Street in Columbia.

I glanced at Darcy. "Do you know where Water Street is? Is there a Water Street in Columbia?"

She shrugged. "I haven't lived there that long."

I'd lived twenty minutes away for two thirds of my life. I'd gone to high school in Columbia. If anyone should know, it should be me.

"Most towns have a Water Street, right?" Even Sweetwater. And even if the only water in town is the tiny tributary of the Duck River that runs through the Bog—or Mallard Meadows now—where Old Jim Collier drowned the year Rafe was twelve.

Not that Columbia boasts a lot more water. Just a lot of tiny creeks that flow into the Duck.

"The combination of the last name Sweet with an address on Water Street is interesting," I said.

Darcy looked at it again. "I didn't think of that."

And it might not mean anything at all. But as Rafe had said, when pretending to be someone you're not, it's always easier to pick a name you'll remember to answer to. One similar to your own. And—if you have to think fast—it's easy come up with information close to your own. Like Sweet instead of your real last name, and Water Street instead of your real address.

If you lived in Sweetwater, anyway.

Was Ora her real name, or had she made that up, too?

The folder had very little information beyond the original birth certificate. The Metro Nashville police had contacted the Columbia Police back in December, and asked them to dig up what they could on Ora Sweet. There was a report in the file, signed by one Officer Lupe Vasquez, that there was no street number on Water Street matching the one Ora had given in the records, and no one currently on Water Street had any knowledge of the Sweet family, or of Ora.

"I know Lupe Vasquez," I said. "Sort of."

Darcy arched her brows, and I added, "There were a couple of murders at my high school reunion in May. She responded to the first 911 call." And had handled my vapors and nausea quite well, considering. "I liked her. And more importantly, she seemed competent. Maybe we can talk to her when we get back down there later."

"About what?" Darcy wanted to know.

"Not sure. But maybe there's something she noticed that isn't in the report."

We put Ora Sweet aside, and moved on to the next file. And the next. Thirty minutes later, another possible biological mother turned up, a single teenager, this one from right here in Nashville.

"Rhonda Fallon," I read. "Eighteen years old. Baby girl, seven pounds, four ounces, born three days after the date on your birth certificate. No father listed."

"There are more papers behind this one," Darcy pointed out, flicked them with her finger-nail. It was painted an elegant watermelon color, gorgeous with her almond skin.

I turned the original birth certificate over to peer at the next piece of paper.

"Looks like the police tracked her down last year, but she had no idea what happened to the baby." I turned over the police report. "Never mind. The police found her. Has her own family now, and lives in Paducah. Not you."

Darcy sighed. We went back to work.

In the end, we finished before lunch, and with just Ora Sweet as a possible birth mother for Darcy. Something about her just rang my bell. Her address, in Columbia; twenty minutes from Sweetwater. Her name, which sounded fake. And the fact that someone from Sweetwater had sent that clipping of a job opening to Darcy in Birmingham, and brought her to Sweetwater.

We had no proof, though. We didn't find a record of Darcy's adoption. There were no paperwork with her parents' names on it, or anyone else whose names Darcy recognized.

"I probably wasn't even born there," she grumbled, as she bundled files together and put them back into the boxes.

"Maybe not." I was using the copier in the corner to copy the few pieces of paper from Ora Sweet's folder. "We knew it was a long shot, coming here. But there is this one possibility we should follow up on."

"How?" Darcy wanted to know. "She obviously used a fake name. The Columbia Police tried to find the address and couldn't. There's no information about what happened to the baby. How are we going to follow up?"

"I'm not sure yet," I admitted, as my phone rang, "but I'll figure something out. I just have to give it a little bit of thought. Hello?"

The number was unfamiliar. The voice wasn't.

"The shit hit the fan in a very big way last night," my husband informed me. "I'm not gonna make it to lunch. Sorry."

"That's all right." I was quite used to this happening, actually. "Are you OK?"

"I'm fine. A couple of guys we were hoping to catch last night caught on that something was going on, and now they're in the wind."

"I'm sorry," I said, while over at the table, Darcy kept cleaning up.

"Me, too." He sounded tired, like he hadn't slept at all. "The good thing is, nobody got hurt."

That was a good thing.

"We caught some of'em before they were able to carry out

any of the shootings. But a couple of'em are still out there, and we gotta get'em off the streets before they come after one of us."

Oh, God. "Do you think they will?"

"Dunno," Rafe said. "Not sure if Jamal and me had anything to do with them catching on. They coulda just smelled it. If it wasn't something we did, we can just sit tight and wait for'em to get in touch. If it was something we did..."

Yes. There was no need for him to spell it out. If he and Jamal had somehow given the game away, they'd be next in line, probably.

"You have protection, don't you?" Knife, gun, surveillance...

"I can take care of myself, darlin'. I've dealt with bigger threats than a couple overgrown boys who think they're hot shit."

His voice was even, but with a cold edge that didn't bode well for said boys when he caught up with them.

"Can't argue with that," I said lightly. "Still, you're only human. And not indestructible."

"I'll be fine," Rafe said.

"How's the meth lab?"

"Still there. One of the vice cops from Metro was gonna move in this weekend, to keep an eye on next door when I leave. That might have to wait now."

I imagined it might. "How long do you expect it to take to find these guys?"

"Not long," Rafe said. "There are APBs out on all three of'em. We've rounded up a lot of their friends, so there's not many places for them to go. And I've got a feeling they're lying low today, but they'll show up when it's dark. I'm hoping, by tomorrow morning, they'll be off the streets."

"I guess this means I'll have to spend another day in Sweetwater."

"Sorry, darlin'."

"I'm not complaining," I said. "I have plenty to keep me

busy." Darcy's adoption, Yvonne's inheritance, Beulah's death. And in the next hour, Alexandra's possible pregnancy.

Maybe it was just as well that Rafe couldn't make it to lunch. "I'll tell Alexandra you said hi."

"You do that. I'll give you a call again when I can."

I told him I appreciated it, and hung up. To find that Darcy had completed the task of putting the files back into the boxes and stacking them neatly without my help.

"I'm sorry," I said. "I left you all the work."

"It's all right. You're doing me a favor, being here. And we may have gotten a lead." She glanced at the phone I was dropping back into my purse. "Is your husband OK?"

"Fine. Things didn't go according to plan last night. They're scrambling to catch up. I'll have to stay in Sweetwater another day or two." Just because Rafe thought the wayward gang members might turn up after dark tonight, didn't mean they would. And if they didn't, I'd have to stay longer.

"Let's go tell Grimaldi we're done," I added, and headed for the door. "If she hasn't been called out, she can come to lunch with us."

Darcy followed me out into the hallway and closed the door to the conference room behind us. I walked down the hall to Grimaldi's office.

The door was open and the room beyond was dark and deserted.

"Huh." I turned to Darcy. "She's gone. She could at least have told us she'd been called out."

"Maybe she had to leave quickly," Darcy said.

Maybe so. Although by the time they got to Grimaldi, the bodies were already dead. Not like time was of the essence anymore.

Then again, there might be evidence that was in danger of being lost, or something like that.

"I'll give her a call when we get outside," I said, "and let her know we've left and all the files are in the conference room."

Darcy nodded.

"I guess it'll be just the three of us for lunch."

Darcy fell into step beside me. "Your husband can't make it?"

I pushed the button to summon the elevator. "He has to work. Law enforcement never sleeps." At least not when there are bad guys on the loose, and there usually are.

I called Grimaldi from the car, as we made our way across the bridge from downtown into East Nashville. "You left."

"Somebody died," Grimaldi said.

"I'm sorry. I was just looking forward to lunch."

She unbent as far as to tell me, "Me, too. Have you heard from your husband yet?"

"As a matter of fact, I have." I slowed down for the light on the corner of Main Street and Fifth, and told Darcy out of the corner of my mouth, "I used to live in that building."

She looked at it.

"Second floor," I added, "where there's a green bike on the balcony."

Darcy nodded.

"He called just before we left the conference room," I told Grimaldi. "We put everything back into the boxes, but we had to leave them there, since we didn't know what else to do."

"That's fine. How's Mr. Collier?"

"Bruised but unbowed. Or actually, he's neither. Things did not go according to plan last night. They lost a couple of the people they were hoping to arrest. He's staying undercover for another day in case they turn up."

Grimaldi didn't say anything, and I added, "Why do you ask?"

"The DB looks like a gang member. Shot execution style through the back of the head sometime last night."

My own head got a little light, and her voice sounded far away when she added, "I thought he might be connected to your husband's operation."

Darcy nudged my arm and pointed to the light, now green. I took my foot off the brake, just as the car behind me sounded the alarm. I resisted the temptation to give him a sign in the back window. It would have been unladylike.

"He might be," I told Grimaldi. "It isn't Jamal, is it?"

"Of course not. I know what Jamal looks like. If it were someone you knew, I wouldn't have broken the news like that."

Good to know.

"Male black," Grimaldi said, "eighteen to twenty-two. Five feet, ten inches, approximately one-eighty. Dressed in a wife-beater shirt, saggy jeans, and with a bandanna in his pocket."

"You can try to call Rafe, but when he called me, it was from a different number. I'm not sure he's using his own phone." And I wasn't sure he'd answer. "You might be better off trying Wendell. Although if you do talk to Rafe, remember his name this week is Ry'mone."

"I have a call in to the gang unit," Grimaldi said. "I figure they'll be able to identify the gentleman. They keep a list of suspected gang members, and this one has the tattoos, so he's probably known to them."

"Let me know how it goes, will you? If there's any connection to Rafe?"

Grimaldi said she would. "How did it go with the hospital records?"

"We found one possibility," I said. "We're going to try to hunt it down this afternoon. But first we're having lunch."

The sign for the barbeque place was up the road on the right. Darcy pointed to it. I nodded.

"Enjoy," Grimaldi told me. "I'll be in touch."

I told her I appreciated it, and swung the car off the road into the parking lot.

Alexandra's bright Miata was nowhere to be seen, so we went inside. And because the barbeque place is run cafeteria style—you place your order at the counter and pay for it, and they bring it to you when it's ready—we found a table and settled in to wait.

"Your friend, the detective, caught a case?" Darcy asked, fiddling with the bottle of hot sauce and the salt and pepper.

I nodded. "Young black male, shot through the back of the head. She said he looked like a gang banger. That maybe he has something to do with the case Rafe's working on."

"That would be convenient."

I suppose it would be. One less gang member to hunt down. Although I knew that part of what Rafe had tried to accomplish, was to save lives, so he wasn't likely to be happy that this guy was dead.

I caught a flash of red out of the corner of my eye, and turned to watch as Alexandra Puckett's Miata zoomed into the lot, narrowly missing a planter full of wilted petunias, and rocketed into a parking space. The door opened and Alexandra bounced out.

If she was bothered by the idea that she might be pregnant, it didn't show. There was no dragging of feet here. And if she was battling morning sickness, it sure didn't show.

She'd always looked a couple of years older than she was, at least when she went to the effort, and she'd gone to the effort now. Her skirt was short, her wedge sandals were high, and she was wearing a low-cut top and enough makeup for two people. The skirt flounced around her thighs, and the black hair—streaked with blue—bounced around her face.

More than one man turned to watch her approach the door, and I wanted to get to my feet and yell, "Jail bait! Jail bait!"

But of course I didn't. It would have mortified Alexandra, and besides, I've been taught never to stand up in a crowded room and yell, unless there's a fire.

Instead, I just waited for her to look in our direction, and waved.

She lit up and headed our way.

"How old did you say she was?" Darcy asked me, *sotto voce*.

I didn't take my eyes off Alexandra, weaving her way between the tables toward us. "Seventeen."

"She's going to get herself in trouble one of these days."

Yes, indeed. And perhaps sooner rather than later. I reached into my purse and touched the plastic bag with the pregnancy test, just to make sure it was still there, before getting up to greet her.

"Wow!" She stopped on the other side of the table, her eyes on my stomach. "You're huge!"

I made a face. "Thank you ever so."

Alexandra giggled. "You know I didn't mean it that way. But you've really popped since the wedding."

Yes, I had. And I had to remind myself to be happy about it, that it would result in a healthy baby. If I didn't, I could really start to feel like the Hindenburg.

"This is Darcy," I said. "You probably saw each other at the wedding."

"Briefly," Darcy said and held out a hand. "Nice to see you again."

They shook.

"Let's order," I suggested, since I was starving, "and then we'll sit down and talk."

We did. Alexandra wanted chicken wings, Darcy barbeque, and I ordered fried catfish, since I'd eaten here with Rafe once and he'd fed me a piece of his, and it had been good. It came with cornbread and a couple of sides, and since one of them was banana pudding, I had that. Dairy is good for the baby. And a side of green beans, so I could feel virtuous.

Then we went back to the table, and I handed Alexandra the pharmacy bag. "Here you go."

"Thank you."

I expected her to put it in her own purse, but instead she started looking around for the bathroom.

"Don't you want to take it home?" I asked. Where she'd be more comfortable than a restaurant restroom. And have more privacy.

She gave me a 'duh' sort of look. "If I take it home, I'll have to worry about getting rid of it again. And my dad might see it. I don't think he goes through my trash, but you never know."

"Right." I hadn't thought of that. It's been a while since I was a teenager living at home. "Of course."

"I'll be right back." She pushed back her chair.

"We'll hold down the fort here," I said, and watched her walk toward the bathroom. Darcy arched her brows at me, and I added, "She thinks she might be pregnant."

"But she's just a kid!"

"Didn't you have a boyfriend when you were seventeen?"

"Yes," Darcy said. "But I didn't sleep with him."

"I didn't, either." Todd Satterfield and I had never had sex. It had come as quite a surprise to Rafe when I told him that. He, of course, had gotten around a lot more than I ever had. Sooner as well as more frequently. My first sexual experience had been with Bradley, and I'd been in college by then.

Rafe's... I'd never even asked. Wasn't sure I wanted to know the answer.

"I hope she's not," I added. "She still has a year of high school left. Her dad's paying a fortune for her to go to Harpeth Hall. Very exclusive girls' school."

Darcy nodded. "How do you think she got pregnant?"

The usual way, I'm sure. "She had a boyfriend when I met her last year. She's probably had a boyfriend or two since then, too. She probably has one now."

"You didn't ask?"

I shook my head. "None of my business."

"Will you tell her dad?"

"If she's pregnant?" She might want me there when she broke the news. She'd asked me to stay last year, while she explained to him that she'd lied about staying at a friend's house overnight and had gone to a party at her boyfriend's place instead. "I don't feel good about ratting her out, but I'll be there to help her through it, if she wants me to be."

"That's nice," Darcy said.

I shrugged. That's what friends are for, isn't it?

Nine

The food arrived before Alexandra. I don't know whether she was in there, psyching herself up to pee on the stick, or worried about what she'd find out, or whether it just took that long for the results to show up. Or maybe she had to wait for a stall, or finish crying over the results—one way or the other—before coming back out. Either way, the food got to the table before Alexandra did.

"Maybe you should go get her," Darcy said, with a worried glance over her shoulder. "She's been in there a long time."

She had. The food was in front of me, though, smelling great, and I was really hungry. "I'm sure she's fine," I said, eyeing my catfish. "If she's not out in five more minutes, I'll go look for her."

Her car was still in the lot, anyway, so she hadn't crept out the back door and left us.

The catfish was crispy and crunchy and delicious, and the tartar sauce the perfect accompaniment. I made myself eat the green beans because they're good for me, and I picked at the fried cornbread, even though it isn't my favorite. All the time, I was counting down the seconds until I could have a go at the banana pudding.

The restroom door opened before I got that far, and Alexandra came out. I watched as she walked across the floor, skirting the tables. She wasn't flouncing anymore. Hard to say whether that was a sign of something or not.

Her face gave nothing away when she sat down on the opposite side of the table. Rather than jumping down her throat with questions, I continued to wield knife and fork. "The food came while you were in the bathroom. You better eat before it gets cold."

Alexandra nodded and picked up her silverware. Whatever she'd discovered hadn't affected her appetite, anyway. She dug in with gusto.

Darcy didn't say anything—probably didn't feel it was her place—and I finished lunch and picked up my cup of banana pudding and my plastic spoon, and dipped one into the other and conveyed it to my mouth. *Mmmm*. My eyes almost crossed as the taste of bananas and whipped cream exploded on my tongue.

"Good?" Darcy asked with a grin.

I nodded. "Delicious. Did you get the banana pudding, too?"

She had, and agreed it was great, even if it did come in a plastic cup. While we were oohing and aahing and savoring every bite, Alexandra caught up, as well. She hadn't chosen pudding as one of her sides, but had a cup of cherry jell-o on her tray instead.

"So how did it go?" I asked finally, after I had scraped the plastic cup clean and talked myself out of licking it. Next time, maybe I'd just get two sides of banana pudding and forego the green beans. Bananas are fruit, right? That's almost as good for you as vegetables.

Alexandra rolled her eyes. "Just what I expected. I'm pregnant."

Shit. I mean... shoot.

"Are you sure?" I asked, and then made a face. Stupid question. Of course she was sure. She'd make sure she was sure and there was no room for doubt.

"I could show you the stick," Alexandra said, "but I left it in the trash can. But it definitely had two lines. Two very solid, pink lines. Does that mean it's a girl?"

I shook my head. "I don't think so. The baseline is pink either way, and if the baseline is pink, then I think both lines are pink. It doesn't have anything to do with the gender of the baby."

Alexandra nodded. We sat in silence a few moments.

"How do you feel?" I asked, and tried to make it sound supportive rather than nosy.

"How do you think I feel?" She did a typical teenage huff. "Scared. Stupid. In shock."

All perfectly natural. Last fall, when I'd found myself pregnant—after, literally, the first time Rafe and I had sex—I'd felt all those emotions, too. Worried about what my family would think. Worried about what Rafe would say. Scared that I'd have to be a single mother, because my baby's father hadn't signed on for fatherhood.

And I hadn't been seventeen and still in high school.

"The father," I said tentatively. "Is he your boyfriend? Or... um... just some guy you fell into bed with?"

It was Alexandra's turn to make a face. "Somewhere in between. We're not dating. Not really. He's a few years older than me."

My eyes narrowed. "How few? How much older is he?"

Alexandra squirmed. "He's twenty. Or maybe twenty-one."

Three or four years older than she. I'd been expecting worse. "That's not bad," I said. "Rafe's three years older than me. Three or four years isn't that much."

Alexandra nodded, and looked relieved. "Anyway, I'm still in high school. I think he likes me, but he thinks I'm too young."

Although not too young to sleep with.

I didn't say it, but Alexandra must have read my mind, or more likely, my expression. It probably wasn't hard. "He thought I was older. I look older. I didn't tell him, not until afterward."

And he'd backed off. Good for him.

"What will he want you to do?" Darcy asked, the first time she'd spoken during this conversation.

Alexandra shrugged jerkily. "Not sure."

"What do you want to do?"

"I don't know." She sounded close to tears. "I have a year of high school left. How can I have a baby just before final exams? How can I go to college with a baby?"

Neither Darcy nor I said anything. We—or at least I—had a hard time imagining it, too. But at the same time, I certainly didn't want to doom the girl to a life of menial labor just because she'd gotten herself knocked up as a teenager.

"Other girls manage," I told her. "There are lots of women who get pregnant in high school, who go on to live happy, successful lives. Look at David's mother."

"She gave David up for adoption!" Alexandra said.

He'd been taken away from her, actually, but there was no need to mention that. "You can't deny that she had a successful career, though. And I'm sure there are other women who had babies in high school who went on to live happy, successful lives while keeping their babies, too."

I could have mentioned Rafe's mother, although LaDonna Collier wasn't really a poster child for either happy or successful. She'd managed to raise a great son, though. Even if he'd probably partly raised himself. Or become who he was in spite of his mother and grandfather and not because of them.

"There are options other than to keep the baby," I said. "You could—you know—get rid of it..."

I had considered that when I first found myself pregnant with Rafe's baby and had no clue whether he'd be happy or the opposite, or whether he'd even care one way or the other. In the end, it hadn't been an option I personally could choose, but that didn't mean it shouldn't be open to Alexandra. Abortion wasn't illegal, and I didn't want the girl to have to keep a baby she didn't want. While life is sacred and all that, who in their right mind would insist that a girl who didn't want to be a mother needed to become one anyway? In custody proceedings, the judge is supposed to make the decision that's best for the child. It should be the same thing in this case. And surely it wouldn't be best for the child to insist that he or she should be born to someone who didn't want him.

"And there's adoption," I said, without looking at Darcy. "David was adopted. He has wonderful parents who couldn't love him any more if he carried their DNA. They couldn't have a child of their own, and David was a gift. If you don't want a baby, you can give a gift to someone who does."

Alexandra bit her lip and nodded. She looked beyond overwhelmed and well into shell-shocked.

I took pity on her. "You don't have to decide now. You have some time to think about it. Get used to the idea of being pregnant first. Talk to the baby's father. Tell your own father, although maybe that can wait until you decide what you want to do. And you'll need to see a doctor. I can give you the name of mine, if you want."

"That'd be great," Alexandra said weakly.

I asked for her phone, and programmed the number in. While I was doing that, Alexandra turned to Darcy. "I'm sorry I'm not better company."

"It's OK," Darcy told her. "I was adopted. My mother might have been a girl like you. It actually helps to see what you're dealing with. It helps me to understand what she might have been going through." And although she didn't specifically say so, it probably also helped her to understand why her mother had given her up, and that it wasn't necessarily just because Darcy wasn't wanted.

Alexandra smiled, a little watery. "Thanks." She dropped the phone I handed over back into her bag. "Thanks, Savannah. I think I'm going to go home and think about this. Can I call you if I need someone to talk to?"

"Sure," I said, with a glance at Darcy. "I think Darcy and I are just headed back to Sweetwater now. Unless there's something you'd like to do while we're in Nashville?"

She shook her head.

"We're stopping in Columbia on the way back," I told Alexandra, since I'd already decided to do that, "but I should be back in Sweetwater by five. You can call me anytime after that."

Alexandra said she might, and took herself off. Darcy and I did the same.

The house on Potsdam Street is only a few minutes from the barbeque place, so I asked Darcy if she minded if we swung by, just to make sure everything was OK. The neighborhood isn't the greatest, as I told her, and it was always possible that someone had taken advantage of Rafe's and my absence to break in.

Not that I really thought anyone had: it was more that while we were there anyway, I could throw a couple more outfits into a bag and take them with me, since I'd have to stay in Sweetwater longer than expected. That way, I wouldn't have to keep wearing the same pairs of panties every day.

Darcy said she didn't mind, so off we went, down Main Street, up Dickerson Road, past the buffalo statues, right on Dresden, left on Potsdam at the Milton House old folks' home, where Mrs. Jenkins had been staying last year, and up the street toward home.

It was Darcy's first time here, and she kept looking left and right, her face registering an expression somewhere between horror and fascination. "Is it safe?"

"Not as safe as where you live. But it's safe enough."

A lady of the night, plying her trade in broad daylight, swayed her way down the opposite sidewalk, while a gaudy

Plymouth with a bunch of teenage boys hanging out of the windows cruised slowly by in the other lane, cat-calling. Darcy eyed her. "Is that...?"

"Looks that way. Although it could just be a woman with bad fashion sense." I shook my head. "The trouble we've had since we moved here hasn't come from the neighborhood. The neighbors pretty much all know Rafe and know that he works for the TBI. The law-abiding ones appreciate the presence of law enforcement, and the ones that don't keep a wide berth."

Darcy nodded.

"That's the house, up there." I pointed to it. Three stories tall, red brick, with a round tower on the corner.

Darcy's eyes widened. "Wow."

"Isn't it great? Mrs. Jenkins, Rafe's grandmother, owns it, but she's in a nursing home now. Rafe put her there to keep her safe last fall, after Marquita Johnson died—Cletus's wife; she was Mrs. Jenkins's nurse—and then Mrs. J seemed to settle in, and we decided we might as well keep her with people who understood her condition and could work with her."

Darcy looked politely inquiring, and I added, "She has dementia. Half the time she thinks Rafe is her son Tyrell, and I'm LaDonna Collier. It got even worse when we brought David into the mix. Anyway, she isn't safe staying at home anymore. We can't stay with her twenty-four/seven, and if we don't, she wanders off and gets lost. She's better off where she is. They're working with her, and she has company and things to do."

Darcy nodded. "It's a beautiful house."

Yes, it was. "You should have seen it the first time I came here." I turned into the circular driveway and heard the gravel crunch under my tires, the same way it had done back then. "The porch was sagging, the roof was caving in, and the weeds were up to my knees. Rafe did a great job of bringing it back to life."

Also, he looked very nice mowing the lawn, muscles moving smoothly and skin glistening with sweat.

Not that I wanted to put that particular image in Darcy's head, so I didn't say anything about it. Instead, I pulled the car to a stop at the bottom of the stairs, and cut the engine. "Let's go inside."

I reached for the door handle.

"Wait." Darcy put out a hand to stop me.

"What?" But I waited.

She was looking at the house. "I saw the curtains move."

"What?" I leaned over, until I was almost in her lap, and peered out the passenger side window. Nothing moved now. "Are you sure?"

"Positive," Darcy said, her voice tight. "Someone's inside."

"Nobody's supposed to be inside." I thought for a second. "Maybe Rafe's back."

Although why would he be back here, if he were hoping that the missing gang bangers would show up at the duplex?

Granted, he had told me he expected them to lie low until dark, but still, it didn't make sense that he'd leave. It especially didn't make sense that he'd come here.

"Go!" Darcy said, the edge in her voice so shrill it was almost a shriek.

I glanced past her in time to see the door start to move.

"Shit! I mean..."

Never mind. Nobody was here but Darcy, and I didn't think she'd begrudge me the curse.

"Hurry!" she told me.

I was doing the best I could. I had taken the key out of the ignition when we stopped, and now my hand fumbled getting it back in. But after what felt like an eternity—but which was probably just a few seconds—I managed, and yanked on the gearshift. The car bulleted down the driveway, spitting up gravel. I looked in the rearview mirror, in time to see a figure come out of the door. Dark skin, oversized T-shirt, baggy jeans hanging low on skinny hips.

And a gun in his hand.

He lifted it and sighted down the barrel, and I braced for impact. But he must have decided to save the lead, or maybe he figured we were too far away and moving too fast to make a good target.

The next second we took the turn onto Potsdam on two wheels and screamed down the road. My heart was beating double-time in my chest, and Darcy was hyper-ventilating next to me. "Go!" she kept telling me. "Go!"

I wanted to tell her I was going as fast as I could, but there didn't seem to be much point in it. And anyway, I couldn't get my voice to cooperate.

The words '*get away*' ran like a refrain through my head. *Get away. Get away.*

So we got away, as quickly as I could get us there. But while my body was shaking like a leaf and my breath sawed in and out of my lungs, I did manage to keep an eye on the rearview mirror. I didn't fancy being in a car chase, and if they came after us, I wasn't looking forward to what would happen.

By the time we reached the light at Dresden, I had lost sight of the driveway. In the time I had been watching, nobody had come out of it. The light was red, and after a quick back-and-forth look—nobody was coming—I tore across the intersection and into the parking lot outside the Milton House. There, I screeched into a parking space between two bigger cars, where hopefully we would be out of sight while I recovered, but where we could see the end of Potsdam Street. If anyone came after us, we'd see them.

"Keep an eye on the road," I told Darcy, who was clutching the handle on her side of the car so hard her knuckles were white. "I have to make a call."

She nodded, although I'm not a hundred percent sure she understood what I'd said. Her eyes were huge, staring straight ahead, but I'm not sure she actually saw anything beyond the fear.

It couldn't be helped. I dug the phone out of my purse with shaking hands, and managed to turn it on. Punching in the numbers took a bit longer, but finally I managed. The phone rang once, twice, then—

"Darlin'? This ain't a great time."

"There's someone in our house," I said.

He was all business immediately. And didn't ask me to repeat it, either. It's nice to be married to someone who doesn't make you reiterate the obvious. "Who?"

"Black guy. Early twenties. Jeans, T-shirt, bandanna. Gun."

I could feel the chill through the phone when he heard that last word. "Did he shoot at you?"

I shook my head, and then realized he couldn't see me. "No. He lifted the gun, but by then we were all the way down the driveway."

"Color?"

"I told you," I said. "He was black. Or brown. More like coffee without a lot of cream. Darker than you, but—"

"Not the guy. The bandanna."

"Oh." I told him the color of the bandanna. "Is he one of the guys you're looking for?"

"Sounds like. Where are you?"

I told him we were down the street at the Milton House. "Sitting in the parking lot. Watching the cars."

Almost like a song lyric.

"Did they follow you from the house?"

"I don't think so," I said. My teeth were chattering less now, and Darcy's grip on the handle had loosened. Her knuckles were no longer white, although she was still hanging on. "We're watching, and we haven't seen anyone."

"Stay where you are. Don't go back."

I told him, with all the sincerity I could muster, that I wouldn't dream of it.

"Or better yet, go home."

"Not sure I want to do that," I said. "Just in case I'm wrong and they did follow us. I don't want them to tag along to Sweetwater. One nutcase this summer was enough."

He didn't say anything to that. There wasn't a lot to say. "Don't move from where you are, then."

"Are you coming?"

He sighed. "I might as well. If they're there, it's 'cause they know who I am and where I live."

They knew the house would be empty because they knew Rafe was somewhere else.

"I'm on my way. And I'm bringing a SWAT team."

"That should be fun," I said, and hung up.

And just sat for a moment with my hands in my lap trying to get my adrenaline under control. We were safe now. No one had followed us. Rafe was coming, and he was bringing reinforcements.

"What did he say?" Darcy asked. She had given up her death grip on the door handle, and was massaging her fingers. They were probably stiff from hanging on so tightly.

"He's coming. And bringing a SWAT-team."

Her eyes widened. "You're kidding."

"I wish I were. But no. Apparently these guys are dangerous."

"I could tell that when he tried to shoot at us," Darcy said.

"It should be quite a show, though. When I see the SWAT car go by, I'm going to follow it."

"Maybe it won't go by," Darcy said.

Well, no. Maybe it wouldn't. If it came from downtown, it would. Dickerson to Dresden was the quickest way from downtown to Potsdam Street. But if the East Police Precinct had a SWAT vehicle, it would come from the north. They were located on the opposite side of the house from where we were sitting.

"Maybe we should go back there and hang out in a driveway across the street. That way we won't miss anything."

"I don't think we should go back there," Darcy said as I put the car into gear. "Didn't your husband say not to go back there?"

He had. But— "They're probably not even there anymore. They knew we saw them. Unless they're stupid, they'll have left by now."

"Then why is your husband sending a SWAT team?" Darcy wanted to know. She was fumbling for the door handle again, and we were barely even moving. Maybe she was thinking of opening the door and throwing herself out so she didn't have to go back to the house. "I don't think this is a good idea, Savannah. I mean, of course they're stupid. They're criminals, right?"

"We're just going to sit across the street," I said. "It's my house. I want to watch." I glanced at her. "Wouldn't you want to watch, if it were your house?"

"Not if there was a chance I was going to get shot," Darcy said as I maneuvered the car slowly out of the parking lot and onto the street.

"They're not going to shoot us."

"They tried!"

"He didn't actually fire." At least I hadn't heard any shots, and they're hard to miss. "If he wanted to shoot us, he would have done it then. And we won't go anywhere near the house. I promise. There's a driveway just up the street, that has a perfect view of our house." The deranged serial killer who had kidnapped and tortured Rafe back in June, had parked there to keep us under surveillance. "The house is being renovated, so nobody lives there. And they're probably not working today." Seeing as it was the weekend.

Darcy sighed, but didn't protest. I waited for a low-slung, black Dodge to take a left onto Dresden, and then turned the Volvo onto Potsdam.

As it turned out, we were just in time. No sooner had we backed into the driveway across the street—where no one was working today—than the SWAT vehicle came lumbering down the street from the north. While it stopped just shy of our property, and a half dozen armored and armed men in black with the letters *SWAT* emblazoned across their backs tumbled out, I kept my attention on the house.

"I don't see anything."

"They're not going to be standing on the porch," Darcy said, a bit waspishly. I guess she really didn't want to be here, even though we now had the protection of a six-man SWAT team.

"I'm sure they're gone. If they have any sense at all, they're gone."

We watched as the SWAT cops swarmed over the low stone wall at the bottom of the yard and made their way toward the house, zig-zagging from tree to tree. Maybe they'd noticed something I hadn't, or maybe they were just being careful.

"Your husband isn't here," Darcy said, "is he?"

I shook my head. "I don't think he would have had time to get here from South Nashville. He drives like a bat out of hell, but there are limits to how fast he can go. And he wouldn't tell the SWAT team to wait for him. He'd know that their best chance to get these guys is to get here quickly."

Darcy nodded. "I guess they have another team in the back, right? So the bad guys can't go out that way?"

I was sure they did. I didn't know how often the Nashville police had occasion to dispatch a SWAT team, but it was frequently enough that they had one on standby.

The group in the front reached the house and swarmed up on the porch like an army of ants, high-powered rifles clutched in their hands. We watched as they peered through the windows into the house.

"Oh, shit," I said. "I mean... oh, no."

Darcy glanced at me. "What's wrong?"

"I hope they won't have to break down the door. It's original to the house. Almost a hundred and fifty years old. Maybe I should have offered them a key."

I reached for the door handle.

Darcy grabbed me. "Don't you dare! The door can be fixed. You can't."

She sounded like Rafe.

"I was just going over to the SWAT car," I said. "There's probably a driver left in it. I was going to offer him the key. They're all wearing earbuds, I'm sure."

Darcy shook her head. "Just stay here."

Fine. I settled in to wait, and then jumped high enough in my seat that the top of my head connected with the ceiling when a figure suddenly materialized next to the car.

Ten

A few seconds passed before I managed to swallow my heart and make sure I hadn't lost control of my bladder. By then, Rafe was scowling and making imperial gestures about opening the window.

I rolled it down. "You scared me."

"Good," my husband said ruthlessly. "You're not supposed to be here. I told you to stay at the Milton House."

"We wanted to see what was going on."

I glanced at Darcy, tacitly trying to communicate to him that this was really her fault; she was the one who had wanted to come back.

She shook her head. "Don't blame me for this. I wanted to go home."

Rafe arched a brow.

"Fine," I said. "I wanted to see what was going on. Not Darcy. Me."

Rafe didn't answer. He knows the value of silence. Makes the suspect—or in this case his wife—babble.

"We figured he'd have left by now anyway," I said. "He knew we'd seen him. He knew we'd seen the gun. He had to figure we'd call the police as soon as we were away from the house. He'd have to be an idiot to stick around."

Rafe nodded sagely. "And you parked in this driveway because...?"

"Nobody lives here," I said. "The house is empty. I knew nobody would bother us."

"Uh-huh. Did it cross your mind that this big, empty house might be a good place for a couple gang bangers on the run to hide, while they watched SWAT search the house they'd been in until five minutes ago?"

Oh... snap.

"No," I admitted, with a wary glance over my shoulder at the empty house behind us. "I didn't think of that."

Darcy turned to look, too, her expression fearful.

"Uh-huh," Rafe said again, dryly.

"Are they there?"

He shrugged. "I don't imagine so. Like you said, they'd be stupid to hang around."

"Then why did you say they might be? Just to scare us?"

"You could do with a good scare, darlin'."

"I've already had one today," I told him.

His face darkened. "You all right?"

"Fine." I glanced at Darcy. "He didn't actually shoot at us. Just looked like he thought about it. And maybe thought better of it."

I looked back at the house. The SWAT ants were gone from the porch and the door stood open. Hopefully no one had destroyed it. "They're inside."

Rafe nodded. "If anybody's left inside, we should start hearing shooting soon."

Great. "I hope they don't destroy our stuff."

"I wouldn't count on it," Rafe told me, and straightened. "'Scuse me, darlin'. I better go introduce myself to the SWAT commander."

He sauntered off across the street, pants hanging low on his butt. Darcy breathed out. I hadn't realized she was holding her breath.

"Does he scare you?" I asked curiously.

She glanced at me. "Doesn't he scare you?"

"Not anymore. Now that I know him, I know he's mostly all bark."

Not true at all, actually. He was plenty dangerous when he wanted to be. He just wasn't dangerous to me. And never had been, although I hadn't realized it at first.

We watched as he stopped and talked to the man inside the SWAT vehicle. He was still standing there, leaning on the window, when one of the SWAT team came out onto the porch and gestured.

I knew he wasn't gesturing to me, but I got out of the car anyway.

Rafe shot me a look over his shoulder and raised his voice. "Don't even think about it, darlin'."

"It's my house! I live here!"

"And now you're gonna stay in your car till I tell you it's safe."

"But it must be empty. Otherwise, he wouldn't be standing there waving."

"No," Rafe said, patience obviously wearing thin. "Sit." He pointed to the Volvo.

"I'm not a dog," I told him, but I opened the car door again anyway. "Can I at least move across the street and up the driveway?"

Rafe rolled his eyes. "Fine. Just don't run over anybody."

I managed to avoid doing that as I maneuvered the Volvo up the same gravel driveway we'd careened down just thirty minutes ago. And then I parked where we'd stood earlier, and waited for approval to go inside the house.

Rafe and the SWAT commander hoofed it up the driveway. "Just stay here until I come and tell you it's safe," Rafe told me on his way past. "Keep the windows up."

And the air conditioning going. "No problem," I told him.

They disappeared up the stairs and inside.

We sat in silence a few seconds.

"What do you think happened?" Darcy wanted to know.

I made a face. "They probably destroyed something. Shot out the TV screen, punched holes in the walls, plugged up the tub and let the water run. Rafe probably wants to look at the damage before he lets me in."

Darcy nodded.

We sat in silence another minute, as the SWAT team started filing out and back to their vehicle to get rid of the heavy armor.

"Does this happen a lot?" Darcy wanted to know.

I thought about it. "Not a lot. We had people break into the house last month. And the month before that, there was the crazy serial killer who was after Rafe. He left a dead prostitute on the bed. But before that, there were several months when nobody but us was inside."

Darcy stared at me. Her mouth was open, but no words came out.

"No," I said. "It doesn't happen much at all."

Darcy snapped her mouth shut. "That's good."

It was. I hated that it had happened now, but hopefully the gang bangers hadn't done too much damage.

The SWAT team went in and out for five or ten minutes, and then Rafe came back outside and down the stairs. He stopped next to the car. I rolled down my window. "How bad is it?"

He shook his head. "Not good."

"Can I go inside and see?"

He nodded, his face set to grim as he reached for the handle. "You, too," he told Darcy, "if you don't mind."

"I don't mind at all." She opened her door and swung her legs out, as I turned off the car and the lovely, cool air conditioning. "I don't want to sit out here by myself."

Hard to blame her for that, even with half a dozen SWAT

cops in the yard.

So we walked up the steps and across the boards of the porch together. No sooner had we crossed the threshold into the house, than my nose wrinkled involuntarily. My steps hitched.

"Oh, no."

Rafe's hand was under my elbow, steadying me. "Afraid so."

"What?" Darcy asked, looked from him to me and back.

"Can't you smell it?"

She scented the air, and her nose wrinkled, too. "It smells like sewage. They didn't ruin your pipes, did they?"

Not quite. The smell wasn't that strong. Thank God. And what there was of it, was mixed with the metallic tang of blood.

The body was slumped over the kitchen table, where two bottles of beer, both empty, were standing next to a bowl of chips and a smaller one of salsa. He had been shot through the back of the head. It was a mess, and his face—what was left of it—was worse.

I felt my knees turn to water. Rafe held me up. Until Darcy took one look at the corpse and crumpled into a dead faint.

"I'm OK," I said weakly, grabbing hold of the back of another kitchen chair for support. "Get her out of here."

"You sure?" He gave me a measuring look. And I must have passed muster, because he bent and scooped Darcy up. I could hear his steps retreat with her. A minute later he came back. "I put her on the sofa in the parlor."

"That'll work."

"I'll take you there in a minute. But first I gotta know... is this the guy you saw?"

I forced myself to look at the body. He wasn't pretty. The bullet had gone into the back of his head, and taken a chunk of his face with it when it exited. Lots of blood and other stuff on the table—and I'm not talking about the beer bottles. It was hard to concentrate, and honestly, hard to get a good idea of what his face had looked like. But—

"I don't think so. I only got a glimpse of him, you know. I mean, he was out on the porch for maybe twenty seconds, between the time when we first saw him and when we turned onto the road. But I wasn't looking at him other than the first second, and the last. I was busy driving. I think, though, that his shirt's a different color. And maybe his skin's a little lighter."

Rafe nodded. "Good enough. So this is someone else."

"As far as I can tell," I said, and looked around. "You've checked the house, right?" This guy's comrade wasn't lying in wait anywhere, ready to jump out?

"It's empty. The SWAT team cleared it. And I went through, as well."

Good to know. "So the last guy made it out of here."

Rafe turned to look at me. "Whaddaya mean, the last guy?"

"Didn't Grimaldi call you?"

He shook his head.

"She caught a case. Dead gang banger. Same color bandanna as this one. She surmised it might be one of your missing guys."

"Shit," Rafe said.

"I don't know for sure. You'll have to talk to her. But it seems like maybe one of them was killed last night. Disagreement over what to do next, maybe. And then this one was killed sometime today."

"Sometime in the last thirty minutes," Rafe said. "The body ain't cold yet."

He might have been alive when Darcy and I pulled up outside. I don't know why that should make a difference to me, since we'd had no idea he was here and there was nothing we could have done to stop him being shot anyway—and besides, he was a gang member and most likely a killer himself, too—but somehow it hit home. He'd been alive, and now he wasn't.

I wobbled.

"C'mere." Rafe scooped me up. "I'll take you in to Darcy."

"Thank you." I looped my arms around his neck and held on. "I'm sorry. It's just... a lot. You know?"

"Sure." He brushed his lips over my cheek. It wasn't quite a kiss, but close enough for jazz. And then we were in the parlor, and he put me down, carefully, on a chair opposite the sofa where Darcy lay.

She was still out cold. I lowered my voice. "Are you going to make her look at him again?"

Rafe squatted next to my chair, and managed to shrug at the same time. "Second opinion. She mighta seen him better than you. She wasn't driving."

And had been closer to the porch than I'd been. I nodded. "She isn't likely to pass out twice, I guess."

"Prob'ly not," Rafe agreed.

"We found a birth record in the St. Jerome files that might be her mother."

He looked skeptical, and I added, "I know. We don't even know that she was born there. She could have been born in any number of other hospitals, or for that matter at home in bed."

He squinted at me. "You ain't gonna wanna give birth at home in bed, are you?"

"Have you lost your mind?" I said. "I know some people want to have natural childbirths in the sanctity of their own homes, etc, etc, but no thank you. Give me drugs, and give me a nice, sanitary hospital with doctors and nurses, and equipment if anything goes wrong. A baby isn't something I want to take chances with."

"Good to know. So you found a record that might could be Darcy?"

I kept an eye on her face as I told him about it. Her eyes weren't open yet, but some of her color was coming back. "The timing works. Just a few days, give or take, from the birth date on Darcy's amended birth certificate. And when Officer Vasquez in Columbia went to Water Street to look for Ora Sweet, the neighbors said there'd never been a Sweet family living there. The house number didn't even exist."

He nodded.

"So I thought about what you told me, about picking information that's close to your own, to make it easy to remember. And I wondered..."

"If she was from Sweetwater," Rafe said.

"Exactly." I beamed. "If you thought of it, too, that means it makes sense, right?"

"Sure. That don't mean it's true, but it's worth looking into."

I nodded. "That's what I thought. So we were planning to stop by Columbia on our way back to Sweetwater. See if there was anything Vasquez thought of, that she didn't put in the report. Just to cover all the bases. You remember her, don't you?"

"From back in May? Sure."

"She seemed competent, didn't she?"

"For a girl cop," Rafe said with a grin.

I was going to chastise him—as he clearly deserved—but then I realized I didn't have to. Grimaldi stood in the doorway, hands on her hips. "I heard that."

"I thought you would." He got smoothly to his feet before gesturing to Darcy. "We got one out cold. Passed out when she saw the body."

"Ugly?"

He shrugged. "I've seen worse. He was shot in the back of the head. Exit wound's messy."

Grimaldi nodded. "You look like hell."

I had my mouth open to tell her thank you very much, that I was six months pregnant, it was a hundred degrees outside, and I'd just seen a dead body, when I realized she wasn't talking to me.

"Thank you very much," Rafe said dryly. "Savannah ain't a fan, either."

"I can see why." She nodded to me. "You all right?"

"I will be. It's hot and I'm uncomfortable. And Rafe's right. The exit wound's messy."

"I'll go take a look." She headed off down the hallway.

"Better go with her," I told Rafe. Just in case she fainted, too. Not that I thought there was any chance she would.

"You gonna be OK here by yourself?"

I wasn't by myself. I had Darcy across from me, and him and Grimaldi twenty feet away. The SWAT team was still combing the yard. I could see them through the window. They had stripped down to short-sleeved black T-shirts, and there were a lot of very nice muscles on display. Not as nice as when Rafe mows the lawn, of course, but enough to keep me occupied.

"I'll be fine," I said. "I'll scream if anything happens."

He nodded and followed Grimaldi down the hall. I sat back, divided my attention between Darcy and the SWAT team outside, and listened to Rafe and Grimaldi talking in the kitchen.

At first it was just a technical discussion about the body. The caliber of weapon used—a 9 millimeter semi-automatic versus maybe a .38 or .45—and also where the shooter must have been standing when he made the shot. (Right behind the guy with the barrel almost touching the back of his head; notice the abrasion collar and tattooing.)

He must have come in from seeing Darcy and me drive off, they surmised, and his buddy was still sitting at the table eating chips and drinking beer. The shooter walked behind him, aimed, and pulled the trigger before beer-and-chips dude even knew what was happening.

They didn't call him beer-and-chips dude, though.

"Robert Lewis," Rafe said, giving the young man's name the French pronunciation.

"How d'you spell that?"

"His mama spelled it Ro'bear," Rafe said. "Like the animal."

There was a beat. "OK," Grimaldi said, and I'm sure she had

her little notebook out and was writing it down. "Ro'bear Lewis. Was he one of the gang members you lost yesterday?"

"We didn't lose'em," Rafe told her, and sounded a bit irritated that he had to. "Just misplaced'em for a while."

"Sure. Well, you've found this one again."

"No offense," Rafe told her, "but I'd rather not have found him like this, here."

I would rather not have, either.

Over on the sofa, Darcy started to stir. First her eyelashes shivered, and her lips pursed. Then her eyes opened. They were unfocused at first, but after a few seconds she started looking around.

Meanwhile, the conversation in the kitchen went on to the other case Grimaldi had caught this morning, and how the victim in that one also looked like a gang banger.

"You shoulda called me," Rafe told her.

"I've been a little busy. And I'm telling you now."

He acknowledged that with something like a grunt. "You gotta picture?"

Grimaldi said she did. And must have pulled out her phone to show him. I took the opportunity to greet Darcy. "How are you feeling?"

"Weird." She pushed herself up on one elbow and swung her feet over the edge, pushing the ends of her short bangs away from her face. "I can't believe I fainted."

"Take it slow," I said. "Put your head between your knees if you feel faint again."

She was still pale. Not as sickly white as she'd been at first, but there was a long way from a rosy glow in her cheeks.

"Have you ever done this?"

"A year ago," I said, "right in this house. In the room across the hall. My colleague Brenda Puckett had been murdered—Alexandra's mother—and was lying in front of the fireplace with her throat cut. There was blood everywhere. Everything went really bright and light. Rafe had to pick me up and carry me outside." And then I really had fainted.

While I talked, Darcy pushed herself upright, and was leaning her head back against the sofa. In the kitchen, Rafe was identifying the body. The one in the picture. "Germaine Wilson."

"Another of the boys you lost last night?"

"I told you," Rafe said tightly, "we didn't lose'em. And they ain't lost now, are they?"

"Two of them aren't. What about the third?"

"We didn't lose him, neither. He ran. He's prob'ly still running."

Probably. Especially after shooting two of his comrades.

"At least we know who he is," Grimaldi said soothingly.

"We always knew who he was. Now he's alone. I dunno whether that'll make him easier to find, or harder."

"You caught a lot of his gang yesterday," Grimaldi pointed out. "With the way he keeps losing his remaining friends, he may not have many places to go."

"I sure didn't expect him to come here."

I hadn't either.

"We can put a guard here tonight," Grimaldi offered. "Make sure he doesn't come back."

"Don't worry about it. I'm staying the night."

"You could use some backup..."

"I'll get some," Rafe said. "I'll call Wendell and the boys. We'll sleep in shifts. Just in case he's stupid enough to come back."

"What about the duplex?"

"I'll let the guy from narcotics know it's all his. And to keep an eye out for our missing boy."

We heard their footsteps coming down the hall toward us. Darcy started breathing faster.

"Don't worry," I told her, and added, when Grimaldi and

then Rafe appeared in the doorway, "now that you've identified him, Darcy won't need to look at him again, will she?"

They both shook their heads. "We know who's still standing," Rafe said. "That's all we need."

"That and knowing where he is," Grimaldi added.

I shook my head. "We can't help you there. So we can go? I think Darcy would probably like to get home."

She nodded.

"If you're staying here tonight," I asked Rafe, "can I drop Darcy off and come back?"

He shook his head. "Hell, no. Not until we've caught him. Wasn't being shot at once today enough?"

Since that's what I had expected him to say, I wasn't even upset. A little disappointed, maybe. And a touch worried. "You'll make sure you're not alone, right? You'll get Wendell and the boys to stay with you?"

"I promise," Rafe said and held out a hand. "C'mon, darlin'. I'll walk you to the car."

On the other side of the table, Grimaldi gave Darcy an unobtrusive hand up, just to make sure she was steady on her feet, I guess.

Rafe stepped through the door first. I don't know if he was holding his breath, but I knew I was. It wasn't likely the missing gang banger would shoot at him in broad daylight when the yard was still crawling with SWAT cops, but stranger things have happened. It was pretty bizarre in and of itself that he was going around assassinating his former friends.

No shots were fired, though, but Rafe still kept me behind him when he walked down to the car, and he made sure to stand in front of me when he put me into the driver's seat, too.

"Don't think I don't see what you're doing," I told him.

"What?" He tried to look innocent. It's way beyond him. He didn't look innocent when he was David's age.

"If you do something stupid like stay here alone to try to flush this guy out, I'll kill you myself."

He grinned. "Don't worry. I may be dumb, but I ain't stupid. If it's just me and him, I'll prob'ly end up killing him, and I'd rather take him alive. I'll call Wendell and get some backup."

"Thank you." I shut the door and then rolled down the window to finish talking to him while Grimaldi got Darcy situated on the other side of the car. "I really don't want to wake up tomorrow and hear that something's happened to you."

"You won't." He leaned down.

I leaned out and gave him a kiss. Grimaldi closed the passenger side door.

"Drive carefully," Rafe told me, straightening.

"I will. You be careful, too."

He stepped back, and so did Grimaldi. I steered the car down the driveway, at a much slower pace than last time, swerving to avoid the SWAT team members still milling about. And then we were on the road, for the second time today, and on our way south on Potsdam Street.

"Do me a favor," I told Darcy. "Just keep an eye on the mirrors. If you see a car staying behind us for any length of time, let me know."

She turned a shade paler. "You think he might follow us?"

"I think he's probably on the other side of town by now. It doesn't make any sense for him to stick around here, especially with all the cops crawling all over everything. And I can't think of any reason he'd be interested in us. But it never hurts to be careful."

Darcy looked apprehensive, but game. She kept staring in the mirror until we were out of the East Nashville area and onto the interstate headed south. For the first several minutes, I'm not sure she blinked.

By the time we got to Columbia, almost an hour later, she was a little more relaxed, and she swore no one had followed us.

I'd been keeping an eye out myself, and hadn't noticed anyone either, so I figured she was right. Not that I'd know what to look for, necessarily—or that Darcy would—but since we were both aware that we might be followed, and we had both been looking for any sign of it, the guy was either very far behind us, very clever, or not there.

We exited east of Columbia and, instead of heading south toward Sweetwater, took the road into Columbia itself. Five minutes later, we were parked outside the police station.

"I can go in by myself..." I told Darcy, who hadn't said much on the way here. I got the very distinct feeling she wanted to get home as soon as possible, and get away from me. She had probably gotten a little more than she'd been expecting today.

She shook her head. "Oh, no. I'm not sitting out here by myself. If you're going in, so am I."

Fine with me. "We may be coming right back out again," I warned her. "Officer Vasquez probably won't be here. Unless it's the beginning or end of a shift, she's likely either home or on patrol."

"I don't care," Darcy said. "I'm coming."

OK, then. We locked the car—just in case—and went inside. If someone had managed to follow us all the way from Nashville, in spite of us both keeping an eye out, he probably wouldn't be stupid enough to do something to the car when it was parked outside a police station, but better safe than sorry, right?

Eleven

There was a desk in the lobby, with a uniformed officer sitting behind it. It wasn't Lupe Vasquez. I asked whether she happened to be in the police station, and was told no, she was on patrol.

"Any chance you can find out where she is? I have a couple of questions about a report she made, a favor to the Nashville PD."

The cop on duty looked skeptical.

"Here." I dug the report out and showed it to him. "See? It's her signature. We just had a question about it."

He scanned the piece of paper.

"I know her," I added. "I was involved in that high school serial killer case this spring. She'll remember my name if you want to call and tell her I'd like to talk to her about something."

He looked reluctant, but he did reach for the phone. "You can take a seat over there," he told me, before he started dialing. I guess he didn't want to give me a chance to see—or guess—the phone number.

'Over there' was a couple of uncomfortable chairs ranged against the wall. Darcy and I sat down on them and waited. I pricked my ears up, but couldn't hear anything of the mumbled conversation. After about a minute he hung up, and turned to us.

"She'll be at the Mexican place on State Street in ten minutes. It's their dinner break. She says you can talk to her there."

I told him I appreciated it, and we headed back out.

"Do you know the Mexican place on State Street?" I asked

Darcy on our way across the parking lot.

She shook her head.

"Do you want Mexican food?"

"Isn't it a little early for dinner?"

Maybe it was. By the time we got there, it would be barely four. Nonetheless, I could eat.

"It's up to you," I said, as visions of chips and guacamole danced in my head.

State Street wasn't hard to find—it ran straight through town—nor was the Mexican place. There was only one: called *Fiestas de Mexico,* all decked out in orange and green, with little flags and lighted signs for Corona and Dos Equis in the windows.

There was a police car parked in the lot.

"That must be them," I told Darcy, a bit unnecessarily.

She nodded.

"You ready?"

"I don't know what you think she'll be able to tell us, but I guess it can't hurt to talk to her."

Her enthusiasm floored me. Then again, she had a point. If Lupe Vasquez had learned anything of interest, chances are it would be in the report.

And anyway, Darcy was probably over the whole thing by now. I'm sure she'd had more excitement today than in the past two years put together. And on top of that, it wouldn't be surprising if she were a little worried about what we might find out. It's one thing to want to find your biological parents, in a theoretical sort of way. It's quite another to come face to face with who they are, or some aspects of them you maybe hadn't anticipated. She might be thinking that it would have been better to just let sleeping dogs lie.

But she followed me through the door and into the restaurant. "We're meeting someone," I told the hostess, who advanced on us with two menus, and looked around. "There they are."

The cops were easy to find, prominently seated in the middle of the room, in their navy blue uniforms. Lupe Vasquez had her hair tied back in a bouncing ponytail again. Across from her sat her partner, Officer Nolan: tall and hawk-like, with a beaky nose and a long neck.

They saw us standing there and beckoned.

"Sorry to interrupt your dinner," I said as we approached the table. "This won't take long."

"Have a seat." Lupe Vasquez nodded to the chair next to her, while Nolan took one look at Darcy and shot to his feet, his cheeks flushed, to pull out the chair next to himself for her.

She simpered at him and sat. I plunked myself onto the seat next to Vasquez without assistance. "We were going through a bunch of hospital records the Nashville police got from St. Jerome's Hospital in Brentwood last fall. They asked you for help trying to find a woman who gave her address as being on Water Street in Columbia thirty-some years ago."

I put the report on the table. She scanned it and nodded. "I remember. And for the record, they didn't ask me specifically. They contacted support services, and the captain gave it to us, since it's part of our beat." She glanced up at Nolan. He was busy getting acquainted with Darcy and didn't even notice.

"You couldn't find her?" I asked.

She shook her head. "Couldn't even find the address. It wasn't there. Never had been. No such number."

"So you talked to the neighbors."

She nodded. "It seemed like the only thing we could do."

"And they didn't know her."

She shook her head. "Some of them have lived there a lot longer than thirty years. There's never been a Sweet family on Water Street. It's just a little stretch of road. Two or three blocks long. They all know one another."

"No indication they were lying to you?"

"None that I noticed," Lupe Vasquez said. "They're not real fond of the police—racial profiling and police brutality and all that. So they were more willing to talk to me than Patrick. Me being female and younger and brown."

Patrick was Nolan, I assumed. I also made the assumption that the population on Water Street was mostly black. And while Lupe Vasquez wasn't, her skin was several shades darker than mine and Nolan's.

"Look at this." I pulled out the birth certificate we'd taken a copy of. And pointed to the checkmark next to 'Caucasian.'

Vasquez shook her head. "She wouldn't have lived on Water Street. You know how it is. There's a white side of town and a black side of town. Or at least there was thirty years ago."

Yes, indeed. Sweetwater had the same dynamic. Black churches and white churches, black neighborhoods and white neighborhoods. Things had started to change, slowly, over the past decade, but back when Darcy was born, Water Street would have been firmly African-American. And the Caucasian Ora Sweet wasn't likely to have lived here.

"Her mother could have been black," I told Vasquez softly, with a glance at Darcy. She and Nolan—Patrick—were talking and weren't paying any attention to what was going on on this side of the table. Darcy looked a lot perkier than she had when we walked in. "Look at her. Black hair, black eyes, skin like yours."

Vasquez nodded. "Hard to imagine the nurses at the hospital wouldn't have noticed a black girl claiming she was white, though."

True. "So maybe it was her father who was black. And Ora lived on Water Street with him."

"Even more likely the neighbors would have remembered her, I'd say."

Probably so.

At that point the officers' dinner arrived. It was probably time for us to go. I started making leaving noises, and Nolan immediately did everything short of holding on to her to get Darcy to stay. "Aren't you hungry?"

"I guess I could eat something..." Darcy said, with a glance at me.

I arched my brows—now she wanted to eat?—but if she'd found a guy she liked, who certainly seemed to like her back, who was I to cut things short?

I turned to the waiter. "I'd like a bowl of guacamole, please. A big one. And a bowl of chips. And an iced tea."

He nodded. "Senorita?"

Darcy ordered a drink and a Speedy Gonzales, maybe because she thought it would be quick and easy to make.

It was kind of awkward sitting here while Vasquez was tucking into her food and while Nolan was trying to decide whether to focus on Darcy or his burrito.

Darcy won out, and I guess that was a good sign. My guacamole arrived shortly, and I got busy scooping it up and shoving it in my mouth. Then Darcy's dinner arrived, and Nolan allowed her and himself to eat, hopefully before his own food had gotten too cold.

"I don't suppose you know anything about Beulah Odom?" I asked Vasquez, mostly just for something to say.

She swallowed. "The woman who ran the meat'n three outside Sweetwater? She died a few weeks ago."

"I know. That's why I asked."

She put down her fork. "I don't know a lot. I mean, I was there, but there wasn't much to see."

"No sign of foul play?"

I'm not sure why I kept harping on that, when the death had been ruled natural by the M.E. and the sheriff had been at the crime scene and told me it all looked as it should.

Lupe Vasquez shook her head. "Not that I could see. Just an older woman who died of heart failure in her own bed. Or out of it."

She waited a second and then added, "Why do you ask?"

I shrugged. "No reason, really. One of her employees told me it happened. And that there's a problem with the will. The employee was supposed to get the restaurant. Beulah had been grooming her to take over, but the Odoms are contesting it."

"That doesn't mean they killed her," Vasquez said.

Of course not.

"If anyone did, I'm sure you realize that it's your friend who had the best motive."

I blinked. No, I hadn't realized that, actually. Or hadn't thought about it, at any rate. "Yvonne would never kill Beulah!"

Nolan stopped mid-sentence to look at me. Darcy did, too.

"Sorry," I said. "But she wouldn't. I know her. She wouldn't kill anyone."

Nobody answered, and I picked up a chip and dipped it into the guacamole just to avoid the silence and the eyes. Then Nolan began speaking again, and Darcy turned to him.

"Listen," Lupe Vasquez said, her voice low. "Nobody killed her. The M.E. said it was heart failure. And he should know."

I nodded. He should.

"The case is closed. The body is buried. She'd lived a good life, good enough that she brought both heart disease and diabetes on herself."

"I suppose."

"And I'm sure your friend will figure out the will. If it's valid, and Miz Odom wasn't under duress when she wrote it, your friend will probably get the restaurant."

I hoped so. But before I could say anything, Nolan's radio squawked. "Dispatch to One-Adam-Four. One-Adam-Four, come in, please."

"That's us," Vasquez said, while Nolan excused himself (to Darcy) and got to his feet. He disappeared outside, already talking into the radio, while Vasquez looked around for the waiter. He must be used to this, because he was on his way to the table with the check. She took it and pushed her chair back. "'Scuse us."

"No problem."

"Sorry I couldn't be more help with the adoption thing."

"Not your fault," I said. "If she didn't live there, she didn't live there. And we have some other strings we can tug. I figured if there'd been anything else, you'd have put it in the report, but it was worth checking."

Especially since I'd gotten a very nice bowl of guacamole out of it. A bowl of guacamole I had to pay for, of course—I wasn't about to stick the officers with it—but still. A very nice bowl of guacamole.

She nodded. "I'll see you around. Nice to meet you." She smiled at Darcy and then walked off, hardware jangling from the belt around her waist, to settle the bill.

Darcy was looking at the front door and pouting. I hid a smile. "He'll find you if he wants to. And you know where to find him, if you get tired of waiting."

She glanced at me, and then blushed. I guess maybe she hadn't realized how obvious they'd been. "Did she know anything more than what was in the report?"

I shook my head. "She said that Ora Sweet never lived on Water Street. Nor did any other Sweets. Nor did anyone, at the address on the report. It doesn't exist."

Darcy nodded.

"Also, she said Water Street is a black neighborhood. If it is now, it would have been thirty-some years ago, too. The race on the birth certificate says Caucasian."

"I've probably got some of both in me," Darcy said calmly. This obviously wasn't news to her. Or anything that bothered her, either.

"Many of us do," I answered, just as calmly. "My great-great-grandfather William was the son of the groom. Great-great-great-grandma Caroline got lonely during the War Between the States."

Darcy's eyebrows rose. "Does your brother know?"

"I think he does. Aunt Regina told me and Catherine. She probably told Dix, too. I'm not sure about Mother, though."

"I won't mention it to her," Darcy promised and looked around for the check.

By the time we got out into the parking lot, the squad car with Vasquez and Nolan was gone. And he hadn't left his card with his phone number on the windshield of the Volvo, possibly because he didn't know it was ours. The way he'd behaved around Darcy, though, I thought it a certainty that he'd be in touch either by the end of the day or sometime tomorrow.

"Let me get you home," I told Darcy when we were in the car and on our way out of the parking lot. "We've had a big day."

She nodded.

"Do you want to drive by Water Street? Since we're here anyway?"

"No sense in that, if the girl didn't live there." She shook her head. "This is crazy. We don't know if she was my mother. We don't even know if I was born at St. Jerome's Hospital!"

No, we didn't. "It's interesting, though. Don't you think? There's a connection between this girl—Ora or whatever her name was—and this area. Columbia at least, but maybe Sweetwater too. And there's someone in this area who sent you a newspaper clipping about the job at Martin and McCall. That someone could be your mother. Or your father."

"So how do we find out more?"

"I'm not sure," I admitted, accelerating as we left the more densely populated areas of Columbia and headed south on the highway toward Sweetwater and Darcy's subdivision, "but I'll think of something. Once I have a chance to sit down and think. I'll call you later."

Darcy nodded, but I had no idea whether she believed me or not.

I dropped her off at her little ranch with the blue door and bright yellow flowers, and waited until she'd gone inside with the door safely shut behind her before heading back to Sweetwater and the mansion.

I wasn't really worried about having been followed. We'd both been keeping an eye out, and while it's fairly easy to get lost among all the other cars on the interstate, it's a lot harder to shadow someone on country roads and in a small town. I hadn't noticed anyone behind us on our way into Columbia earlier, or on our way out again now. But the least I could do was make sure Darcy got safely inside, after everything I'd put her through today.

It had been quite a day. Darcy had held up pretty well, considering. And I couldn't really blame her for passing out at the sight of the body, when I'd come close to passing out at the sight of my first one, too. And this had been a particularly gruesome one, with half its face missing.

Not that Brenda, with her throat cut, had been a pretty sight.

I hadn't heard anything from Alexandra since we left the barbeque place. Hopefully she was all right. She'd had a big day, too. Although she'd been prepared for the results of the pregnancy test. She'd already suspected she was pregnant.

I remembered, quite vividly, the confused mixture of my own feelings last fall, when I first discovered I was pregnant with Rafe's baby. Alexandra must be experiencing all of them, plus a few more that hadn't been applicable to me. Like, how was she going to finish high school and get an education with a baby in tow?

But there'd be time enough to figure that out once she decided what she was going to do next. Hopefully she'd call later, if she wanted to talk.

I glanced in the rearview mirror. There was still no one behind me. The ribbon of the Columbia Highway stretched in my wake, empty and steaming with heat.

When I pulled up in front of the mansion, Mother was on her way out. "Dinner with Audrey," she told me brightly.

"Good for you." Audrey has been Mother's best friend since Mother settled in Sweetwater as a young bride, before Catherine was born. They're as different as can be—Audrey unmarried, Mother a widow with grown children and grandchildren, not to mention the totally opposite ways they look—but they're like two peas in pod when they get together.

"You're welcome to come along," Mother offered. "Unless you've already had dinner."

I hadn't. Not unless you counted the guacamole at *Fiestas de Mexico*, and I didn't.

"I don't know..." I demurred.

On the one hand, it had been a long day and I was tired. I didn't want to intrude on their girl-time, and I was hoping that Alexandra and/or Rafe would call.

On the other, it had been a crazy day, and just in case I was wrong about nobody following us from Nashville, I wasn't sure I wanted to be alone in the mansion.

"It'll be good for you," Mother coaxed, patting my arm. "Unless you're too tired?"

"No..." I wasn't too tired. And—I realized—it would give me an opportunity to pick Audrey's brain. Unlike Mother, who had moved here after marrying my father, Audrey was a native. She'd grown up in Sweetwater. She'd been around when Ora was pregnant and Darcy was born. Audrey might have known the real Ora, or at least be able to give me some kind of direction for where I could look.

And she might know Beulah Odom's sister-in-law and niece, too. Maybe I could get some dirt on them I could share with Yvonne.

"I suppose I could come with you," I told Mother. "If you don't think Audrey would mind."

"Of course not, darling." She tucked her arm through mine and propelled me back down the steps to the Volvo. I guess I was driving. "Audrey is always happy to see you. And I'm sure she'll be happy to hear that everything is fine with you and Rafael."

"About that," I said.

"Oh, dear." Mother stopped at the foot of the steps and dropped my arm. "What happened?"

"Nothing, really. I saw him when I was in Nashville. He's back home at the house."

"That's wonderful," Mother said warmly, opening her door. "I guess that means his undercover case is over and he can get rid of that awful hair and the teeth?"

I walked around the car. "Unfortunately not. The case isn't over. One of the bad guys is still out there. And he has figured out who Rafe is, and where we live. So I'll be staying in Sweetwater a few more days."

"Oh, dear," Mother said again, sliding into the passenger seat. I think she might have turned a shade paler, even, although that could have been my imagination. "Rafael is safe, isn't he?"

As safe as he ever is. "He said he'd get Wendell and the boys over to stay with him."

Mother had met Wendell and the TBI rookies before, both at our wedding and before that, when we were all busy turning Middle Tennessee over to find Rafe after he was abducted.

"I expect they'll probably sleep in shifts. Just in case the guy comes back. I don't think he will, and Rafe doesn't think so, either, but it's better to be careful."

"Certainly," Mother nodded. "He can take care of himself, darling. Don't worry."

It was weird, to say the least, to have my mother reassure me about my husband's capabilities. Two months ago, she'd have done everything she could to disparage him.

"I know he can," I said, as I steered the car off the mansion's property and back onto the Columbia Highway in the direction of town. "So can the others. I'm sure they'll be just fine."

"And this way we get to keep you a little longer," Mother said, reaching over to pat my hand. "We're going to the Wayside Inn, darling."

Of course we were. I was already headed that way, having anticipated the destination.

Twelve

The Wayside Inn is what it sounds like, an old roadside inn from the days when the road south to the Gulf went this way. It's built of huge, old logs, with authentic chinking made from clay, lime, and sand, mixed with straw. Since it's two-hundred years plus, and the oldest building in town—older than the mansion by thirty or forty years—it's been updated many times, but it still has the original log walls inside, with a polished concrete floor that looks like it might have been there for a hundred years, and a lot of dark, atmospheric booths along the perimeter.

It's the nicest—read: most expensive—restaurant in Sweetwater, and Mother loves it. She had probably been here with the sheriff just last night.

The last time I could remember being here, was the day before my ten-year reunion, when my best friend from high school, Charlotte, and I were going to have dinner, and ended up running into two other old classmates, Tina and Mary Kelly.

Audrey had already snagged a table, and a glass of white wine, and was sitting there, looking for all the world like a middle-aged, Americanized, Coco Chanel. She's tall and angular, with cheekbones for days, a severe, black, stacked bob, and bright red lips, always dressed in dramatic primary colors. No soft pastels for Audrey; she leaves those for Mother, who is a little shorter and a lot softer, with champagne-tinted hair and an elegant, ladylike wardrobe mostly made up of pale blues, greens, and corals.

Audrey lit up when she saw us. "Margaret. And you brought Savannah!"

We air-kissed, and I slid into the booth opposite while she and Mother did the same thing. "I hope you don't mind," I said, when Mother had taken her seat next to me. "I have to stay in Sweetwater another day or two. Mother thought I might like the company for dinner."

"Of course, darling." Audrey is pretty much always happy to see me. Having never been married or had children of her own, I'm sort of like a niece, I guess. "And how's your handsome husband? That's was quite a kerfuffle at the party the other night."

"He's fine," I said. "We worked it out. And he still has the dreadlocks and gold teeth. But I'm getting used to them." Earlier today, I hadn't even really noticed they were there. He was just Rafe, and I'd been delighted to see him, dreads and all.

Mother shuddered delicately. "He's not thinking of keeping them, is he?"

"I hope not. The hair gives him a headache, he says. It's heavy. And I don't imagine he'll keep the gold teeth when he doesn't have to."

"Good to know," Mother said. "He's quite handsome, you know. Without all of it."

Yes, I did know. I had no idea Mother knew, though. This was the first time she had said anything complimentary about my husband's looks.

I didn't comment, of course. "I'm happy the two of you are getting along better these days," I said instead, blandly. "I know he was worried about his welcome into the family. I'm glad we were able to work things out."

"But of course, darling," Mother said. "If he's your choice, then I'm happy for you."

Sure.

Audrey gave me a knowing look across the table. I'm sure she'd been privy to more of Mother's feelings on the matter than I ever had. Mother and I hadn't ever talked a lot about Rafe. After I'd informed her that he was the one, and that if he wanted me, he could have me, and I didn't much care what anyone else thought about it, she'd kept mostly quiet. To me, that is. Audrey had probably gotten an earful on more than one occasion.

"So what did you do today," she asked me, once the waiter had come and left after taking our orders.

"I'm glad you asked. I went to Nashville with Darcy Corcoran. She's trying to find her biological parents, so we went to look through the records the police confiscated from St. Jerome's Hospital after Sheila died."

Audrey blinked. "They let you see those? Aren't they privileged?"

"I guess they probably are. But I have a friend with the police." I smiled complacently.

"How is Detective Grimaldi?" Mother asked. Like Audrey, she had ordered a glass of Chardonnay for her dinner beverage, and was swirling it around in the glass. I'd like to say I wasn't envious, but I enjoy a good glass of wine, and the Wayside Inn has an excellent cellar. But of course in my current condition, wine was not on the menu. I took a sip of my tea and tried not to feel deprived.

"She's fine. Busy. Caught a case this morning. A dead gang banger who was one of the three Rafe lost last night."

Mother nodded. I wondered if she had noticed the relationship between Grimaldi and Dix, and was curious. She wasn't stupid, so it was likely she had. She'd had occasion to observe them together during my wedding in June, after all.

On the other hand, she can be obtuse, so maybe she didn't realize what kind of relationship it was they had.

Or maybe it wasn't the kind of relationship I thought it was. Maybe they were just friends and I was the obtuse one.

"So did you find anything in the police records?" Audrey wanted to know.

I shrugged. "Yes and no. I don't know if it has anything to do with Darcy. We don't even know if she was born at St. Jerome's Hospital. But we did find the record of someone born at the right time, that the police hadn't been able to trace."

"That's wonderful," Mother said warmly, and likely didn't mean it the way it sounded.

"The mother was a young woman from this area, who gave her address as 4521 Water Street in Columbia."

They both nodded.

"There is no 4521 Water Street in Columbia."

"There is a Water Street," Audrey pointed out.

I nodded. "But it's only a couple of blocks long. There's a 600-block, an 800-block, and a 900-block. Nothing above 1000."

They both looked nonplussed. "Did you go there?" Mother wanted to know.

"I didn't have to. Officer Lupe Vasquez with the Columbia police went there instead. Last year. The Nashville police asked the Columbia police's help with tracking Ora Sweet down, and Lupe Vasquez got the job. I have her report in the car. But the bottom line is, there's no such number and no such woman. No Sweet family on Water Street. Ever."

I waited to see if they'd pick up on what I'd picked up on—Sweetwater—but it didn't look like either of them did.

"So what are you saying?" Mother asked.

"I'm saying that Ora Sweet gave a fake name and a fake address when she checked into the hospital to have her baby. And now we have no idea how to find her. Or who she was."

Mother wrinkled her brows. Audrey looked distressed.

"You've lived here a long time," I told her. "Your whole life, right?"

She nodded.

"You'd have been living here when Ora—or whatever her name was—was pregnant. She'd be around your age. Can you remember anyone like that? Someone who was pregnant, but didn't come home with a baby?"

"That was a long time ago, Savannah," Audrey said. "Darcy is what? Thirty-four, thirty-five years old? Before you even came to Sweetwater, Margaret."

Mother nodded. "You know who you should talk to?" she told me.

"Who?"

But by then Mother had seen the waiter approaching the table with his big tray of dishes, and she shushed me. *Not in front of the servants.*

I rolled my eyes, but kept quiet as he deposited various nicely presented and delicious-smelling plates in front of each of us. Mother had ordered the mountain trout and Audrey the stuffed flounder. I had fallen into temptation and asked for the seared potato gnocchi with mushrooms and brown butter sage sauce. Not as many healthy Omega-3s, plus I'd be paying for it later, with an extra five pounds to lose after the baby was born, but it would be worth it.

Mother, remarkably, didn't say a word. Normally, she would have eyed my food and my waistline and told me something like *"a moment on the lips, a lifetime on the hips,"* but since I became pregnant the second time, she's been biting her tongue a lot. It's appreciated, even though I don't actually say anything about it. I'm sure she'll start mentioning my weight again as soon as the baby's born.

The waiter withdrew, with hopes that we'd enjoy our food. I lifted my fork and turned to Mother. "Who?"

"What?... Oh." She picked up her own fork and used it to pick at her fish. It flaked very nicely, and she must have been satisfied with its consistency, because she used the fork to convey a morsel to her mouth. After swallowing, she said,

"Denise Seaver, dear."

"Denise Seaver is in prison," I said. "I put her there."

"Yes, dear. I know that. But she's about our age." She glanced across the table at Audrey. Audrey had her mouth full, and her flounder must not have been up to the same standard as Mother's trout, because Audrey looked like she had a mouth full of sawdust. However, she nodded.

"And she was practicing female medicine in Columbia at that time," Mother added. "She had been doing it a few years already when I came to her with Catherine."

Since my sister is thirty-two, give or take a few months, that would have been thirty-three years ago. Ora Sweet—might as well call her that, for lack of another name—if she was from this area, and it seemed she was, might have gone to see Doctor Seaver. A young, female doctor close to her own age... it must have seemed a much more comfortable proposition than visiting one of the old guard male practitioners with her dilemma of pregnancy out of wedlock.

Had Denise Seaver been involved in the illegal adoption ring that long ago? Was she the one who had told Ora to give birth at St. Jerome's? Or was this the case that had started Denise Seaver down the road to selling babies?

"She's in prison," I said again.

"They have visiting hours, don't they?"

I had no idea how Mother would know that, seeing as we've certainly never had anyone in the family having been incarcerated. Except Rafe, of course. Two years in medium security at Riverbend Penitentiary. Where they do indeed have visiting hours. I had visited Walker Lamont there once, at his request. That had been after the first time he'd tried to kill me, but before the second. He'd apologized. I didn't think he'd apologize again if I went back.

"She's in Southern Belle Hell," I said thoughtfully. "At least I think she is. I could call and make sure. And ask if she can have visitors."

Mother and Audrey both looked at me with arched eyebrows.

"The Tennessee Women's Prison," I clarified. "They call it Southern Belle Hell. It's located somewhere in Nashville."

I'd never been there. But I thought it likely that it was in the same area as Riverbend. Group your criminals together and make the other areas of town safer for everyone else.

"If anyone in Sweetwater would remember a young pregnant woman from thirty-five years ago," Mother said, "I think it would be Denise Seaver."

I forked up some gnocchi and mushrooms while I thought about it. "I should call Darcy and ask if she's up for a trip to prison tomorrow." And make sure she was safe at the same time. Just in case. "But first I guess I should find out whether they're open for visitors."

"After dinner," Mother said firmly.

I resisted the urge to salute, and devoted myself to my food.

By the time we got home, it was dark, and Alexandra hadn't called me. Nor had Rafe, or for that matter Darcy. I couldn't call Rafe, who was surrounded by other men and no doubt having a great time while they were waiting for their missing gang member to stop by and start shooting. He'd call me when he was ready. And I didn't want Alexandra to feel like I was nagging her. She'd call when she was ready, too.

But Darcy I could call. So I did.

It took a couple of rings, and then she answered. "Hello?"

"It's Savannah," I said. "Are you all right?"

"Fine." I could hear rustling noises, as if she'd been lying down. She hadn't been asleep, though. The TV was on in the background, and now she muted it. "What's up?"

"I wondered whether you were up for another trip

tomorrow."

She sounded a little suspicious. Probably wanted to ensure she wouldn't have another experience like today. "Where?"

"Back to Nashville. To prison."

"Prison?"

"I was having dinner with my mother and Audrey," I said, "and they suggested that we talk to Denise Seaver. She was an OB-GYN in Columbia for many years, until—"

"I remember," Darcy said. "I heard the story last fall."

"Then you know that she helped to facilitate many of the illegal adoptions at St. Jerome's. But she was also, legitimately, a doctor here in Maury County, and Mother thought that if anyone would remember Ora Sweet—or whatever her name really was—Denise Seaver would."

"And we have to go to prison to talk to her?"

"You don't have to," I told her. "I can go on my own. I just thought maybe you'd like to come. Just in case there's something you'd like to ask her."

She hesitated, and I added, "She might not want to talk to me. I'm the reason she's in prison, after all. I could get there, and have her refuse to see me. But she might be willing to talk to you."

"I don't know..." Darcy said.

"I checked their visiting hours. They're open for visitors from eight-thirty to three-thirty tomorrow."

"I suppose it might be worth a try..."

It was definitely worth a try. Mother was right: if anyone remembered anything, it would be Denise Seaver. We just had to find out if she could be persuaded to talk.

"If you'd like to think about it before you tell me one way or the other," I told Darcy, "you can get back to me later. Or tomorrow morning. The checkpoint closes at ten and opens again at eleven-thirty, and then closes again between one-thirty and two-thirty. We'd have to get there at a time when it's open. I was thinking of getting there by ten, just to get the visit out of the way," and because I was curious and didn't think I could wait any longer than I had to. "But I could be talked into making it later, if you didn't want to leave that early. It'll take us more than an hour to get there."

"No," Darcy said. "Let's go early."

Sounded like her mind was made up, then.

"I can pick you up again," I suggested. "We'll get there before ten. It's just on the other side of Nashville."

Darcy allowed how that would work.

"Any problems on your end?"

"What kind of problems?"

"Just making sure you're all right," I said soothingly. "I don't think anyone followed us from Nashville, but it doesn't hurt to be careful."

I'm fairly certain I heard a faint gulp.

"If you get worried," I told her, "you could always call the Columbia PD and ask someone to drive by." Someone like Patrick Nolan. "Just to make sure you're safe."

"Yes," Darcy said, sounding like she was catching on, "maybe I could do that."

"Good luck with it. I'll see you at eight-thirty tomorrow."

I disconnected, so she could call the Columbia PD and ask for Nolan if she wanted to. And then I leaned back against the pillows—I was in my room, on the bed—and thought about the last time I'd seen Denise Seaver.

She had been standing in her kitchen with a gun in her hand. Marley had been out cold on the floor, from being hit with a frying pan—or maybe it was a wok—and Doctor Seaver had been ready to shoot her. That's when I had stumbled in, and she had ended up shooting me instead, when I doused her with pepper spray. I still had the scar, small and round and a little sunken under my fingers.

What if she refused to talk to us? She had no reason to want to help me with anything. I was responsible for putting her in prison, for a couple of counts of murder, a couple more counts of attempted murder, and a long string of adoption offenses, not to mention kidnapping. And it wasn't like talking to me would help her in any way. If I could promise her a couple years off for good behavior, that would be different, but I couldn't. She was going to die in prison, unless she lived to be well over a hundred.

Maybe we should bring her a gift. She wasn't likely to have a vase in her cell, so flowers were out, but maybe a nice box of chocolates?

But no, she was in prison. She probably wasn't allowed to have chocolate. Surely that must be part of her punishment.

We'd just have to throw ourselves on her mercy, then, and hope for the best. And even if she wasn't willing to tell us anything, maybe she'd let something slip, that would be worth going on with.

At that point, the phone rang. I rolled over and grabbed it. I was hoping for Rafe, but it was Alexandra.

"Sorry," she told me. "I had to have dinner with my dad and my brother."

"No problem. I just came in from having dinner with my mother and her best friend."

"What did you eat?"

"Gnocchi," I said.

"I had chicken."

There was a moment's pause.

"I don't know what to do," Alexandra said.

The small-talk portion of the conversation was clearly over.

"You have some time to figure it out." She hadn't looked at all pregnant when I saw her, and surely she would have noticed that she wasn't getting her period if it went on for months and months. "How far along are you?"

"Seven weeks," Alexandra said. And amended it to, "More or less."

That made sense. Seven weeks is long enough to realize you aren't getting your period as regularly as you should, but not so long that you look like an idiot for not realizing it sooner.

"Did you tell your dad?"

"No," Alexandra said. "With Austin sitting right there? I don't think so."

No, I wouldn't have wanted to have that conversation with Dix sitting across the table, either. Although back in the fall, when I was pregnant with Rafe's baby, Dix was the first person I'd told. I guess it's different when you're an adult, and I knew Dix wasn't likely to judge me. Mother hadn't known about the pregnancy until I miscarried. Nor had Rafe, for that matter.

"What can I do to help you?"

"Right now I just want to talk," Alexandra said. "I'll call the doctor on Monday."

And he would present the options for going forward. So no need for me to do that again.

"Shoot," I said.

There was a moment's pause. "I don't know where to start."

I remembered that feeling. It was part of the reason I had never broached the subject with Rafe. The other part was that I had no idea how he'd take the news. This was before I knew he loved me, and wanted to marry me. Back then, I hadn't been sure whether he'd cared about me at all, or whether I'd been nothing but an amusing diversion, and once he'd gotten Savannah Martin into bed and out of his system, he was ready to move on.

"Let me help you out," I said. "The father... is he your boyfriend?"

She hesitated. "Not really."

"A friend? Someone you go to school with?"

"I go to a girl's school," Alexandra said. "There are no boys there."

"Sorry."

"It's not your fault," Alexandra said. "And he's just a guy. We kind of hit it off. And then when we got back to Nashville, we met again. A couple days later. And then we ended up in bed. And now I'm pregnant."

Admirably simple and clear. "Back from where?"

Between you and me, I had a bad feeling about this. Eight weeks ago had been the weekend of my wedding. A wedding Alexandra had attended. Here in Sweetwater. She'd gotten pregnant a week or so later. To a guy from Nashville, whom she had met somewhere else.

I didn't want to think that she'd gotten knocked up by someone I had put in her path, but it didn't come as a surprise to hear her answer.

"Back from your wedding."

My wedding. There had only been so many single men at my wedding. Most of the guests had been from Sweetwater, except for the ones we had brought down from Nashville with us. Like Grimaldi, and David, and Wendell. And the TBI rookies.

José had brought a girlfriend, so it wasn't likely to be him. That left Clayton or Jamal.

Neither of them would make Steven Puckett happy. Jamal was black. And Clayton had a criminal record. Like Rafe, the TBI had taken him on straight out of prison.

They were both gainfully employed now. Clayton and Jamal, I mean, although of course Rafe was, too. Engaged in keeping the rest of us safe. That had to count for something. But maybe not with a father whose seventeen-year-old daughter had been knocked up by the man in question.

Maurice Washington, last year's boyfriend, had been black.

"Jamal?" I ventured.

Alexandra didn't answer, but I could hear her squirm. And yes, I know that's impossible. But I swear to God I did.

"Your father isn't going to be happy about that."

"My dad wouldn't be happy about me sleeping with anyone," Alexandra said, with some justification.

"I'm not real happy about it, either. I realize you're just a kid, but he should have known better."

"He thought I was older," Alexandra said.

And in a court of law, that might help. She did, in fact, look older than seventeen. But with a baby on the way, Alexandra's age or Jamal's knowledge of it had nothing to do with anything. She was just as pregnant whether he'd known her real age or not.

"I have to talk to Rafe about this," I said, more to myself than to her.

"God," Alexandra moaned.

"No, listen. I have to. They're neck-deep in an undercover investigation right now. People are dead." And Rafe had some very important matters to take care of. But I had to make sure he understood that he had to keep Jamal alive to deal with this.

Not that he wouldn't do whatever it took to keep Jamal alive otherwise too, but now it was even more important.

Rafe could take care of himself. He'd had a lot of practice. But Jamal, for all his bravura, was really just an overgrown kid. And he needed to be kept alive so Alexandra could tell him that he was on his way to becoming a daddy.

Thirteen

I knew Rafe wouldn't be happy to hear from me, but it couldn't be helped. As soon as I got off the phone with Alexandra, I dialed his number. And waited.

There was no answer. Part of me had expected that, so I wasn't upset, although I will admit I was disappointed. I still got to hear his voice, but the recording on the phone wasn't the same as when he actually spoke to me. "This is Rafe. Leave a message."

"It's me," I said. "Listen. I have something to tell you, and I know now's not the time, but I need you to do me a favor. I need you to make sure Jamal makes it through the night OK. I'm sure you'd do that anyway, but just make sure of it. And call me when you can."

There wasn't anything more to say, really—not without going into details, and I wasn't about to tell him about my plans for tomorrow—so I told him I loved him, and then I hung up and went to sleep.

When *Hot Stuff* went off on the bedside table, it was pitch black outside. I rolled over in bed—or tried; I could only make it halfway before the stomach got in the way—and grabbed for the phone. "Rafe."

"You've got some 'splaining to do," my husband informed me, in his best Ricky Ricardo voice.

I was too tired to catch on. "What do you mean? Why?"

"Make sure Jamal makes it through the night? What about

me? You got something you wanna tell me, darlin'?"

"Oh," I said. "No. Of course I want you to make it through the night, too. But I really wasn't worried about that. You can take care of yourself."

"Uh-huh." His voice was just about as dry as kindling. "What's going on, darlin'?"

The *'darlin'* told me he wasn't really upset. When something important is going on, he calls me by my given name. The rest of the time it's darlin'. It can be snide or sarcastic, exasperated or tender, but it isn't particularly heartfelt. When he has something... for lack of a better word, *real* to say, he calls me Savannah.

"Alexandra Puckett is pregnant," I said.

"Yeah?" It took less than a second for him to move from the fact to the reason I mentioned it. If it had been during the day, it probably would have taken less. "Oh, for Christ's sake!"

"Is he there?"

"No," Rafe said.

My heart gave a single, heavy beat. "Do you know where he is?"

"No." His voice was grim.

"Have you tried calling him? Or didn't he answer?"

"I called. He didn't answer."

"Have you gone out looking for him?"

"A couple hours ago," Rafe said. "Wendell and José went to his house. They're back now."

So he hadn't been home. I wasn't sure whether that was good news, or bad. On the one hand, they hadn't found him shot to death on the floor. On the other, he could be anywhere, in God only knew what straits.

"I'm sure he'll turn up," I said, in the most chipper tone I could muster. "He's probably just lying low."

"Sure." Rafe sounded about as untroubled as I felt. Not at all, in other words. "Go back to sleep, darlin'. I'll call you if I see him."

"I'd appreciate that. I love you. Take care of yourself."

"You, too. And take care of my baby."

I promised I would, and went back to sleep.

He didn't call again. Not during the rest of the night, and not in the morning. I got up, showered and put on clothes, and headed out to pick up Darcy.

She was wearing peach today, with a skirt and strappy sandals. Sunday church wear doubling as prison-visitation wear, I guess.

"Any problems last night?" I asked when she was in the car and we were headed north.

She shook her head.

"Did you end up calling Nolan?"

"There was nothing to call about. Nobody bothered me. And if I called and there wasn't anything wrong, I'd look like one of those batty old women who believe aliens are listening to their phone conversations."

Not the best way to impress a guy you liked, who seemed like he liked her back. I could see that.

"He'll get back in touch," I said, since I'd definitely gotten the impression that Nolan was as smitten with Darcy as she seemed to be with him. "If he hasn't come looking for you by tomorrow night, I'll track down Lupe Vasquez and ask her why."

"Why tomorrow?"

"Because he knows where you work," I said. "You must have told him you work for my brother and Jonathan. But you probably didn't tell him where you live. So it's most logical that he'll come looking for you at the office. You just have to give him a little more time."

Darcy looked cautiously optimistic. "That makes sense."

It did. I left her thinking happy thoughts about Patrick Nolan showing up tomorrow to sweep her off her feet, and concentrated on driving.

Traffic was light on a Sunday morning, and we made good time from Columbia to Southern Belle Hell.

The Tennessee Women's Prison is located on the west side of Nashville, near the Ashland City Highway, and across from the Southern Services garbage dump: a great big mound of trash with several tractors driving around on top of it. The temperature had been in the nineties for several weeks, basically cooking the garbage in the dump, and even with the air conditioning blasting inside the car, there was no escaping the odor. Darcy's nose wrinkled.

"Just be glad you don't live here," I told her, pointing out the other window, where several squat brick buildings sat surrounded by tall wire fences topped with barbs. The fences curved inward at the top, so they were impossible to climb. By the time you got to the top, you'd be hanging on by your fingernails, quite literally, and gravity would do the rest.

"Grim," Darcy said.

I nodded. Even under a bright, blue sky—and if I imagined it without the pungent odor of garbage—it looked like a place you didn't want to live. It didn't even particularly look like a place I wanted to visit.

"I hope this isn't a waste of time."

"We're here," Darcy said, "so we might as well go in. And inside, it probably won't smell like garbage."

It was a hopeful thought.

We followed the signs to the visitor's parking lot, and slotted the car into an empty space between an old Pontiac with a peeling top and a pickup truck with oversized tires and a painted beach scene that included a buxom young woman in a bikini on the tailgate.

"We have to leave everything in the car," I told Darcy. "All we can bring inside is one key—I have to take the house keys off the chain and leave them in the car—and our driver's licenses for identification. No wallet, no purse, no money."

She looked pained, but started to remove her ID from her wallet.

"You can keep your watch and two earrings. If you have more, you'll have to take them off. I get to keep my wedding ring and one other ring." My pre-engagement ring, the one Rafe gave me last Christmas, with the blue stone. He'd told me I wasn't ready for him to propose—he'd been wrong about that; I'd have accepted on the spot if he'd popped the question on Christmas Day—but he'd still wanted me to wear his ring. So I did. And would continue to.

"There are strict rules for behavior once we're inside," I continued, from my vast experience and the reading I'd done on the computer last night. "We can't hug her—not that we'd want to. We can't give her anything. No passing anything across the table. We can't touch her, or she us."

So at least I didn't have to worry about her throwing herself across the table to try to strangle me. And if she did, there'd be someone on guard to stop her, since it was against the rules.

"We can't really leave the table—unless it's to go to the vending machine, and I don't plan to buy a vending machine card. This isn't a social visit."

Darcy nodded.

"We'll have to pass through a metal detector on our way in. They are allowed to frisk us, so don't be upset if they do."

"You've been through this before," Darcy said. "Was it your husband?"

Not at all. "Rafe went to work for the TBI ten years before I met him again. But I went to visit my old boss in Riverbend Penitentiary last year. He had some paperwork he wanted to give me. I guess he must have gotten special permission to pass it over the table."

"Was it uncomfortable?"

"The prison? Quite. And I don't expect this to be any easier. Although they're all women, so maybe that will make a difference."

At least they wouldn't be looking at me as if I were lunch, the way some of the men at Riverbend had done. Although the inmates being female could mean that most of the visitors were male, and that might be another version of awkward.

I squared my shoulders. "Let's get this over with."

Darcy nodded and fell into step beside me.

We joined the line at the checkpoint, where we explained to the big, beefy (male) guard that we were there to see Denise Seaver.

No, we'd never been to see her before, so we weren't on her list of visitors. Was that a problem?

It wasn't.

Did she have a list of visitors? Could we see it?

We couldn't, but the guard said he'd get Inmate Seaver down for us. And then we were processed in, though the ID check, the metal detector, and the frisk search.

The meetings took place in a big room full of tables. We were directed to one, and sat there and waited for Denise Seaver to be brought down. Around us, other families were waiting, too, or chatting with their incarcerated members and friends. Here and there, subdued children sat kicking their legs while they waited to be set free. Running and playing was not allowed in the visiting area.

All the inmates were dressed in the same blue shirt and pants. They were similar to scrubs, and maybe that made Denise Seaver feel at home.

She walked in a couple of minutes later, accompanied by a female guard. They stopped just inside the door to look around. I saw Doctor Seaver scan the room, and there was no mistaking the change of expression on her face when she saw me. Her eyes narrowed, and her lips compressed to a line.

She said something to the guard; I assumed it to be along the lines of not wanting to see or talk to me.

Was that allowed? For a prisoner to refuse to talk to someone?

It probably was. It's not like we were anyone official.

I pasted what could probably pass for a friendly smile on face—at least from a distance and to someone who didn't know me. In truth, I had no more desire to talk to Denise Seaver than she obviously had to talk to me. However, she might have information about Ora Sweet, information we needed, and for that, I could make nice for the time that I had to.

The guard must have laid down the law, or maybe just convinced Doctor Seaver to give us a chance, because they came toward the table.

"You have an hour," the guard informed us as Denise Seaver took a seat on the opposite side of the table. "No touching. No passing anything across the table. No profanity."

Sheesh, I wasn't sure about that last one. I already wanted to swear, just looking at her.

"I don't think this will take an hour," I told the guard, "but thank you for the information."

She nodded and stepped back. As she headed for the door, presumably to bring the next inmate down for a visit with her loved ones, I turned to Denise Seaver.

"Doctor."

Her lips twisted. "Savannah. I see you got yourself in the family way again."

Denise Seaver had been my OB-GYN the last time I was pregnant. I'd ended up in Skyline Hospital in Nashville when I had the miscarriage, but she'd seen me both before and after that, in Columbia. She knew all about it, and about Rafe. Once upon a time, she had considered taking him away from LaDonna and selling him to some couple somewhere who couldn't have a baby of their own. But as she'd explained, thirty-one years ago, there'd been less demand for a mixed-race baby. If he'd been the Swedish supermodel type—blond and blue-eyed—things would have been different.

"Rafe and I got married," I told her, lifting my hand with the wedding band. "Two months ago."

"Your mother must be thrilled." The implication was that Mother would be having kittens.

I smiled. "Actually, she is. I didn't think she would be—she wasn't at first—but now that she's gotten to know him, I think she likes him better than she likes me. We're very happy."

The conversation obviously wasn't going the way Denise Seaver had hoped. She'd always been adept at taking jabs at people, and now the jabs weren't working. She looked at Darcy instead. "Who's your friend?"

I made the introductions. "Darcy works for Dix and Jonathan at the law firm."

"Of course." Denise Seaver smirked knowingly.

"We're trying to find Darcy's biological mother," I said. Might as well just spit it out, right? Nothing ventured, nothing gained, and so on. And besides, I didn't want to stay here any longer than I had to. Sitting across the table from her made my skin crawl. "We believe Darcy was born at St. Jerome's Hospital to a young woman who called herself Ora Sweet. She gave her address as 4521 Water Street in Columbia."

Doctor Seaver nodded pleasantly.

"There's no such address. And no one named Ora Sweet ever lived on Water Street in Columbia. Or for that matter anyone else named Sweet."

"Of course not," Denise Seaver said pleasantly. And yet not pleasantly as all, if you know what I mean.

"I would have brought a copy of the birth certificate to show you, but they don't let us bring anything in here other than car keys."

She nodded.

"But we thought you might remember her."

"Oh, I remember. Of course I do."

She sounded very complacent about it. Darcy straightened on her chair.

I gave her a warning glance and turned back to Doctor Seaver. "Are you sure? It was a long time ago." And a dose of healthy disbelief might get us more information than breathless anticipation. Darcy had enough of that for both of us. I might as well provide the counterpoint.

"I had just finished medical school," Denise Seaver said, "and come home to practice. She was one of my first clients."

You always remember your first. Or something.

"So I assume you knew her name wasn't really Ora Sweet?"

"Of course," Denise Seaver said. "We'd gone to school together, after all. She was a year ahead of me, but I knew her quite well. I was the one who told her to give a fake name at the hospital, so her real one wouldn't show up on the birth certificate."

Good to know. "So then you can tell us her real name."

Denise Seaver shook her head, her lips shaped into a superior little smile. "Oh, no."

"No?"

She leaned back, plump little hands folded over her plump stomach. She has a very earth-motherly look about her, with long gray hair and a comfortable sort of figure, and the best part of a year in prison hadn't changed her looks overmuch. Nor her attitude. "There's something called doctor-patient confidentiality, my dear."

"I'm aware of it," I said. *Condescending witch.* "But you're in here, and for all we know, she might have been the victim of a crime. Elspeth was. She was told her baby was dead, and instead you took David and sold him."

"Those were adoption fees, dear."

Her composure wasn't the least bit ruffled.

"And you might have done the same to Ora Sweet." Or whatever her name was.

Denise Seaver shook her head. "It was her decision. She was of age, and capable of making her own choices. Unlike Elspeth, who was underage, and whose father made the decision for her. There was nothing illegal about it."

"There certainly was," I said. "You took her baby and told her he had died. If that isn't illegal, it's immoral, at the very least." And directly opposed to the Hippocratic oath. *First, do no harm.* If harm hadn't been done to Elspeth Caulfield, I didn't know what had.

Denise Seaver just smirked. I reined in my emotions, since this was ancient history, and I couldn't let it interfere with what we were trying to do here today. We had to find out about Ora Sweet, and antagonizing Denise Seaver wasn't likely to get us the information we wanted.

While I restrained myself, Doctor Seaver turned to Darcy. "I'm so sorry, my dear. I know it must be hard to hear these things."

I wondered whether Darcy picked up on the delighted maliciousness in her voice, or whether I was able to just because I'd heard it before.

"But your mother didn't want you," Denise Seaver said, twisting the knife. "She was of age. Mid-twenties. She was more than capable, mentally and financially, of caring for a baby. She just didn't want to."

"That's a horrible thing to say!" I said. "You don't know what her life was like. You might have gone to school with her, but that was years earlier. And you had no idea what was going on in her life when she came to you. She might have been very reluctant to give Darcy up!"

Doctor Seaver giggled. "She seemed happy enough to sign the papers, dear."

Sure. "So you're not going to tell us who she was."

Denise Seaver shook her head. "I told you. Doctor-patient confidentiality."

"Of course." There was nothing more we could do here. I got to my feet. "Let's go, Darcy."

Darcy got to her feet, too, but reluctantly. "I just want to know where I come from," she told Doctor Seaver.

Denise Seaver nodded, and managed to look like she understood and sympathized. "I'm sorry I can't help you, dear." If she had been allowed to reach out and touch, I'm sure she would have leaned over to pat Darcy's hand.

I turned to signal the guard who had brought Darcy in earlier that we were ready to go, only to catch the back of her head as she opened the door into the visitation room for another inmate. The newcomer was dressed in the same boring blue scrubs as everyone else. Except on her, they looked—if not like high fashion, at least somewhat elegant.

She was short, with coloring similar to Darcy's. Long, straight, black hair was scraped back from a stunning face with flawless caramel skin and exotic almond-shaped eyes.

The last time I'd seen her, she'd been wearing a short, tight cocktail dress, and her lips had been lacquered red. Now they were pale, but still perfect. Even without makeup, she was gorgeous. And not just that, but she glowed.

Pregnancy hormones.

"She looks ready to pop," Darcy said, and woke me.

I glanced at her, and then at Denise Seaver. The doctor was looking at me, her expression calculating. "She's due in couple of weeks," she said.

I swallowed and tried to make sure my voice was steady, and

that I sounded untroubled. "At least by the time I get that big, it won't be so hot outside."

Not that she looked like she was suffering. Not from heat, or acid reflux, or swollen ankles, or anything else. None of the things that were bothering me. She glided across the floor without looking right or left—thankfully that meant she didn't notice me—and took a seat at a table on the other side of the room, across from a couple of Hispanic women. One about her own age, with a similarly pretty face, and one older. A mother and a sister, maybe.

"What will happen to her baby?" Darcy asked, and saved me from trying to come up with something coherent to say. My mind was busy calculating due dates and conception dates. Nine months from September 1st, give or take...

"She will keep it with her for the first few months," Denise Seaver said. "After that, her sister will raise it. Until she's released."

"When will that be? What is she in here for?"

"Organized crime and a host of other things," Denise Seaver said. "That baby will be going to high school by the time she gets out."

She sounded gleeful. I wasn't surprised. Her excuse—what she'd always told herself to justify her need to take other people's children away—was that she'd been providing them with better homes. The fact that this baby wouldn't be brought up by a criminal mother, in a penal institution, was one of those things that would totally float Denise Seaver's boat.

"That's a shame." Darcy looked at me, probably wondering why I just stood there like I'd been turned into a pillar of salt. "Did you want to leave, Savannah?"

I did. I really, really did.

"Yes. Let's go." I didn't wait for Denise Seaver to make another snide remark, or for the guard to turn and notice us. I just headed for the door and let Darcy play catch-up behind me.

Fourteen

"That was a waste of time," Darcy said when we were outside the checkpoint and on our way across the parking lot to the car. The hot air combined with the stench from the dump across the highway conspired to make me feel nauseated, or maybe it was just the shock. "We didn't learn anything."

She stopped by the passenger door of the Volvo.

I unkeyed it so she could get in, and then walked around the car and opened the driver's side door. "I'm not so sure. I think we learned a few things."

Like the fact that Carmen Arroyo was pregnant, and that her conception date coincided with the time last winter when she and Rafe had rolled around under the blankets.

But that wasn't what Darcy was talking about. I turned the key in the ignition and cranked the AC up to high. While we waited for the car to cool down, I pushed the thoughts of Carmen and Rafe to the side and continued, "We learned that Ora Sweet—or whoever she was—really was your mother. It sounded like Denise Seaver confirmed that, right?"

Darcy shrugged.

"We learned that you were born at St. Jerome's Hospital. We learned that Denise Seaver knew Ora. We learned that Ora was Doctor Seaver's patient. We learned that they went to school together before Ora was pregnant. High school, I assume, since I doubt Ora went to medical school."

Darcy nodded reluctantly.

"That's all information we can use." I wasn't sure exactly how yet—I wasn't thinking straight—but once I did, I'd come up with something.

"She didn't want me," Darcy said.

I pulled on the gear shift and took my foot off the brake. "You don't know that. Just because Denise Seaver said so, doesn't mean it's true."

"She had no reason to lie," Darcy said.

"She doesn't need a reason. She's mean. And angry. And in prison, probably for the rest of her life. She has no incentive to tell the truth."

"So what do we do now?" Darcy wanted to know.

That was the question, wasn't it? As we rolled out of the parking lot and onto the road, putting Southern Belle Hell behind us, I asked myself the same question.

What did I do now?

Call Rafe and tell him I'd seen Carmen, and she was carrying what might be his baby?

Go home, to the house on Potsdam, and tell him face to face?

Think about it, before I did anything?

Or just pretend I hadn't seen her? She might have been sleeping with other men too, around that same time. It wasn't like their affair had been a love affair. For him it had been business. She had expected him to be seduceable, so he'd let himself be seduced. To do anything else would have put his life and the mission in danger. I'd come to terms with that.

Mostly.

Hell—heck—he and I hadn't even been involved then. He'd left Nashville for Atlanta after the miscarriage, believing the baby I'd lost had been Todd Satterfield's. Not like he'd feel any kind of loyalty to me after that. There had been no reason to say no to Carmen and every reason to say yes.

I had no idea whether their fling had meant anything more to her. It might have. I knew just how easy it was to fall in love with

Rafe. I'd done it even when I knew better. And I wasn't the only one who had, not by a long shot. He'd left a long trail of broken hearts and besotted women behind him.

Carmen might have had feelings for him. She hadn't gotten in touch when she found out she was pregnant, though. And if she were carrying his baby, you'd think she might have.

Then again, by then, she would have known that he wasn't who he'd said he was; that the man she'd slept with was responsible for putting her in prison.

Or rather, her own actions were responsible for putting her in prison. She had committed criminal acts; Rafe had just caught her for them. But she might not see it that way. And it could be a reason why she wouldn't want to contact him and tell him he was about to become a daddy.

Or maybe it wasn't his baby at all.

Without my conscious decision, the car made the choice to go east on Briley Parkway. East, toward Nashville.

Darcy didn't say anything about it. She probably didn't even realize we weren't on our way home.

She caught on when we got off the interstate and turned onto Dickerson Pike and then up Dresden Street, though. I heard her quick intake of breath. "This isn't the way back to Sweetwater."

"I just want to stop by the house for a minute," I said. "I want to see Rafe."

And reassure myself that he was alive, and more than that, that he was mine.

Not that there'd ever been a question about him preferring Carmen. He'd done what he'd had to do, and that was all it had been. He probably hadn't thought about her since.

It would be nice to keep it that way. And tempting to leave well enough alone. If she hadn't told him, maybe it was because it had nothing to do with him. Someone else's baby, not his.

"It's perfectly safe," I told Darcy. "Nothing like what

happened yesterday is going to happen today. The house isn't empty. Rafe's been there all night. So has Wendell, and a couple of the rookies. There won't be anything ugly there."

"I hope you're right," Darcy said.

I hoped so, too.

The house looked calm and quiet when we pulled up in front of it. No windows were shot out or boarded up, and there was no yellow crime scene tape in sight. They must have passed a quiet night.

Rafe's Harley was parked at the bottom of the stairs, along with a pickup truck with a picture of the Virgin Mary on the back window that I knew belonged to José.

I didn't want to accidentally startle him—or anyone else who carried a gun for a living—so I knocked on the door before I inserted the key in the lock. By the time I had the door open, José was standing in the foyer, gun in hand. Down the hall, in the door to the kitchen, I spotted the skinny frame and skin-head buzz-cut that belonged to Clayton.

I smiled and shut the door behind me. "Hello, boys. Is Rafe here?"

They both shook their heads. "He gotta call," José said, in his accented English. "He and Wendell took the Town Car down to the duplex."

I was familiar with the Town Car. Wendell had picked me up for my first date with Rafe in it a year ago.

"Do you know why?"

"It's on fire," José said.

"The duplex? Is on fire?"

They nodded.

Oh-kay. "Any problems last night?"

They both shook their heads. Clayton had ambled up from the kitchen now, and was standing next to José. He was a bit taller and a lot thinner, his muscles ropey, while José was a little fireplug with the sleeves of his polo shirt rolled up above his biceps, not to show them off but because the fabric likely wouldn't stretch that far.

"Any word from Jamal?"

They both shook again, and shadows crossed both their faces. They were in competition with each other constantly, but they were also a team, goading and helping each other through TBI training. To lose a part of the team and not know where he was or what he was doing, must be hard for them.

"We'll drive down to the duplex and see if we can catch Rafe and Wendell there," I said, with a glance at Darcy. "It's on the way home anyway."

Sort of.

"If they come back," I added, "please tell them we stopped by. And ask Rafe to call me."

The boys both nodded.

"Carry on."

We withdrew back out the door. I heard the locks and bolts slam before we'd turned to go down the stairs.

"What's the duplex?" Darcy asked when we were back in the car and on our way down Potsdam Street.

I glanced at the dashboard clock, and then at her. Still a bit too early for lunch. "It belongs to the TBI, I think. In a roundabout sort of way. It's a little house Rafe used to stay in when he'd blow through town during the years he spent undercover. Every once in a while, they put it to use for something else. Something like this. Otherwise, it just sits there."

And the ownership must be deeply hidden, if someone had decided to set up a meth lab next door. Either that, or they'd figured setting up shop next to a building owned by the TBI would make a dandy front, since no one would suspect them of being that stupid.

"It won't take long," I added.

"I'm not doing anything else," Darcy said with a shrug, and settled into the seat.

We were still a mile away when we saw the spiral of smoke reaching toward the sky.

"That must be it," Darcy said.

I nodded. "I wonder what happened." There were only so many options, and I didn't think a lightning strike was likely. "It would have to be either an accident or arson, I guess. Rafe said the people next door were cooking methamphetamine. Maybe their place exploded."

I hoped they'd made it out in time. I know they were criminals, and in a sense murderers, but I didn't want them dead. Behind bars was good enough.

"Yikes," Darcy said and turned pale. "Is it safe?"

"If Wendell and Rafe went down there, I'm sure it is. And it's not like we're going to crawl through the debris. And anyway, if we're not supposed to be there, there'll be barricades."

Darcy nodded, but bit her lip worriedly.

The closer we got, the thicker the smoke became. And the thicker the traffic was, too. By the time we turned onto the street where the duplex sat, there were people everywhere, gawking at what was going on. Lights flashed where a big fire engine was parked crosswise in the middle of the street, stopping anyone from going further.

I pulled over to the side and slotted the Volvo in, carefully, between a couple of parked cars, and cut the engine. "Looks like we'll have to walk the rest of the way."

"Are you sure we should?" Darcy asked, although she did open her door.

"You don't have to. You can wait here. But my husband's up there. I want to see him."

Darcy didn't say anything, but when I struck out for the other side of the fire truck, she followed.

On the far side of the fire engine, a couple of firemen in

heavy gear were busy coiling hoses. The street ran with water along both sides, and a burned-out truck sat in the driveway of the meth house. The house itself was gone: just a patch of burned grass was left, and about half a chimney. Debris was everywhere, and what had to be investigators were crawling all over the ground, dressed in Hazmat suits. I gulped, and then coughed. The air was thick with the smell of fire and floating ash.

"It looks like the house in the *Wizard of Oz* during the tornado," Darcy said softly. "Like it was just scooped up and carried off."

I nodded. "I don't think it was. This debris is all that's left of it, I bet."

Burnt pieces of wood, charred beams, roof shingles, all were strewn across the road in front of us and the grass of the neighbors' lawns.

"I think it exploded," I added.

"That wasn't the duplex, was it?"

I shook my head. No, thank God. "The duplex is up there. To the right. Or maybe *was* up there is better."

There wasn't much left of it, either.

Or perhaps I shouldn't say that. The walls were standing, and some of the roof was intact. The windows had blown out, but the door was still there, even if it was hanging open. And there were investigators going in and around it, too, but they weren't wearing hazmat suits. Just good old firemen in T-shirts and uniform pants.

"There's your husband," Darcy said, and pointed.

I nodded. There he was, in a huddle with Wendell and one of the firemen, an older gentleman with an impressive walrus moustache.

"Must be the fire chief."

"Or the arson investigator," Darcy said.

Yes, maybe so. "Let's go see what happened."

They were standing at the bottom of the driveway, well away from the shell of the house. We had to jump over fire hoses and detour around puddles to get there. And we had only gone about half the way when Rafe looked up and saw us.

He scowled. I smiled brightly and waved. He scowled harder. I ignored the expression and kept coming.

"You shouldn't be here," he told me when I was close enough to be able to hear him, with Darcy a step or two behind. His scowl seemed to work better on her than on me.

"We stopped by the house on our way home from the Tennessee Women's Prison. José told us what happened."

I turned to look at the duplex.

"Tennessee Women's Prison?" Rafe said, moving close to me. I had thought that might get his attention off the fact that we were here and onto something different.

"We went to talk to Denise Seaver. To see if she'd be willing to tell us anything about Darcy's mother."

"That the woman who killed your sister-in-law?"

I grimaced. "Yes. And took David away from Elspeth. And kidnapped Oliver Cartwright. And killed the other doctor, the one we met at St. Jerome's when I took you there. Remember?"

Rafe nodded. "You thought she might wanna help you?"

"As a matter of fact, I didn't expect her to be willing to help me. And she wasn't. But she let slip a couple of pieces of information we might be able to use."

"You shoulda told me you were going there."

"It wouldn't have made any difference," I told him. "You couldn't have come with us. You had more important things to do this morning." I glanced around, at the big mess surrounding us, and all its implications. And then I looked back at him. He still had the dreadlocks and the gold teeth, but at least he'd dug out a pair of jeans that fit—very nicely, I might add—and a T-shirt that stretched tight across his chest and shoulder and tapered to his waist. "And anyway, I'm not about to take you into a room full of man-starved female prisoners. They'd fall on you like a pack of wolves."

He grinned. "It's a curse."

"Sure it is." I leaned into him, my head on his shoulder. His arm settled more firmly around me. "So what happened here? Did the meth lab explode?"

"No," Rafe said, and changed his mind. "It did. Later. But that wasn't what started this. Someone threw a firebomb through the window of the duplex, and the fire spread next door. The place went up like fireworks."

"Casualties?"

"Two in the lab. One in the duplex."

"Someone was living in the duplex?"

"The cop I told you about," Rafe said. "From narcotics. He moved in yesterday to keep an eye on the folks next door."

"And now he's dead?" How horrible!

Rafe shook his head. "He's fine. He made it out. That's how we know what happened. He was on the other side when the bottle went through the window in the part I'd been using."

"Someone thought they were going to get you?"

He shrugged.

"So if the cop made it out, who's the dead body?"

"Dunno yet," Rafe said.

"Do you think..." It wasn't a very pleasant thought, but— "We didn't overlook a set of remains back at the beginning of the summer, did we?" When we'd been scouring the woods behind the house for the bodies of dead prostitutes.

"I don't think so. And anyway, they were down to bones."

They had been. Several skeletons of young women dumped in the woods behind the house.

But if this was a real body, one with flesh on the bones, it wasn't likely to be one of them.

"So who—?" And then I realized what he was very carefully

not telling me. "Oh, no. He wouldn't have been stupid enough to come here, would he?"

"He mighta thought I'd be here," Rafe said. "And when I wasn't, he decided to spend the night."

"You haven't heard from him?"

Rafe shook his head, his expression grim.

"You've tried to call him again, I assume? And told him he needs to answer because you're worried about him?"

"Yes, darlin'." His tone said he didn't need me to tell him his business, but he didn't actually say so out loud. I snuggled into his side and tried to give what comfort I could as we both stared up toward the duplex and the van from the morgue making its slow way up the driveway.

Fifteen

Darcy and I didn't stay long after that. There was literally nothing I could do to help, and Rafe had important things to deal with. So we said goodbye and got back in the car. Rafe promised he'd let me know as soon as the M.E. determined whether the remains were Jamal's or some other unfortunate soul who had gotten mixed up in this mess.

"Here's what I think we ought to do," I told Darcy as we headed west on Bell Road to meet up with the interstate toward Sweetwater.

"Yes?"

"If Ora Sweet was a patient of Denise Seaver's, there's a record of it somewhere. The birth records at St. Jerome's went back more than thirty-four years. I bet Doctor Seaver's records did, too. And speaking of St. Jerome's Hospital..."

"Yes?" Darcy said.

"This road we're on passes within a couple of minutes of it. Would you like to take a look? There won't be anything to see other than the building itself—it's still in operation, so we could walk around in it, I suppose, although I'm not sure what purpose it would serve. But you could at least see where you were born. If you wanted. It isn't far out of the way."

"Yes," Darcy said. "Please."

"I'll turn off when we get down there. But in the meantime... Doctor Seaver probably has records of Ora Sweet. Or whatever her real name was."

"How would we know what her real name was?" Darcy wanted to know. "I mean, if we could get access to the records, how would we know which woman was Ora Sweet? If she went by her real name when she saw Doctor Seaver? And she must have, if they knew one another from before."

It was a good question. I thought for a minute, and then ventured, "By the due date? She was a young woman, mid-twenties, whose baby was due within a week or so of the day you were born. And your weight at birth indicates a full-term baby, so you weren't more than a few days early, if you were early at all. One week in either direction should do it."

"That makes sense," Darcy allowed. "How do we get access to the records?"

That was going to be the tricky part, and I told her so. "Doctor Seaver was part of a medical practice in Columbia. It had several other doctors in addition to Doctor Seaver. They're all still in business, and I'm sure they have good security." Doctors' offices keep drugs and things like that on hand, don't they? "We can't just waltz in there and start digging through their files. And anyway, they might not have records going that far back on the premises. They probably have a storage facility somewhere, where they keep them. If they even exist anymore. They could have turned them into electronic files and pulped the paper. And it's going to take a better hacker than me to access those."

"Me, too," Darcy admitted.

"But Denise Seaver strikes me as someone who'd keep personal records. Unless the police confiscated them, and unless her house has been packed up and sold in the time she's been in prison, we might find them there."

Darcy's eyebrows rose so far that they disappeared behind her spiky bangs. "Break into her house?"

"It's not like she'll be there," I said reasonably. "We know where she is, and it isn't anywhere near Sweetwater."

"No..." She sounded shocked, but intrigued, too. "Do you know where she lives?"

Indeed, I did. Denise Seaver's kitchen was where the incident with the gun, the pepper spray, and the frying pan had taken place. "One of the subdivisions on the outskirts of Sweetwater. Dix lives in Copper Creek. Denise Seaver's house is in the one that backs up to it."

"A subdivision full of McMansions," Darcy said. "Those houses are built close together. Won't there be people around who'll see us?"

"Not if we're careful. Denise Seaver's house backs up to a band of trees. And Marley Cartwright's house is on the other side. We could park in Copper Creek, near Marley's house, and walk through the trees."

That was how I'd ended up in Denise Seaver's kitchen that night last November. Marley had realized what had happened, that Doctor Seaver had stolen Oliver, and had taken off through the trees. I hadn't had a choice but to follow. And a good thing I did, because Denise Seaver would have finished her off if I hadn't.

"If we go after dark," I added, "I don't think anyone would see us."

Marley would probably give us access to her property if we asked. We could park in her driveway and walk through her yard.

Although I wasn't sure I wanted to involve her. If she didn't know anything, she couldn't give anything away. Just in case someone asked.

"Don't worry," I told Darcy, "I've broken into lots of places."

Most of them with Rafe, who knows how to pick a lock, but a few on my own, too. We'd manage. Somehow.

"And you haven't gotten caught?"

I've gotten caught a few times. But it was probably better not to mention that. And anyway, it was by cops who knew me, so they'd let me go with a warning.

I wondered whether, if Sheriff Satterfield caught me breaking and entering, he would be as gracious?

Seeing as he was dating my mother, maybe he would.

But there was time enough to worry about that later. For right now, I needed to take Darcy up the hill to St. Jerome's Hospital, so she could see where she was born.

The hospital is located in Brentwood, up a winding road from Old Hickory Boulevard, just a couple of miles from the interstate. We pulled into the parking lot and stopped in front of the big brick building.

"It's old," Darcy said after a moment. "And small."

I nodded. "It's a private hospital. Religious. And it's been here a while. More than a hundred years, judging from the architecture."

She glanced at me. "So I was born here?"

"That's what it looks like. Ora Sweet—whoever she is—came here from Sweetwater to give birth." And had probably gone back home again after.

"Do you want to go inside?" I asked.

She hesitated. "I don't know what the point would be. The records aren't here anymore. We saw them yesterday at the police station. And I'm sure things have changed in the past thirty-four years. They probably don't look the way they did when I was born."

"I wonder if there's anyone left who was working here then? Denise Seaver practiced medicine thirty-four years ago, and she'd still be practicing now if she hadn't gone to prison. It's possible there's a nurse who was a young woman when you were born."

"She probably wouldn't remember me," Darcy said, although she sounded intrigued.

"It can't hurt to ask." I reached for my door handle. On the other side of the car, Darcy did the same thing.

The desk in the lobby was occupied by the same redhead who'd been sitting there last November. The tag pinned to her top still said her name was Molly Murphy. I remembered her, and when she looked up and I saw her eyes narrow, I realized she must remember me, too.

"You've been here before, haven't you?"

I nodded. "I saw Doctor Rushing for a few minutes last fall. I was pregnant, and worried that I'd miscarry."

Molly glanced at my stomach. "What happened?" This obviously wasn't the same stomach as back then.

"I lost the baby," I said, my voice steady. "That same night, I think."

"I'm sorry." The corners of her mouth turned down. "But it looks like you're doing well now."

"Six months along. Everything's great."

"Who are you seeing?"

I told her the name of my OB-GYN, and she nodded. "She's good. Especially with high risk pregnancies. So what can I do for you? Doctor Rushing is no longer here."

I was aware of that. He'd been killed pretty much at the same time I was having my miscarriage. We'd visited his murderer in prison this morning.

"My friend Darcy was born here," I said. Molly nodded a greeting. "We were wondering whether you had anyone still on staff who was working here thirty-four years ago. Obviously not Doctor Rushing..."

Although that would have been great. He had probably delivered Darcy. One more disappointment we could chalk up to Denise Seaver, for having put him beyond our questions.

Molly hesitated. She probably didn't want to help us—confidentiality and all that—but at the same time, she had to know that there had been things going on at St. Jerome's that hadn't been on the up and up, and she didn't want to seem like she was trying to hide anything else.

"Maybe a nurse who worked the maternity ward back then...?" I coaxed.

Molly made a decision. "I'll check and see if Sister Bridget is working."

"Sister?" Darcy mouthed while Molly got busy on the computer.

I shrugged.

Sister Bridget was working, as it turned out, and Molly told us to go up to the third floor, where she'd be waiting. "She won't have a lot of time to talk," Molly warned, "so try to make it quick."

"That was easier than I thought it would be," I whispered to Darcy as we waited for the elevator.

She nodded. "She probably won't remember anything."

Maybe not. But maybe we'd get lucky and Sister Bridget was one of those people with long memories who never forget the details.

I expected a nun. I'm sure Darcy did, too. But Sister Bridget was dressed in the same pink or blue scrubs as everyone else on the maternity floor. They brought to mind the prison uniforms we'd seen this morning.

She did keep her hair covered, under a modified wimple that was really just a scarf tied over her head. Little wisps of gray stuck out at her ears and over her forehead.

She was probably ten years older than Mother, in her late sixties or maybe even early seventies, but she moved like a young girl, bouncing back and forth on rubber clogs. Her face was as wrinkled as a dry apple, however. No Botox injections or fancy face creams for Sister Bridget.

When we got off the elevator, she was standing there waiting. A quick glance at the both of us, and she knew who was here to see her. It could have been because Molly Murphy had told her 'not the pregnant one,' but I don't think so.

"You must be Darcy." She reached out a hand. Darcy took it. "I don't have a lot of time, but we can take a couple of minutes in the break room. This way." She squeaked off on rubber soles, pulling Darcy behind her. I brought up the rear, looking around at the closed doors. Halfway down the hall was a big window into the nursery, and my steps slowed as I peered in at all the wrinkled newborns, swaddled in pastel cloths with little color-coded caps on their heads.

Before much longer, one of those would be mine.

Not here, though. There wasn't enough money in the world to convince me it would be safe to have my baby at St. Jerome's. What if I woke up the next morning and found that someone had taken him or her?

Granted, with Doctor Rushing dead and Denise Seaver in prison, I'm sure the baby-ring was disbanded. But still. It wasn't a chance I wanted to take.

More to the point, thirty-four years ago, one of those sleeping or squalling infants had been Darcy. And Sister Bridget might be able to tell us something about that time. I abandoned the view and hustled to catch up.

The break room was a small area behind the nursery. It boasted a sink, a refrigerator, a microwave that had seen better days, a couple of kitchen cabinets, and vending machines for soft drinks and snacks. I was happy to see that nurses didn't seem any more immune to the lure of sugar than the rest of us.

At the moment it was empty—the room, not the vending machine; that was fully stocked, and calling my name. Sister Bridget sank down on a chair with a little grunt—probably happy to be off her feet—and Darcy took a seat on the other side of the table. I bee-lined for the machine. We still hadn't had lunch, and the baby was letting me know it.

"Anyone want anything?" I asked over my shoulder.

"No," Darcy said. "Thank you."

Sister Bridget shook her head. "I have some yogurt in the fridge I'll get it in a minute. But you go ahead. Gotta keep that baby fed."

Yes, indeed. I dug in my purse for coins and fed them into the machine. A few seconds later, a Kit-Kat bar tumbled into the slot. Chocolate, yes, but also crispy wafers. I could almost talk myself into believing it was good for me.

While I tore off the paper and bit in, the other two started talking. "Molly said you were born here," Sister Bridget said.

Darcy nodded.

"Thirty-four years ago," I added, around the chocolate. "Denise Seaver in Columbia was her mother's obstetrician."

Sister Bridget's face darkened. "You know what happened to Doctor Seaver?"

"She's in prison," Darcy said softly. "We went and saw her this morning."

If Sister Bridget was surprised, it didn't show on her face. At her age, she'd probably seen enough—of everything—that nothing much surprised her anymore.

"She remembered Ora Sweet," I added, "but she wouldn't tell us anything about her. Cited doctor-patient privilege."

Sister Bridget nodded. "And that's a real thing. Can't blame her for that."

Actually, I could, but it was probably better not to say so. "Darcy just wants to try to find her birth mother," I said. "Her parents passed on—" Darcy glanced at me, but didn't interrupt, "and now she wants to know where she came from. And whether she has any biological family who might be interested in getting to know her. Thirty-four years is a long time, and her mother might have changed her mind about not wanting her baby. We think that maybe her mother was responsible for getting Darcy the job she has right now, in Sweetwater."

"How's that?" Sister Bridget wanted to know.

We told her the story about the newspaper clipping and the Sweetwater postmark, and she nodded. "Sounds like your mama might have wanted a look at you, precious."

"And if so," I said, "her mother did kind of make the first move. So it's OK for us to try to figure out who she was."

That was more of a stretch, since Ora—or whatever name she went by these days—hadn't made a move toward telling Darcy the truth. But it made sense. From where Darcy and I were sitting, anyway.

"I can't tell you much," Sister Bridget said. "It was a long time ago. I've rocked a lot of babies since then."

She undoubtedly had.

"But I remember her. You look like her."

"I do?" Darcy sounded surprised. I was, too. If Darcy's mother lived in Sweetwater, she must be someone I knew. And if I knew her, I should have noticed the resemblance.

"She was younger than you," Sister Bridget said, "but not as young as some of our girls. Not married, or if she was, her husband wasn't with her."

It hadn't even crossed my mind that Ora might have been married. I guess because most people who are married, especially when they're in their mid-twenties, wouldn't give up a baby for adoption.

Unless she hadn't. Maybe I'd been right and Denise Seaver had taken it away without Ora's permission, like she had done with David.

"Did she... was it her choice to put Darcy up for adoption, or did Denise Seaver and Doctor Rushing do that?"

Sister Bridget's expression was sympathetic. "She did it herself, dear. I'm not sure she wanted to—she was crying when she signed the papers—but she did it herself."

Bummer.

"Do you remember the baby? Darcy?"

Sister Bridget smiled at her. "You were a pretty little thing. Lots of black hair, like your mama. Your new parents came and got you the next day. They looked like a nice couple."

"They were," Darcy said softly. "I had a good life. I'm just... curious, I guess. Especially since my mother—if it was my mother—made sure I got to Sweetwater."

"Anything else you can tell us?" I asked Sister Bridget. "How long did Darcy's mother stay here?"

"Another day after the baby left. We kept them forty-eight hours in those days, for a vaginal birth."

Hearing the word 'vaginal' come out of the mouth of a seventy-year-old nun was a little disturbing. Maybe it shouldn't have been, but I wanted to squirm.

"And you don't know her real name, right? Did anyone come to visit her while she was here?"

Sister Bridget shook her head. "I'm afraid not. Or if they did, it wasn't while I was working." She glanced at the clock above the door. "And speaking of work..."

"We'll get out of your hair and give you some time to eat your yogurt in peace," I said, as Darcy got up from the table. "Thank you for your time."

"My pleasure." The smile she gave us looked like she meant it. "Your mother loved you, precious. I don't know why she decided she couldn't keep you. She must have had her reasons. But it wasn't because she didn't want to. I could tell."

Darcy's eyes welled up. "Thank you," she managed.

Sister Bridget nodded briskly and turned her attention to me. "Nice to have met you. You take care of that baby."

I promised her I would, and then I took Darcy's arm and led her out of the break room and over to the elevator, since I wasn't sure she was able to see the way without a little help.

Rafe called when we were halfway to Sweetwater. Neither one of us had said much—Darcy was still processing the information we had learned, and I was thinking about that, and also still about Carmen, and wondering what reason a twenty-five year old woman might have for not wanting to keep her baby.

The car was quiet, and the tones of *Hot Stuff* cut through the air like a drill sergeant's whistle. Darcy jumped, and I did, too.

It took me a few seconds to fumble the phone out of my purse. "Hello?"

"It's me," Rafe said.

"I know it's you. I have you programmed."

There was a beat. "You sound grumpy."

"I'm hungry," I said. We still hadn't stopped for lunch, and the effects of the Kit-Kat had long since worn off.

"Sorry, darlin'. Go get yourself something. Where are you?"

"Halfway down the interstate to Sweetwater. We stopped by St. Jerome's Hospital on the way and spoke to an old nun who was there when Darcy was born. She remembered Ora."

"Good for Darcy," my husband's voice said in my ear. "Now take care of yourself, and my baby. He needs food."

Or she.

"I'll stop and get some once we get off the interstate," I promised. "What can I do for you?"

"It ain't Jamal," Rafe said.

"Great!" He didn't answer, and I added, "It's good, right?"

"Yes and no," Rafe said.

"How can it not be good? If it isn't Jamal, then Jamal's alive." And if Jamal was alive, then he would still be able to do the right thing as far as Alexandra was concerned. Whatever 'the right thing' in that situation turned out to be.

"So far as we know," Rafe said.

Well, yes. But surely this was a positive sign? "So who's the dead person?"

"That's the bad part," Rafe said. "Remember the jackass who

shot at you yesterday?"

"He didn't actually shoot. Just sighted. But yes. I remember. He also shot somebody else and left him in my kitchen."

"That's the guy."

"The dead body? He's the last of your missing three gang members?"

"Uh-huh," Rafe said.

"But if he's the dead body, who threw the firebomb through the window? It wasn't him. Not if he's dead."

"That's what we gotta find out," Rafe said grimly.

Sixteen

We ended up at Cracker Barrel again. It looked like Darcy and I had found ourselves a place to call our own. Over salad for Darcy and a chicken sandwich for me—I needed something more sustaining than lettuce—I asked her, "How do you feel?"

She shrugged, sort of helplessly. Probably hadn't sorted it out in her head yet.

"She seemed nice. And sincere."

Darcy nodded. "But Denise Seaver was right. My mother didn't want me."

"That's not what Sister Bridget said. She said Ora was crying when she signed the papers. I think she did want you, but for one reason or another, she couldn't keep you."

"I don't know why," Darcy said. "She was of age. She probably had a job. And it didn't happen so long ago that women were ostracized for having babies out of wedlock."

Depends on your family. Me getting pregnant out of wedlock last year, at a year or two older than Ora had been when she had Darcy, certainly hadn't made my mother happy.

Then again, we were Martins. We had to set an example.

So was Ora's family one that had to set an example, too? And having a baby without a husband was a no-no? Was that why she had given Darcy away?

Hell, maybe Darcy's mother was my brother's sister Regina. She's short and dark—Darcy was tall and dark, but she could have gotten the height from her unknown father—and I didn't think Aunt Regina had been married thirty-four years ago. Maybe she'd gotten pregnant out of wedlock and my grandparents had made her give the baby up for adoption. It would even explain the darker cast to Darcy's skin. Aunt Regina looks like the Martin side of the family, dark-haired and a bit sallow; a heritage from great-great-grandfather William, the son of the groom. Stuff like that can lie dormant for generations and then suddenly show up out of nowhere.

Naturally I didn't mention that possibility to Darcy. I'd have to investigate a little more in depth first. I was really just making a wild guess here. One without any foundation in... never mind fact: no foundation in anything expect my imagination.

"We don't know anything about Ora's situation," I said instead. "Maybe when we find her, and ask, it will make sense."

Darcy nodded, her eyes downcast, picking at her salad.

"Even if she couldn't keep you then," I added, dredging a French fry through ketchup and lifting it to my mouth, "she must want to get to know you now. She made sure you came up here and got a job."

At least it made the most sense, with what we knew now, that it was Ora who had sent the clipping to Birmingham, and not some other entity, like a potential boyfriend. I could probably forget looking into Dix's client, the one who had asked Darcy for a date repeatedly. If we found Darcy's biological mother and she denied having sent the clipping, there'd be time enough to look into him later.

Darcy glanced up. "That's true."

"I'm sure when you meet her, she'll explain everything."

Darcy shrugged, but she looked a bit more cheered.

"I need to go see my aunt this afternoon," I said, "but tonight we can go over to Denise Seaver's house, if you want, to look for those records. It'll be better to do it after dark, anyway. Less chance of anyone seeing us. Or if you just want me to go on my own, that's OK, too. I don't mind. That way you don't have to make the drive from Columbia."

"I don't mind," Darcy said. "I'd like to be there."

Good. Breaking and entering is always better with company. We arranged to meet in front of Dix's house at eight—since Darcy knew where it was—and then we'd move on from there. And after that, I took her home and dropped her off so I could deal with a couple of other things.

One of them was Aunt Regina. But on my way over to my aunt's house, I gave some thought to what Rafe had told me earlier.

The dead body in the duplex wasn't Jamal. That was good news.

The fact that Jamal was still missing was the bad news.

And I wasn't sure whether it was my imagination or something else, but Rafe had seemed worried. And not just about Jamal being missing—although that was worrisome enough. But I'd gotten the distinct vibe that he was worried about something else. Like, about Jamal having killed the gang banger in the duplex, and Jamal having lobbed the firebomb through the window to hide the evidence.

The gang banger hadn't done it, after all. So someone else must have.

Or there was a mastermind behind the whole thing, and that mastermind had instructed the now-dead gang banger to eliminate his comrades. Now-dead gang banger had complied, and had reported to the mastermind that the job was done. And the mastermind had gone to the duplex and eliminated the last of the gang bangers.

I liked that idea better. All Rafe had to do was figure out who the mastermind was, and make sure he didn't kill Jamal, and all was well.

And in the meantime, I had my aunt to talk to.

Aunt Regina and Uncle Sid married later in life. They never had children; I don't know whether that was by choice or by nature. It had never occurred to me to ask, to be honest. Could be that they were too old when they got married—or thought they were. Could be that Aunt Regina shared my problems, and after a few miscarriages they gave up. Or they could just have decided they preferred to focus on one another.

Dad inherited the Martin Mansion from his father. Aunt Regina, meanwhile, moved into the small but choice Victorian cottage Uncle Sid took over from his parents. They retired to Arizona at some point, to get away from the humidity, and Aunt Regina and Uncle Sid moved in.

I parked outside the white picket fence—shades of Tom Sawyer—and just sat there and watched the house for a moment.

It's a Folk Victorian cottage with just two bedrooms; one for the master and mistress of the house and the other for Aunt Regina's office. Uncle Sid spends most of his time on the golf course now that he's retired.

The house is pale pink with white trim, and looks like a frosted cupcake. The yard behind the pickets burgeons with flowers, since Aunt Regina enjoys gardening when the weather isn't too hot.

It was much too hot now, but on a steamy Sunday afternoon, she was sitting on the porch sipping lemonade and fanning herself. After a few seconds, when I didn't get out of the car, she got to her feet and waved.

I waved back—not sure she could see me through the window—and opened the door. The heat hit me like a wall, and the walk to the porch was like wading through molasses, the air so thick it took effort to move through it.

I collapsed into one of the wicker chairs. "Hi."

"Savannah." Aunt Regina smiled and handed me a glass of lemonade, so cold the condensation burned my fingers. "You look like you could use this."

"It's hot. And the baby makes it feel worse." I stretched my legs out and looked at them. "I have swollen ankles."

"So do I," my aunt said comfortably and settled back again with her own glass.

We sat in silence a minute and just enjoyed the cool liquid. It had thin slices of lemons floating in it.

"Is Uncle Sid golfing?" I asked eventually.

Aunt Regina nodded. "Can't imagine why he'd want to, in this heat, but it's an obsession with him. Don't know what he'll do while we're on the cruise."

"I think they have driving ranges on cruise ships," I said, although I had no idea, really. "I'm surprised he didn't offer to take you somewhere with a lot of golf courses instead."

"He wanted to go to Scotland," Aunt Regina said, with a grimace. "Cold and damp."

But with a lot of golf courses. And interesting architecture, fascinating history, and men in kilts. I would have done that before I went on a cruise.

Not that Rafe is particularly interested in golf. Or cruises. Or for that matter, men in kilts. He'd happily go back to the beach, though. But he likes getting in the water, not just being on top of it.

"Everything all right with you and your young man?" Aunt Regina asked.

"Fine, thank you. He's working a lot."

"Undercover," Aunt Regina nodded. "I heard."

"I spoke to him about an hour ago. He's fine." Apart from being worried about Jamal, and what Jamal might have done.

"I'm glad you were able to work things out." She leaned forward and put her glass on the table. "So to what do I owe the honor?"

I must have looked confused, because she added, gently, "You don't usually stop by out of the blue on a Sunday afternoon, Savannah. What do you want to talk about?"

Well, that was getting straight to the point, anyway. So I might as well do the same, and not beat around the bush.

"I've been helping Darcy look for her biological mother," I said. And kept a close eye on my aunt as I said it, in case her expression gave something away.

It didn't. "Your brother's receptionist?"

"She was adopted. Her parents are dead. She wants to know whether her biological mother is still alive."

"Here?"

"We're thinking she might be here," I said, and explained about the newspaper clipping and the Sweetwater postmark, as well as Ora Sweet and how she'd been Denise Seaver's patient. "She would have been around your age, I guess. Maybe a little younger."

"Definitely a little younger," Aunt Regina said. "Unless she lied about her age."

"Denise Seaver said Ora was a year ahead of her in school. I assume high school and not medical school."

"I think you can safely assume that," my aunt said. "I was a couple of years ahead of Denise. Robert was a year ahead, I think."

Robert being my late father and Aunt Regina's brother. He passed away a few years ago, so it wasn't like I could ask him.

"Did you know anyone named Ora?"

"No one that comes to mind," Aunt Regina said. And if she was trying to hide that she was Ora and had had a baby out of wedlock in her twenties, she was doing a masterful job of it. I didn't get any indication that she was involved in any way. No sense of guilt, or worry, or even surprise.

But I could still pick her brain.

"What about someone who was pregnant? This would have been before you married Uncle Sid."

"A few years," Aunt Regina nodded. "Some people find their

soul mates early in life, and some people take a little longer."

Nothing wrong with that. I'd found mine, but I hadn't been particularly quick about it. It had taken me a fair amount of time to accept the truth, I guess.

That's if you believe in such things as soul mates, of course. But Aunt Regina and Uncle Sid had been married for thirty years, so whether they were soul mates or not, they'd obviously found something that had lasted.

"And I don't remember anyone who was pregnant out of wedlock," Aunt Regina added. "Except for LaDonna Collier, of course. Bless her heart."

Of course. "This would have been before LaDonna. About three years before. Darcy's thirty-four." And LaDonna had been eleven when Darcy was born, so there was no chance she could have been Darcy's mother. Bad enough she'd become pregnant with Rafe at fourteen. "And Darcy's mother would have been at least ten years older than LaDonna."

Aunt Regina shook her head. "No one comes to mind. Lots of women were pregnant, of course, and had babies, but I can't recall anyone being pregnant and then not showing up with one."

"Some people are able to hide that they're pregnant," I said. "I guess if they're tall. Or big already. And the babies are small..."

Aunt Regina shrugged. "If she didn't look pregnant, I wouldn't have known."

"Not unless she told you."

"I'm certain no one told me," Aunt Regina said firmly. "I would remember that."

OK, then. "We went to Tennessee Women's Prison this morning and talked to Doctor Seaver."

"Oh, dear," Aunt Regina sighed.

"It was OK. A little strange, but not too unpleasant. The

worst thing—" Other than the pregnant Carmen, and she wasn't something I wanted to share with my aunt, "was the smell from the city dump across the highway. I'm glad I don't live out there."

Aunt Regina wrinkled her nose in sympathy, and for a moment we both sat in silence and enjoyed the smell of the flowers and the buzzing of the bees.

"Anyway," I said, "she wouldn't tell us anything. Although she did confirm that Ora was Darcy's mother and that she was from this area. But on our way home, we stopped at St. Jerome's Hospital—where Darcy was born—and talked to a nurse who had worked there back then. She remembered Ora and the baby. And she said that Darcy looks like her mother."

Aunt Regina tilted her head sideways, like a plump bird. Those twelve pounds Mother had mentioned, hadn't made much of a difference as far as I could tell. "I've seen Darcy."

I nodded.

"I can't think of anyone she particularly resembles."

I couldn't, either. Although there had been times when I'd looked at her and caught a glimpse of something familiar. Not familiar enough to pin down, unfortunately. But it was enough to make me think that Ora was someone I knew. Or maybe not knew personally, but someone I saw around town on a regular basis. The waitress at the Café on the Square, the check-out clerk at the drugstore or library, Beulah Odom.

Although most of the waitresses at the Café on the Square were younger than Darcy and the check-out clerk at the drugstore was Yvonne McCoy, who was my brother's age.

"Did you know Beulah Odom?" I asked my aunt.

She nodded. "Of course. Beulah's Meat'n Three has been a fixture around here since I was a girl. We ran her obituary in the *Reporter* a week ago."

And then she shook her head. "She's too old, Savannah. She would have been closer to forty thirty-four years ago."

"I know. This is about something else."

"What's that?" Aunt Regina asked, and settled in to listen to gossip.

"Well, before she died, Beulah wrote a will in favor of Yvonne McCoy, one of the waitresses at the meat'n three. Do you know Yvonne?"

"Big-chested redhead," my aunt said. "She went to school with your brother."

"That's her. Beulah wanted Yvonne to take over the restaurant after she was gone. She was teaching her how to run it. But Beulah's sister-in-law and niece are contesting the will. I told Yvonne she should hire Catherine to represent her."

Aunt Regina nodded approval. "Your brother is too much of a gentleman to go after a couple of women. Catherine won't let that stop her."

No, she wouldn't. While my sister had received the same upbringing I had, she'd turned out a lot tougher. At least in a courtroom.

"Do you know them? The sister-in-law and niece?" If anyone would, it was my aunt. The society reporter.

Aunt Regina shook her head. "I'm afraid not. They're from Franklin, I think. Or Leiper's Fork. Somewhere in Williamson County. Beulah's brother settled up there. And rarely came back down this way. They're too good for us simple folk, I guess. Or think they are."

In that case, it was even harder to imagine why they'd want Beulah's Meat'n Three.

"I don't suppose you've heard any rumors about Beulah's death?"

"No," Aunt Regina said, perking up. "Are there rumors?"

"If you haven't heard any, probably not. Sheriff Satterfield and Officer Vasquez with the Columbia PD both said it looked like a heart attack. And the M.E. ruled natural causes."

"Then I'm sure that's all it is," my aunt said, looking disappointed.

I pushed to my feet. "I should go home and lie down for a bit. See if I can get my ankles back to normal before tonight."

"What's happening tonight?" my aunt wanted to know.

I hesitated, and then decided I might as well tell her. If something went wrong, at least someone would know where we'd gone. "Darcy and I are going over to Denise Seaver's house to see if we can find any records she may have kept from thirty-four years ago."

My aunt's eyebrows arched. "Do you have a key?"

I shook my head.

"You're breaking in?"

"I'm hoping we'll find a hide-a-key or something, so we don't actually have to break anything. But yes. I guess we are."

"Be careful," Aunt Regina said.

It was my turn to arch my brows. "You aren't going to tell me not to do it?"

She stretched her legs out. "I'm a reporter, Savannah. You think I haven't been in that position before? You go where the story takes you."

I hadn't realized that being the society reporter for a local newspaper in a small town in Middle Tennessee involved quite so much excitement, but as long as she didn't threaten to rat me out to Mother or Bob Satterfield, I was good with playing along. "That's what I thought."

"Make sure you bring a flashlight and wear dark clothes."

I said I would. "I should probably call and tell Darcy that, too."

"That would probably be a good idea," Aunt Regina nodded. "Have a good time."

I assured her we would, and took myself off in the car, while I wondered at this side of my aunt I'd never seen before. It was good advice, however, so I did slip into a pair of black yoga pants and a dark T-shirt before heading out that night. No sense in tempting fate by stepping out in high heels and a sundress. We'd be pushing our way through the woods behind Marley Cartwright's house to get to Denise Seaver's place, so good footwear would be helpful, and besides, I didn't want my favorite maternity dress snagged on a tree branch. And if something went wrong and we were arrested, the yoga pants and T-shirt would be a lot more comfortable for a night in jail than my usual attire.

Darcy was already there when I pulled up in front of Dix's house in Copper Creek. Unfortunately, so was Dix. Out in the street outside the house, leaning on Darcy's window.

She looked very uncomfortable.

"What are you doing?" I asked my brother after turning off the Volvo and getting out.

"Talking to my receptionist. What are you doing?"

I had to think fast. "We're going to exercise. By walking around your subdivision. It's safer to walk here than on the other roads."

Dix looked skeptical. "Now?"

"It's less hot after the sun goes down."

He couldn't very well argue with that.

"We thought we'd park our cars here at your house," I said, "since Darcy knew where it was, and then we'd exercise for thirty minutes or an hour."

"Is exercising for an hour in this heat good for you?"

"We won't walk fast," I said, and glanced at Darcy. "We should probably get going before it gets any later. Ready?"

She nodded, and opened her door. Dix moved out of the way, obligingly. "What's that for?" He nodded to the flashlight in my hand.

"In case the street lights go out," I said. "And in case we get attacked by a rabid dog and I have to hit it with something. This will be easier than looking around for a handy tree branch."

And anyway, in the unlikely event that that happened, blinding it with the light might give us enough time to get away. Behind a handy fence, or something.

Dix looked doubtful, although I don't know why. It was a reasonable explanation.

"We'll be back for our cars by nine at the latest," I told him. Darcy had also changed into comfortable shoes and what could pass for exercise clothes. And they were dark. *Good*. "Make sure no one takes them."

"We don't have a big problem with grand theft auto around here," Dix said. "At least not since Collier left town." He turned toward his house. "Walk carefully. Stop by to let me know you got back here safely."

I told him we would, and then we set off down the street, with me swinging the flashlight in athletic fashion. When we reached the corner and I glanced over my shoulder, Dix was no longer anywhere to be seen. Gone inside to watch Disney Princess movies with his girls, no doubt.

Darcy and I continued walking, just as if we were exercising. In fact, I guess we were exercising, and not just looking like it.

"There's Marley's house," I told Darcy after a couple of minutes. "The one with the... hmm."

She looked at me. "The one with the what?"

"The SUV in the driveway." An SUV that wasn't Marley's. I didn't know what she was driving these days, but it wasn't this SUV. I'd seen it before and knew who it belonged to. "That's Todd's car."

"ADA Satterfield?"

I nodded.

"Didn't he put her on trial for murder last year?"

He had. And had been all set to slam the cell door behind her, until it was discovered that Denise Seaver had stolen little Oliver, and Marley hadn't killed the baby and hidden the remains. Once that came out, Todd had had to drop the charges and grovel.

He must have groveled very nicely to find himself here now. I'm not sure I could have been as forgiving.

"I hope they aren't sitting on the deck," I mumbled. It would make it tough to sneak through the yard without being seen.

"Surely not," Darcy said. "The mosquitoes."

They were out in full force. I'd be covered with red bumps tomorrow. And the longer we stood here, the worse it would be.

"C'mon." I set off up the driveway to the gate.

We slid through—quietly; Marley kept the hinges oiled—and along the wall of the house. I hoped we looked like two shadows, but I wasn't sure.

At the corner, I motioned Darcy to a stop, and we stood and listened. There were no voices coming from the deck. They must be inside. *Lucky break.*

I gestured to Darcy, and we flitted into the backyard. Or at least Darcy flitted. She was tall, but lithe. I felt more like a lumbering elephant, leading with the stomach. As I thundered along, I kept one hand under it so the baby wouldn't bounce up and down. The other hand still clutched the flashlight.

We made it across the lawn without being told to stop. And then we were into the band of trees separating Copper Creek and Marley's house from the subdivision beyond.

"Slow down," I panted, while Darcy ran like a gazelle. "I can't keep up."

She slowed down, and we spent a few minutes pushing through the brush while I struggled to catch my breath. Now was when the flashlight came in handy. I figured we were far enough away from all the houses that it was safe to turn it on, so I did. And it did help us navigate the tree roots and branches and brush littering the ground among the trees.

Then we were out on the other side, and crossing the lawn

toward Denise Seaver's house, looming dark and forbidding in front of us.

My heart was thudding, I admit it. And not only because I'd been running. It had been a while since I'd done much breaking and entering. I was out of practice.

But we'd come this far. I wasn't about to turn back now.

Back in November, Marley had thrown a terra cotta flower pot through the glass in the back door before sticking her hand through the hole to unlock the door. I had assumed the glass would have been repaired by now, for safety's sake if for no other.

Of course, Denise Seaver hadn't been home to do it, but I had thought someone else would. Imagine my surprise when we got to the house and saw that all that stood between us and entrance was a piece of cardboard taped over the hole.

"Looks like somebody's broken in," Darcy whispered. And added, "someone other than us."

I shook my head. "Marley did that. It's been sitting here like that since November. I can't believe nobody's fixed it."

"I can't believe nobody's broken in," Darcy said.

"We don't know that they haven't. The TV and everything else of value might be gone. But they wouldn't have been interested in her medical records."

"If she kept them on her computer..." Darcy began.

"If she did, we're out of luck. But we're here. Let's look around for hardcopies."

And since the door was already open—sort of—maybe we wouldn't go to jail if we were caught.

We approached the door.

"Flashlight or door?" I asked Darcy.

"I'll hold the flashlight." She held out a hand for it. I handed it over and waited for her to train it on the door before I stuck a fingernail under the bottom edge of the cardboard and lifted.

It came away too easily for it not to have been lifted before.

"I don't think we're the first people to have been here," I told Darcy. "Here. Stick the light under the cardboard so I can see the glass. I don't want to cut my wrist accidentally."

I slipped my hand between the jagged pieces of glass still outlining the hole in the door, and stretched for the door knob. And came damn close to severing an artery when there was the scuff of a foot behind me.

Seventeen

"I knew you weren't exercising!" my brother said triumphantly.

I drew my hand back out of the broken window and turned to him. "Holy crap, Dix. You almost scared me into cutting my wrist!"

He ignored me, of course, in favor of looking around. "What are you doing here? No one's lived here since Doctor Seaver was arrested."

"That's why we're here," I said. "We're looking for the medical records of Darcy's birth mother."

Dix looked at her.

"It's a long story," I added.

And not one that Dix cared to go into at the moment, it seemed. He shook his head. "I can't let you do this, Sis."

"You can't stop me," I pointed out.

"You wanna bet?" He didn't wait for me to answer, just went on. "The cops are keeping an eye on this place. Bob Satterfield knows it's sitting empty, so they do drive-bys a couple times a night, to make sure nobody's squatting or carrying things out."

"But we need those records!"

Dix eyed me. "Do you even know there are records?"

I didn't. "But it's worth a look. We can't get into the clinic where she worked, and she wouldn't give us any information."

Dix's eyebrows rose. "You spoke to her?"

"This morning," I said. "We went to see her in prison. She wouldn't tell us anything helpful."

Dix looked torn, but he still shook his head. "We can talk to the sheriff tomorrow—" his glance included Darcy, "and ask permission to go through the place. I'll go with you."

"You think that will make a difference?"

"Yes," Dix said.

"What if he says no? We're here now. And the door's open. Look." I pushed it.

It opened, into the same tiled mudroom I remembered from last year.

Dix's eyes narrowed. "You did that!"

"I didn't. I swear. I didn't have time before you startled me. Someone else has been here. The least we can do is go in and see if anything's been stolen. As good neighbors."

"We aren't neighbors," Dix said.

"It's a figure of speech. As in 'love your neighbor.' Not just the people in the house next door to you, but everyone."

"I know what it means," Dix said. "I went to Sunday School too."

"Then why did you ask?" It was my turn to shake my head. "We're wasting time. All I want is ten minutes to go inside and see if there are any medical records. Less than that. Five."

Dix vacillated. I could see it. Years of practice.

I pressed the advantage. "We know exactly what we're looking for. A nine-month period before Darcy's birthday, thirty-four years ago. Once we find the records, it'll be very easy to check the ones that might apply. Three minutes."

"If you keep going, you won't have any time at all," Dix said. "Fine. Go. But if the cops come and catch you, don't say I didn't warn you."

"Maybe you should leave," I told him. "If you get arrested too, there won't be anyone to bail us out."

"We'll call Catherine," Dix said and gave me a shove. "Go on. Clock's ticking."

I went. Through the door and into the mudroom-cum-laundry I remembered from last fall. Into the kitchen I also remembered—where at least someone had cleaned up the vegetables Denise Seaver had been chopping when we walked in on her back then, so they hadn't turned to rot on the cutting board—and then into parts of the house I hadn't seen before.

I was looking for a home office. It was a big house for one person—one of the McMansions similar to Dix's house. A bit smaller, since Denise Seaver had been single and Dix had been married with two little girls when he bought the place. But still, plenty of room for an office. She'd been a professional. She must have had one.

"Spread out," I told the other two. They'd come in behind me, of course, instead of staying outside and letting me do the reconnoitering. "Look for an office. Or filing cabinets. Or filing boxes, or anything like that."

"Maybe one of us should keep an eye out the front," Dix suggested. "In case we get company."

Sure. We wouldn't want Sheriff Satterfield to sneak up on us unannounced. "Flip a coin."

"I'll do it," Darcy said.

Neither Dix nor I bothered to argue. We had little enough time as it was. If one of the neighbors had noticed us standing outside the back door arguing, the police could already be on their way.

Dix went one way, I went the other. Darcy walked to the front door and positioned herself off to the side, so she could peer out at the—hopefully—quiet residential street, but not be seen by anyone on the outside.

It didn't take long. Dix found the office upstairs. "Here it is!" he called down the stairs.

I walked to the bottom of the stairs and whisper-called up. "Are there files?"

"There are filing cabinets," my brother said.

"I'm coming." I started up. Darcy looked at me over her shoulder, but didn't budge from the front door. "You can probably come up," I told her. "I'm sure there's a window up there you can look out of."

She hesitated, but by the time I had navigated half the staircase, she was on her way up, too, two steps at a time.

There were, indeed, filing cabinets. And the not-so-good doctor had kept meticulous—and meticulously organized—records.

Organized by last name, not year.

We shuffled through to the S drawer, but of course there was no Ora Sweet. Proof, if we'd needed it, that Ora Sweet was not Darcy's mother's real name.

I straightened and looked around. "This can't be all of it. There are just four file drawers here. That's not enough for thirty-five years of patients."

Dix shrugged. "It's all there is."

"There has to be more somewhere else. Let's look around. You check the closets in the other rooms on this level, and see if there are attic stairs. If it's just a pull-down ladder, I don't think we have to bother with it. She wouldn't have carried any files up there."

"We should get out of here soon," Dix said, but he headed for the closet. I guess the life of crime we were living was growing on him.

The house had no basement, and I didn't find anything of interest during the cursory search I did of the downstairs. Everything of value was gone, by the way. There was no TV, no stereo, no computer equipment... and a couple of walls looked bare, too, like they ought to have a painting or something on them, that wasn't there.

I was just reaching for the garage door when I heard Darcy's voice from upstairs.

"Sirens!"

I pricked up my ears, but couldn't hear anything. Not from outside. From upstairs came the sound of scrambling feet as Darcy and Dix made for the stairs.

"Coming closer!" Darcy called from the upstairs hallway.

I yanked open the garage door and saw what I was looking for: stacks of file boxes. And—*Yes! thank you, God!*—they were sorted by year.

"We have to go!" Dix yelled. He turned up in the doorway from the house to the garage. "C'mon, Sis!"

"Grab this box!" I was wrestling with it, and probably shouldn't be, since it was heavy.

"We have to go!"

"It's what we came here for. I'm not leaving without it!"

Dix cursed, but loped across the floor and hoisted the box. "Move!"

I moved. I really wanted the second box, too, the one that covered the couple of months of the year before Darcy's birth in the spring, but I had to content myself with opening it, grabbing a couple of handfuls of files, and thrusting them at Darcy. "Take them and go!"

I took the last handful myself and ran for the back door. The sirens were definitely louder now. I mean, I could hear them. And they were coming closer. Not much doubt they were on their way here. Any second, the car would come to a screeching halt in front of Denise Seaver's house.

I crunched across the glass on the tile floor and out through the back door. With both hands full, I couldn't stop to shut it, so I didn't. Up ahead, Darcy was loping across the grass, gaining on Dix, who was struggling with the heavy box. The were both getting close to the tree line. I hurtled after, just as flashing blue lights illuminated the area between Denise Seaver's house and the one next door.

Dix and Darcy disappeared into the trees. I scrambled after, clutching my handful of folders against my chest and the flashlight in my other hand. In front of the house, the sirens went suddenly silent, and I heard the slam of a car door, and then another.

And then I was under cover, too, stumbling over roots and brush as I tried to keep up with Darcy and Dix. They were making as much noise as buffalo up ahead, crashing through the trees. There was no way the cops, if they came into Denise Seaver's backyard, could avoid hearing them.

"Stop!" I hissed.

We all stumbled to a stop and listened.

At first I couldn't hear anything but my own ratcheting heart and the sound of everyone's breathing. Then came noises from the house, and the beam of a flashlight.

Two shadows approached the back door, and I could hear the excitement in their voices when they discovered that it was open.

There was a moment or two of discussion and gesticulating, and then they pulled their guns and slipped inside, one after the other.

"Now," I told the others. "Go. Quietly."

We moved forward, careful where we put our feet, crunching over dry sticks and last year's leaves. I didn't envy Dix, carrying the heavy box. I was having a hard enough time juggling my own flashlight and the few files I was responsible for.

It felt like an eternity, but eventually we made it out on the other side of the trees and onto Marley's lawn.

Only to be met by a bright beam of light that left us standing in the middle of the yard on display.

"What's going on here?" Sheriff Satterfield's voice asked.

Uh-oh.

I smiled sweetly into the glare. "Good evening, Sheriff."

There was a pause. "I should have known," the sheriff said, resigned.

"Any way you could get that light out of our eyes?"

"In a minute." But the light moved away from me and swung toward the others. "Dix?"

The sheriff sounded surprised. Maybe he'd expected someone else. Rafe, probably. "And... Darcy, is it?"

"Yes, sir," Darcy said, her voice subdued.

Finally, the light went away. "What are you three up to?"

"Exercising," I said brightly.

"Uh-huh."

"That's what they said they were doing," Dix said, "when they parked in front of my house. I didn't want them going off on their own in the dark, so I went after them."

"And got roped into breaking and entering?" The sheriff's voice was dry.

There was no real point in denying the obvious. We were standing there holding the evidence. Caught red-handed, as the saying goes. All the sheriff had to do was take a look at the files to know we'd been inside Denise Seaver's house.

A couple of silhouettes were standing a few feet away, behind the sheriff, and I peered through the dark. "Hi, Marley. Did you call the sheriff?"

"Sorry, Savannah," Marley said. "We didn't realize it was you. When we saw you go through the yard earlier, Todd called his dad."

Of course he had. "Hi, Todd," I said.

Todd nodded. Things have been awkward between us ever since I turned him down in favor of Rafe. This was even more awkward. And not just that he had called the cops on me, but that he was here, at Marley's house, at night.

I turned back to the sheriff. "Can we go sit down somewhere? So I can explain? My feet hurt."

"Make it good," the sheriff said.

Yessir. I made it as good as I could, once we were on the deck and seated in Marley's patio furniture. I emphasized how we'd gone all the way to the Tennessee Women's Prison to speak to Denise Seaver, and how she had been unwilling to help us, and how we'd reasoned that she might have old records at her house. "It's not like we were stealing anything valuable. We weren't trying to profit. Just find out who Darcy's biological mother is."

The sheriff looked at her. "You were born here?"

"Nashville," Darcy said. "But my mother was from this area."

"Denise Seaver admitted that Darcy's mother was one of her patients," I added. "But since she used a fake name at the hospital, we don't know who she is. But Denise Seaver went to school with her, so she would have her real name on her medical records here."

"They went to school together?"

"That's what Doctor Seaver said. That Darcy's mother was a year ahead of her in school."

"I was a year ahead of her in school," the sheriff said.

"Good for you," I said. "Although you're not Darcy's mother." And presumably not Darcy's father, either.

Although someone had to be. He was tall and lean. So was Darcy.

He wasn't dark, though. Like his son, the sheriff has fair hair—more silver now that he's sixty—and grayish-blue eyes.

So maybe Darcy's mother had the dark hair and eyes. Light hair and eyes are recessive, aren't they?

I peered into the sheriff's face, searching for a resemblance. There wasn't one, not that I could see. Then again, I don't look much like my father, either. Dix and I take after Mother's family.

While I'd been thinking, the sheriff had turned to Dix. "You're a lawyer. How did you let yourself get talked into this?"

"They walked off in the dark," Dix said. "I followed them

because I wanted to make sure they were safe."

"Where are the girls?"

That was my interjection, not the sheriff's. Dix shot me a glance. "They spent the evening with Catherine. She's bringing them home at nine."

"We might not be back there by then." Certainly not if the sheriff arrested us. It was getting close to that time now.

"She has a key," Dix said and went back to explaining what had gone wrong. "I didn't catch up until they were opening the door into Doctor Seaver's house. And then I didn't want them to go inside on their own."

"You do know that breaking and entering is a crime?"

"Misdemeanor trespassing," Dix said. "Empty house, no weapon."

He turned to Marley. "Will you be pressing charges for us crossing your lawn?"

"Of course not." Marley smiled at him. Todd scowled, and then straightened his face when he realized I was looking at him.

"If Denise Seaver wants to press charges from prison," Dix told the sheriff, "feel free to arrest us. But until then, I don't think you can."

The sheriff gave him a steely stare. "I'm the sheriff. I can. I might not make it stick, but I can throw you in jail for the rest of the night."

"Catherine would have us out on bail tomorrow morning," Dix said calmly. "And just imagine what would happen when Aunt Regina got hold of the story of how you jailed your ladyfriend's son and pregnant daughter. Not to mention what Mother would say about it."

The sheriff looked harassed, but certain that he didn't want to bring that particular nightmare down on his own head. I guess we weren't getting arrested tonight.

"I'll have to take the files."

"You can't!" I said. "They're our only shot at trying to find

Darcy's mother. Darcy has a right to know who her mother is. Especially if her mother is the one who brought her here."

"What?" Both Dix and the sheriff asked simultaneously. I explained about the newspaper clipping, for what felt like the thousandth time.

Dix shook his head. "I don't remember anybody pushing Darcy at us. We had three or four applicants for the job, and she was the most qualified. But it was me, Jonathan, and Catherine making the decision. Sheila had some input, I guess..."

There was a moment's pause while we all stopped to remember Sheila and that she was no longer with us.

"But I don't remember talking to anyone else about it. You weren't here." He looked at Todd, who shook his head. Todd had still been working in Atlanta then. And he'd been married to Jolynn, who was—pardon the callousness—as dead now as Sheila.

Dix turned to me. "And you were in Nashville. I think you were in the process of divorcing Bradley. Or struggling to get back on your feet again after the divorce. I offered you the job, didn't I?"

"Mother did. I said no. I didn't want to crawl back to Sweetwater with my tail between my legs."

And that's what it would have amounted to.

"We need those files," I told the sheriff. "After all this, you can't take them away from us. It would be different if Darcy's mother didn't want to get to know her, but I think she does. She's probably just worried that Darcy doesn't want to get to know her."

I glanced at Darcy, who nodded.

The sheriff looked from her to me and back. His gaze lingered. "Fine," he said after a moment. "I can get them from you tomorrow. Afternoon."

"Thank you." I shared a triumphant look with my partners in

crime. Not only would we have the chance to go through what we'd found, but the sheriff would take on the trouble of returning the evidence to Doctor Seaver's house. It was like a double win.

"I'll hang onto them until tomorrow," Dix said, "and bring them to the office in the morning. We can go through them there. Together."

If he had thought that would deter me, he was very wrong. "I'll be there at nine."

"Get outta here," the sheriff growled. "And take your files with you. And when you're done with'em, call me so as I can get them back where they belong."

So Dix hoisted the box, and Darcy and I carried the extra files, and off we went. The sheriff could have offered to drive us, I thought, but maybe he wanted to spend some more time with his son and the woman who looked like she was getting under Todd's skin.

Or maybe he just couldn't wait to get rid of us. He might even be reassessing his relationship with Mother based on her criminal relatives.

"Are you sure we couldn't just take a peek tonight?" I asked Dix as we trudged along the sidewalk.

"No." He was adamant. "It's late. Catherine is dropping the girls off in a few minutes. Darcy's tired. And you look ready to drop."

I was ready to drop. But I could drop into a comfortable chair in Dix's house with a stack of files and be just fine.

"Maybe we should just put them in my car. It's parked outside your house."

"No," Dix said again. "I don't trust you. If you take them, you'll stay up all night and go through them."

So?

"That's not fair to Darcy," Dix said. "It's her mother. The choice should be hers. What do you want to do, Darcy?"

Darcy looked overwhelmed. And wrung out. Unlike Dix and me, who were just caught up in the excitement of the chase, this was personal for her. "I guess it's OK if we wait until tomorrow. It's getting late."

And destined to become later, at least if I were any judge. As soon as we turned off Marley's street and onto Dix's, a police car slid up to the curb next to us and kept pace. The window rolled down.

I expected to see Cletus Johnson or one of Bob Satterfield's other deputies. Instead, Lupe Vasquez's face peered out at us. "Whatcha got there?"

"Files," I said. Should have taken a closer look at the car. It wasn't a sheriff's vehicle at all, but a Columbia PD squad car.

One that had no business being here, incidentally. We were well outside the city limits. Unless Bob Satterfield had called on the Columbia PD for help.

"Officers Vasquez and Nolan," I added, in an effort to be friendly, "my brother, Dixon Calvert Martin."

Vasquez nodded. "Pleasure. Those wouldn't be files you took out of the residence of Doctor Denise Seaver, would they?"

"The sheriff let us go," I said. "And you're out of your jurisdiction, Officer."

Lupe Vasquez grinned. "I'm just giving you a hard time. When we heard about a robbery in progress at Doctor Seaver's house, we thought it might be you. We figured we'd take a look."

She was very careful not to glance at Nolan, which gave me the impression that coming here might have been his idea.

"Darcy's on her way back to Columbia in a few minutes," I said. "If you want to hang around and give her an escort."

"We can do that."

"That's her car right up there." I turned to Darcy. "Go ahead and give me your files. I'll put them with the ones Dix has. And we'll see you tomorrow."

Darcy nodded. "Thanks, Savannah." She sounded exhausted. Emotionally as well as physically.

Tomorrow, God willing, she'd find out who her biological mother was. And right now she must be wondering whether she really wanted to know. Once she knew, she couldn't go back to not knowing. And what if the information wasn't what she wanted to hear?

"Go home and get a good night's sleep," I told her. I didn't add, "*If you can,*" but I thought it. "We've had a long day. I'm ready to drop, too."

Darcy managed a weak smile. "I'll see you tomorrow. Dix." She nodded, and then headed for her Honda. The squad car waited until she'd reversed and was going in the right direction for home, and then glided out of the subdivision after her.

"That was interesting," Dix said.

I assumed he meant the officers, and not the whole evening, so I told him about the visit to *Fiestas de Mexico* yesterday, and how Patrick Nolan had seemed quite taken with Darcy.

"They'll make sure she gets home safely." And this time I wasn't worried that anyone would come after her. At the moment, I was more concerned that she was so tired and distracted that she'd run off the road from simply not paying attention.

"Come on," Dix said and led the way to his own front door, where he put the file box down long enough to dig the key out of his pocket and unlock the door. "Let's just put this in the car."

"Are you sure you don't want to take a quick look first?"

I certainly did. And I had assumed, when Darcy left, that Dix would agree to a peek.

He looked at me. "We're looking for Darcy's mother. Not yours. You already have a mother. The sheriff's probably called her and told her you were caught breaking into Doctor Seaver's house."

I grimaced. I wouldn't be surprised.

"This is about Darcy's life. Not yours. You don't get to walk into my office tomorrow morning already knowing what she has yet to find out."

"Fine," I said. Since he put it like that. "I'm curious, OK? It may be Darcy's mother, but it's probably someone we both know. Someone we've seen our whole lives. Hell... heck, I went to Aunt Regina's house this afternoon to see if maybe she'd had a baby out of wedlock a year or two before she married Uncle Sid!"

Dix gave me an astonished look over his shoulder as he led me down the couple of steps from the kitchen into the garage. "Why Aunt Regina?"

"She's a couple of years older than Denise Seaver. Aunt Regina wasn't married when Darcy was born. She didn't meet Uncle Sid until later. I can't imagine our grandparents being happy about their only daughter getting pregnant out of wedlock, can you? And you've looked at Darcy, right? One of her parents, if not both, had to be part black."

Dix dumped the file box into the back of his SUV and turned to me. "How did that make you think of Aunt Regina, for God's sake?"

"She's a Martin," I said. "She looks like Catherine. And like great-great-grandfather William."

Dix shook his head. "The fact that great-great-grandfather William was half black would make Aunt Regina something like one-sixteenth black. She wouldn't have a child who looked like Darcy. It would take more than that."

Maybe. Maybe not. "It wasn't her, anyway. She didn't seem guilty at all, when I asked her. And she didn't remember anyone else who was pregnant at the time. No one who didn't end up with a baby later."

Dix nodded and took the lid off the file box and turned it

upside down. "You can put those in here."

I off-loaded my files where he said to and watched him close the rear of the car. "Are you sure you won't come out here later and go through them on your own?"

"Positive," Dix said. "I have more patience than you. And anyway, Catherine is bringing the girls home soon. I'll be busy getting them ready for bed. When they're asleep, I intend to sit down with a beer and forget this night ever happened."

"Until tomorrow."

He sighed. "Yes, Sis. Until tomorrow."

Eighteen

The sheriff had indeed called to inform Mother that he had caught both Dix and me breaking and entering. You'd think we were still in grade school, getting ratted out by the sheriff.

Mother talked at me about it for a while—setting a good example, being above reproach, how dare I drag my brother into my wild schemes... never mind the fact that he was the one who had followed me after I'd specifically lied to him so he wouldn't.

When she could see that I was dead on my feet and wasn't really paying attention to whatever she was saying, she let me go to bed. I crawled upstairs and collapsed, and I didn't even have time to lament the fact that Rafe hadn't called again before I sank into oblivion.

When I woke up, it was morning. The sun beat against the windows, and the world was already steaming. There was pretty much no point in drying off after my shower, since I'd be damp the moment I set foot outside the door again.

I made it to the law office by nine o'clock. Darcy was already there, looking worse than I did.

Oh, she was nicely dressed, in an elegant summer-weight skirt and elbow length white blouse that probably would have set off her complexion beautifully on any other day. But she was paler than usual, and had dark circles under her eyes that even the makeup she had put on couldn't hide.

We locked eyes across the desk for a silent acknowledgement that we both looked like something the cat dragged in, and we might as well not mention it.

I glanced at the door to the inner sanctum. "Is Dix here?"

Darcy nodded. "He's setting up in the conference room."

"Setting up what? You mean he's started looking at the files already?" I made to head that way, but she shook her head.

"He's just carrying things in from the car. He said we wouldn't start until you got here."

OK, then. "How about some coffee?"

I couldn't have any—not good for the baby—but that didn't mean she couldn't.

Darcy shook her head. "No, thank you. My stomach's a little upset."

And no surprise. Nerves, no doubt.

I tried for a bright smile. "Well, I'm here now. How about we go in?"

"Just let me get Catherine out here." Darcy reached for the phone.

"Catherine?"

She nodded. "Your brother talked to your sister last night. She's going to sit at the desk for the time that it takes us to do this."

You'd think that Jonathan would be able to do that, but OK. The kids were probably all in school of some sort today, anyway. Mother's Day Out for the little ones who hadn't graduated to real school yet.

"She's coming," Darcy said and put down the receiver. "We can go."

We headed down the hallway toward the conference room, and ran into Catherine halfway there. "You look like hell," she told me on the way past.

"Thanks ever so. Do you remember being pregnant?"

"I glowed," Catherine said, in blatant disregard of the truth. There had been times when she'd looked as much like a limp dishrag as I did right now. I remembered them.

She grinned at me over her shoulder. "Yvonne called. I'm meeting with her at one."

"Good for you." And Yvonne. "Do your best for her, OK? I'm sure she would have rather had Dix."

"I'm sure Dix would rather she work with me," Catherine said before she disappeared around the corner into the reception area. "And I always do my best," floated back to us, disembodied.

We walked the few steps to the door of the conference room, and pushed it open.

As Darcy had said, Dix had already carried the files in from the car. He had also taken them out of the box and piled them in three equal piles: one on each end of the long table, and one in the middle.

"I didn't look at the files," he informed us. "I have no idea which stack has Darcy's mother in it. I don't know who Darcy's mother is. It's all random. I guess we just pick a stack and start. Darcy?"

"I'll take the one over here," Darcy said, and walked to one end of the table.

"Savannah?"

"I don't care. I can take the other end. You get the middle. You're already there."

Dix shrugged. "Tell me again what we're looking for."

"Caucasian female," I said, pulling out my chair and taking a seat, "mid-twenties, pregnant, with a due-date sometime during the first two weeks of April. Let's start there. If you find one, pull it out of the stack and set it aside. Then we'll go over those together when we've eliminated everyone else."

Dix nodded. So did Darcy. I pulled the first file off the top of the stack and went to work.

With the three of us, the job didn't take long. Less than twenty minutes later, we had eliminated all but a handful of the files.

"Three," Dix said, fanning them out on the table before leaning back on his chair. "You ready for this?"

He looked at Darcy. She was watching the folders as someone would watch a snake coiled to strike, but she nodded.

Dix pulled the first one toward him, and flipped it open. But before he could read the first name, there was a quick rap on the door. Catherine pushed it open.

"Sorry." She avoided looking at any of us, just came inside, and suddenly the whole world stepped in. First came Audrey, with Mother right behind. The sheriff made up the rear, although at the last second before the door closed, Jonathan squeezed through, too. Catherine sent him a look that said clearly, "You're supposed to be holding down the fort," and Jonathan shrugged sheepishly, but didn't leave again. Although he did find a spot as far away from Catherine as he could, and leaned against the wall.

Dix took charge, after looking from one face to the next. "What's going on?"

I was glad he could speak, because I couldn't. Maybe the sheriff had changed his mind and was going to arrest us after all. And when she couldn't talk him out of it, Mother had brought Audrey for moral support.

"Let's all have a seat," the sheriff said.

At least we weren't in imminent danger of being hauled off to the slammer. *Good*. If he arrested all of us, there'd be no one left to bail us out.

Everyone sorted themselves into chairs. All except Jonathan, who stayed in the corner. Catherine came around the table to sit next to me, leaving the three of us and Darcy facing off against the sheriff, Mother, and Audrey on the other side.

There was a moment of silence as we sized each other up. It felt like the showdown at the OK Corral. It also felt like I wanted to be somewhere else. Anywhere else. Because whatever was going to happen, didn't feel like something I was going to like.

"What's going on?" Dix asked again. And since the sheriff hadn't answered him the last time, he turned to Mother.

She seemed game, if confused. "They asked me to be here, darling."

So no help there. But at least Mother wasn't about to confess to being Darcy's mother.

Not that I had thought she was.

"After we spoke last night," the sheriff said, "I contacted Audrey. And this morning, the two of us got your mother. She should be here for this."

Uh-oh. Maybe I'd been right last night. Maybe the sheriff was going to tell us he was Darcy's father, and he wanted Audrey here as moral support for Mother when she found out about it. It would be a shock to her, no doubt. I mean, Darcy clearly wasn't Pauline Satterfield's child. She didn't look anything like Todd.

Had the sheriff cheated on Pauline? Or had Darcy been born before the Satterfields had gotten married?

"I'm your mother, Darcy," Audrey said.

What?

My head whipped from the sheriff to look at her, so fast I courted whiplash.

And yes, I could see the resemblance, now that she'd said it. Something in the eyes and the cheekbones. Darcy's were less chiseled than Audrey's, her face rounder and softer, but she might get there in another twenty-five years. And they were both tall and lanky, with long legs and slim figures. Audrey's hair was also jet black. I'd always assumed she dyed it, but maybe not. Or if she dyed it now, maybe she hadn't had to when she was younger.

"You're Ora?" fell out of my mouth.

Audrey's lips trembled into something that came within throwing range of being a smile. "I was telling them my name.

At the hospital, when I was checking in to have the baby."

Her eyes flickered across the table and back, and she corrected herself. "To have Darcy. And at the last minute, I remembered that Denise had told me not to put my own name on the birth certificate. I'd already started talking. So I changed Audrey to Aura. They spelled it O-R-A, and I didn't correct them."

"And you took the last name Sweet and Water Street from Sweetwater?"

She nodded. "Denise said it was to be a closed adoption, so I shouldn't put my real information anywhere."

Of course she had. I wasn't even surprised. What she'd really done, of course, was safeguard herself against anyone changing their minds later. Once the baby was adopted, she didn't want the mother to be able to show up and stake a claim, and maybe be able to back it up. False information on the birth certificate ensured that the mother couldn't prove it was her baby.

I knew it was wrong, but I thought I might just hate Denise Seaver a little.

"Why didn't you want me?" Darcy asked from the other side of the table. At the sound of the question, Audrey's eyes filled with tears.

Mother took her hand and held it. Best friends for more than thirty years. Audrey having had a child out of wedlock before she even knew Mother wasn't likely to change that.

"You were of age," Darcy continued, her voice shaking. "You must have had a job. You could have supported us. And women weren't stoned for being single mothers thirty-four years ago."

Audrey shook her head. "It wasn't that. But your father..."

She trailed off, with a glance at the sheriff.

Mother glanced at him, too.

Uh-oh. If the sheriff had had an affair with Audrey while he was married to Pauline, I didn't think Mother would find that particularly endearing.

Audrey turned back to Darcy, her eyes steady. It was easy to see that she was uncomfortable, but she also seemed determined to see this through. "Your father and I were friends. We grew up together. We went to school together. I was a bit of a tomboy as a child, so we fished together and climbed trees together. And as we got older, I fell in love in him."

Mother patted her hand.

"He didn't feel the same way about me," Audrey said. "I always knew that. But we started a relationship anyway. We were both twenty-five. Neither of us had found anyone else. We were afraid of growing old alone, I guess. We got along well. It made sense."

"What happened?" Darcy sounded reluctantly sympathetic.

Audrey's eyes filled with tears. "He met someone else. From one day to the next, everything changed. He took one look at her and knew she was the one."

"What did you do?"

"I told him I was happy for him," Audrey said, and now it was her voice that was shaking, "and wished him the best. And then I stepped aside. Two weeks later I found out I was pregnant."

"Did you tell him?"

Audrey shook her head. "He was back in Nashville by then. Back in school. This all happened during the summer. He was there, with her, and I was here alone. So I made the decision not to say anything to him about you."

"And he never found out?"

"When he came home for Christmas," Audrey said, "he brought her. His girlfriend. They were engaged by then. Nobody thought it was strange that I stayed away. When I gained weight, everyone just thought it was because I was depressed and overeating. It was fairly easy to hide the pregnancy."

There was a moment's pause.

"I understand why you couldn't keep me and stay here," Darcy said, "but didn't you think about going somewhere else? Keeping me and settling down somewhere, just the two of us?"

Apparently not, because Audrey stared at her for a moment as if she couldn't quite process the question. "This is my home. My parents were here. I had just taken over my grandmother's business. I couldn't leave."

She probably could have, to be honest. But some people don't think about it. I'd gone to Nashville to study and had ended up marrying Bradley Ferguson, and when that ended I had stayed. Going back to Sweetwater hadn't crossed my mind. Or let's say I hadn't considered it, because Mother had certainly made sure to bring it up plenty.

But Catherine had also gone to Nashville to study, and had married Jonathan, and they had ended up back here. Dix hadn't considered living anywhere else, either, as far as I knew, after college. And of course Dad had done it first. Studied law at Vanderbilt, and then come home to take over the family business.

But I was digressing. Badly. I couldn't imagine Audrey living anywhere but Sweetwater, and she obviously hadn't been able to, either.

"I didn't want to give you up," she said. "I was there when they... when your parents came and took you away. Watching them walk out with you is one of the hardest things I've ever had to do."

Her voice broke, and I, for one, believed her. I have no idea whether Darcy did. She was on the same side of the table as I was, and it was hard to get a good look at her. Catherine and I exchanged a glance, though, and I think she believed Audrey, too.

"So you sent me the Help Wanted ad from the local newspaper," Darcy said.

Audrey nodded. "It took a while before I found you. At first I didn't want to. You had a new mother and a new father, and you were better off. I tried to forget about you, but I couldn't. So when you were eight or so, I started to subscribe to a couple of the local papers in Alabama. The nurse at the hospital wouldn't tell me the names of your parents, but she said they were from Mobile. When you were eleven or twelve, I found a picture of you. You looked just like I did at that age. And I found your name." She smiled through the tears. "I was going to call you Rose, after my grandmother. Darcy's better."

I had to agree. Darcy looked nothing like a Rose. Not that it isn't a pretty name, but it wouldn't have suited Darcy at all.

"After that," Audrey said, "I tried to keep up with what went on in your life. I found some more pictures, and I also took a vacation and went to Mobile for a few days."

"You were there?"

Audrey nodded. "I saw your house. I saw you, and your mother and father. You looked happy. You had friends you spent time with. But I didn't stay long. You weren't mine anymore."

I think by now they had both forgotten that there were other people in the room. They were just talking to one another.

"I saw where you graduated from college," Audrey said, "and when your engagement was announced. I saw that your parents died. But you were married by then. You were starting a family of your own. And you needed time to grieve. So I didn't contact you. And besides, I was afraid. You had no reason to want anything to do with me. I gave you up."

Her eyes brimmed over, and tears trickled down her cheeks. Catherine pushed a box of tissues down the table.

"But when I realized you were getting divorced," Audrey said, "I sent you the advertisement from the *Reporter*. I was afraid you'd go back to Mobile, and I wanted you here, where maybe I could get to know you—and you could get to know me—before I told you the truth. Maybe by then—if you'd gotten to like me a little—you wouldn't mind if it turned out I was your mother."

There was silence after that. Audrey reached for a tissue to blot her face. Mother patted her arm. We all waited to hear what Darcy was going to say.

"I don't mind that you're my mother," she said eventually. It wasn't a ringing endorsement, certainly, but at least it was neutral instead of negative. It could have been worse.

Audrey sniffed and smiled through it. Everyone else started breathing again.

Then Darcy turned to the sheriff. "So are you my father?"

Bob Satterfield flushed. Mother stiffened. Audrey looked surprised. "No," she said. "Of course not."

It was Darcy's turn to look surprised. "He's not?"

Audrey shook her head. "Not at all. When I got pregnant with you, Bob was already married to Pauline. We were friends. I would never have interfered with that."

"I wouldn't have let you," Bob Satterfield informed her. She almost smiled, and he looked a little better, too. A little less grim.

"So who is he?" Darcy asked. She looked around, as if expecting him to materialize out of thin air.

"No one you've ever met," Audrey said firmly. "No one you know. No one who's here anymore."

"Did he move? Do you know where he went? Can we find him?"

"He passed away," Audrey said. "A few years ago now. I'm sorry."

This time, it was Darcy's eyes that filled with tears. "So I won't be able to meet him?"

"I'm afraid not." Audrey's voice was gentle. "There's just me."

"You said he was engaged. Did he get married? Did he have children? Do I have..." She hesitated before the last word, "—siblings?"

Audrey looked away from her, over at Catherine, Dix, and me, ranged together on the other side of the table. Siblings can be a pain in the posterior, but we all had each other's backs. Darcy had grown up alone. So had Audrey, it sounded like. I wondered whether Darcy's question had hurt Audrey. Whether, maybe, she thought it meant that she, Darcy's mother, wasn't enough. Or wasn't as good as having siblings.

And I didn't think that was the case at all. Darcy had been without family for a few years now. Without anyone she was related to. It was hard to blame her for being excited about the possibility of more relatives.

"Yes," Audrey said, and it sounded like she had to squeeze the words past an obstruction in her throat, like she didn't want to say them. "He had other children."

"More than one?"

"Three," Audrey said. "You have two sisters—half-sisters—and a half-brother."

Darcy's eyes widened and her mouth dropped open. Mine did, too, but probably not for the same reason. Next to me, Catherine gulped.

"I'm sorry, Margaret," Audrey said, turning to her. "It was before he met you. Once he did, there was nobody else for him."

Mother didn't say anything—she didn't look like she was even breathing—and Audrey added, "It has nothing to do with you."

Mother's pale cheeks flushed. "Nothing to do with me? My husband and my best friend had a child together that I knew nothing about, and it's not about me?"

"Robert didn't know, either," Audrey said. "He couldn't have told you. He didn't know."

"But you did! How many years have we been friends? And you never told me you'd had my husband's child?"

Audrey alternated between deathly pale and flushed. "You

were pregnant yourself. Was I supposed to tell you, while you and Robert were over the moon about Catherine, that she wasn't his first daughter? That he already had a daughter somewhere else, growing up with strangers, and he'd never get to meet her?" She shook her head, her eyes full of tears. "I couldn't do that. To either of you."

"And you!" Mother turned to—or on—Bob Satterfield. "You and Robert were close. The four of us spent a lot of time together. You never told me he had another child!"

"I didn't know," Bob said. "While you and Robert were courting, Pauline and I were newlyweds trying to start a family. But we had a hard time of it. She had a couple of disappointments around that time."

Disappointments being a euphemism for miscarriages, I assumed. Bob was too delicate to use the word. And I knew all about what that was like, having had two of my own.

Audrey nodded. "I didn't say anything to you or Pauline. She was struggling to stay positive. And I was carrying a baby I wasn't going to keep. Telling her that I was giving up what she would give anything to have, would be like rubbing salt in her wounds."

Mother looked from one to the other of them. It was easy to see that she was fighting for composure. She was most likely close to tears, but refused to give in to them. I think she probably understood where Audrey was coming from, but she also felt betrayed, and who could blame her? It would be like finding out, when Rafe and I were pushing sixty, that Tamara Grimaldi had had his baby thirty-five years ago, and neither of them had told me.

Mother evaded Bob Satterfield's hand and pushed away from the table. "Excuse me." She didn't look at anyone when she got to her feet and headed for the door.

"Mom," Catherine began. Mother didn't turn around, but she lifted a hand. Catherine subsided.

I think we were all a bit floored, to be honest. Not to diminish Mother's shock and pain, which were very real, but I hadn't expected to come face to face with a sister I never knew I had. Or to learn that the woman I'd always thought of as an honorary aunt had had a child with my father back in the recesses of time, and hadn't told any of us about it.

Bob made to get up, and Audrey put a hand on his arm. "I'll go." She glanced at Darcy across the table. "Well talk more later."

Darcy nodded, and looked as shell-shocked as the rest of us. I examined her face for any resemblance to Dix or myself, but I couldn't see any. To Catherine... maybe a little.

Audrey swept out, leggy and elegant on fire-engine red heels. After a moment, the sheriff excused himself and followed.

The door shut after them.

Nobody spoke.

Jonathan withdrew himself from the corner where he'd been standing—I had forgotten all about him being there—and wandered over to the table, where he pulled out Audrey's chair and sat down in it. Opposite from Darcy. He looked at her for a moment. She looked back.

"Welcome to the family," Jonathan said.

And Darcy put her head down on her arms and burst into tears.

Nineteen

"You'll never guess who Darcy's parents are!" I told Rafe an hour later, on the phone.

"I don't even wanna try. Lay it on me." He sounded a bit stressed out, to be honest, but I couldn't keep the news to myself any longer.

"Audrey!"

There was a beat of silence. Then— "I can see that."

I could, too. Now. Funny how it hadn't struck me as a possibility before it had hit me in the face, so to speak. "I know. I can't believe I never noticed before. Too close to both of them, maybe. But that's not the worst of it."

"What's the worst of it?"

"Her father!"

"What about him?"

"He's my father, too!"

This time there was a longer beat. Then— "You're fucking with me."

I winced. He usually censors those words when he's talking to me. He must be quite shocked to have forgotten. "I'm not. My dad and Audrey had a fling just before he met Mother. Then he dropped Audrey like a hot potato as soon as Mother showed up. He and Mother got engaged and then married. Audrey never told him she was pregnant, and because he was in Nashville and she was in Sweetwater, he never figured it out."

"Shit," Rafe said.

"I know. Darcy's my sister. Half sister."

"Shit." He pondered for a moment. "Does your mama know?"

"She was there when we found out. We broke into Doctor Seaver's house last night—"

"You committing B&E without me now?"

"With Darcy and Dix," I said. "It was going to be just Darcy and me, but then Dix followed us. And then the sheriff caught us coming back with the files. He realized we were close to figuring it out on our own, so he contacted Audrey and, I guess, told her she had to tell Darcy the truth. So this morning the two of them showed up at the law office. They brought Mother, too. At first I thought it was because the sheriff was going to confess to being Darcy's father, and he wanted Audrey there as moral support for Mother when she found out. Then, when Audrey confessed, I thought Mother was there to support her. And then Darcy asked who her father was. And I realized that Mother wasn't there for any of those reasons."

"Shit," Rafe said again. Still taking it in, I guess. I was still taking it in myself, if it came to that. "How'd she handle it?"

"About as you'd expect. Shock. Anger that nobody had told her. That she and Audrey have been friends for thirty-three years, and Audrey never told her she'd had my father's child. That Mother and Bob Satterfield and Pauline and Dad were friends for years, and none of them told her he'd had a thing going with Audrey. Never mind the fact that nobody knew about the baby." Except Audrey, of course. "And then she got up and walked out. Mother, I mean. Audrey went after her. Then the sheriff left, too. I have no idea whether either of them caught up to her."

They hadn't been outside on the square when I came out an hour later. Not that I'd expected them to be. It was hot.

They hadn't been inside Audrey's store, either—it had been shuttered and dark, with the 'Closed' sign in the window. And although I'd checked the Café on the Square, I hadn't seen any of them inside.

So now I was on my way back to the mansion. I came to an intersection and looked both ways before proceeding, steering the car with one hand and holding the phone to my ear with the other. "All the others stayed at the law office. Dix offered to let Darcy go home, but she said she wanted to stay. If she went home, she'd have too much time to think, she said. And Catherine and Jonathan have appointments. Besides, it'll give them some time to work things out while going about their normal business."

I pondered for a second, and added, "I guess Dix will have to give Darcy a pay raise now."

Rafe chuckled. "How do you feel?"

"Numb," I told him, honestly. "I didn't see that coming. I realized she looked familiar. And now that I know, I can see Audrey in her. But I didn't realize she looked like us!"

"She don't." After a second he changed it to, "Not much. A little in the mouth and chin, maybe."

Maybe. I'd have to find a picture of my dad when I got back to the mansion, and take a closer look. I still remembered him—of course; he hadn't been gone that long—but actually looking at the picture would make the similarities easier to find.

"This is crazy," Rafe said.

"I know. I'm still taking it in. It'll be while until we process it, I expect."

The mansion was coming up ahead, and I turned on the signal to go into the driveway. So far, I couldn't see anyone's car parked outside. Not even Mother's.

"I'm sorry to call and dump all this on you," I added. "I know you've got your own troubles to deal with."

"Sure." His voice was dry. "You just keep that kinda thing to yourself, darlin', 'cause your very important husband's way too busy to listen."

"Sorry." I hadn't meant it that way. "I knew you'd want to know. And that you'd care. I just meant that you've got your hands full. And you're worried about Jamal."

He didn't say anything, and I added, "Any word from him? Any news?"

"Nothing so far. When I get my hands on him..."

But he didn't finish the sentence. Maybe it was the idea that when—or if—he got his hands on Jamal, it might be Jamal's body and not the living Jamal he found.

"Go back to work," I told him. "I just wanted to tell you what happened." And now I had. "The rest of it can wait. Nothing's going to change if we wait until tomorrow to talk about it."

But such was not the case with the situation Rafe was in. A delay in finding Jamal could mean the difference between life and death. Jamal's life and death.

"And anyway," I added, and pulled the car to a stop at the bottom of the stairs, "I'm home now."

"Home?"

"Back at the mansion. Go to work. Find Jamal. I'll call you later."

"Good luck." He didn't wait for me to wish him the same, just hung up in my ear. A lot more worried than he let on, it seemed. I turned off the car and opened my door.

At first glance, the house seemed dark and empty. There were no sounds of activity when I opened the door. I shut it behind me and looked around the foyer. "Mother?"

No one answered.

That wasn't necessarily anything to worry about. Audrey could have caught up with her outside the law office, and they could have gone somewhere together. Like to Audrey's house or even the office behind the store. Or Bob Satterfield could have caught up with them, and they could have gone somewhere together. Like Bob's house, or the Wayside Inn. It was a bit early for lunch, but Mother might have needed a Mimosa.

Or Mother could have refused to talk to either of them, and could have struck out on her own. I'd gotten the impression they had all arrived together at the office this morning, so she might not have had her car there. And cabs are few and far between in Sweetwater. But Mother knows everyone in town. She could have found someone to give her a ride. And I hadn't passed her on the road, hoofing. At least I hadn't noticed, and I think I would have.

Or maybe she had walked to the cemetery to yell at my father's grave. Under the circumstances, I'd have been tempted to do just that.

"Mother?" I tried again, just to make absolutely sure she wasn't here. And this time I heard a soft sound from the parlor.

I headed in that direction, and stopped in the doorway. My mother was sitting on Great-Aunt Ida's velvet loveseat with a squat glass of brandy in her hand and a bottle on the table in front of her.

Let me just make sure you understand the significance of that. Brandy isn't my mother's usual choice of drink. She likes white wine. She'll drink sherry. She probably wouldn't turn down a martini, if someone tried to press one on her. She likes mimosas for brunch. But I don't usually see her drink anything stronger. Certainly not before lunch, alone in her house.

I took a couple of tentative steps into the room. "Mom? Are you OK?"

The look she gave me was positively vicious. "What do you think?"

And that didn't sound like my mother at all. Her normal response would be, "Of course, darling," whether she was OK or not.

"I'm going to guess you're not," I said, taking a seat opposite, "since you're sitting here before eleven in the morning drinking."

"You can assume that." She tossed back the brandy and coughed, before filling the glass again.

I raised my brows. "I'm not sure that's a good idea." And to make sure it didn't happen again, I moved the bottle off the table and onto the floor. On my side.

"I'm your mother," my mother informed me, with careful attention to the vowels. "If I want to get drunk before eleven in the morning, I can do that."

"Of course you can. And I can't stop you. But is that really what you want?"

"Yes!" Mother said, and knocked back a slug of the brandy. And coughed. When she put the glass down on the table, some of the brandy sloshed over the rim and splashed onto the hundred-year-old wood. I winced. Mother didn't even seem to notice.

"I can't believe it," she told me. "My best friend! And my husband!"

"He wasn't your husband when he slept with your best friend. And she wasn't your best friend, either. That came later. You hadn't met either of them yet."

"Whose side are you on?" Mother wanted to know, shrilly. Brandy-breath wafted across the table toward me.

I had to think about it. "Darcy's, I guess. None of this is her fault."

"Your sister!" Mother said darkly.

I shrugged. "That isn't her fault, either. And Audrey can't help it that she was in love with Dad. You should understand that. You were in love with him, too. Or so I assume."

"Of course I was!" Mother said with a sniff.

"It happened before he met you. He couldn't have known you were going to come along just when you did. And you heard

Audrey. As soon as he saw you, there was no one else for him."

"I'm not upset with *him*!" Mother said.

I would hope not. He hadn't done anything wrong, unless you consider it wrong to sleep with a woman you're not in love with. If so, Rafe was guilty of the same thing.

And who knew, if Mother hadn't happened along at that time, maybe Dad would have ended up marrying Audrey after all, and they'd have had a long, happy life together. With more children following Darcy.

That was a little strange to think about. My dad having children other than Catherine, Dix, and me.

Not Darcy. I was OK with Darcy. But others. Hypothetical children with someone who wasn't our mother. While Catherine, Dix, and I weren't born.

I shook it off. "Who are you upset with?"

She looked at me as if I were the stupidest individual in the world. "Who do you think? Audrey, of course. And Bob. How could they do this to me?"

"They explained that," I said. "Bob didn't know. Audrey didn't tell him, because he and Pauline were having a hard time getting pregnant and she didn't want to make it harder on them. And do you really think Audrey should have told you that she once slept with Dad and got pregnant and had a baby she gave up for adoption?"

"Yes!" Mother said. "I had a right to know! Your dad had a right to know!"

I couldn't really argue with that, since I agreed. At least that Dad had had a right to know. Just as Rafe had a right to know if Carmen was carrying his baby. However— "How would it have made you feel?"

"Like they weren't keeping secrets from me," Mother snarled and tossed back the rest of the brandy. She slammed the glass down on the table and looked around for the bottle.

I pretended I didn't notice. "What about how Audrey felt? It was her baby." And Mom's husband she'd been in love with. Talk about laying yourself bare. "I think she had the right to keep that to herself. It was private. None of your business."

Until now, anyway. Now, Audrey's affair with Dad had become all of our business.

Mother snarled at me. Wordlessly. "Where did you put the bottle?"

"I think you've had enough," I told her. "You just showed teeth. You need to take a break."

"My house," Mother informed me. "My brandy. If you don't like it, you can leave."

My mouth dropped open.

My mother was kicking me out of the house?

Then I closed it again. Maybe I would leave. I had a home to go to, after all. And what had kept me here—Darcy's quest for her birth mother—had come off in spectacular fashion.

And to be honest, I could understand why she was prickly. Mother, I mean; not Darcy. Although Darcy might be prickly, too, and that would be understandable, as well. But Mother had a lot to process. And while I might not feel that brandy was the best way to deal with it, it made sense that she might prefer to come to terms with all these revelations without anyone underfoot. Especially one of the children she'd had with the man she now learned had had another child with someone else first.

If I'd come face to face with my husband's love child after more than thirty years of marriage—instead of, say, coming face to face with my boyfriend's love child after sleeping with him once—I might not have wanted company around, either.

Mother went for the brandy bottle, and instead of getting into an undignified tussle over it, I got up and left the room instead. If Mother wanted to drink herself into oblivion, that was her prerogative. If she thought a hangover would be easier to handle than reality, more power to her.

So I went upstairs and packed my bag and used the bathroom and made sure the bed was made, and then I headed back down the stairs again, bag in hand. I left it on the bottom step and walked over to the parlor door.

When I showed up in the doorway, Mother gave me a look of active dislike. She was pouring herself another couple of fingers of brandy. I had no idea whether it had taken her this long to retrieve the bottle and twist the cap off, or whether this was the second serving since I left the room.

At this point I wasn't sure I cared. "I'm going now."

"Good riddance," Mother said. "You do realize that if it hadn't been for you sticking your nose in where it didn't belong, we wouldn't be here now?"

That hurt. Even in the moment, I realized she only said it because she was halfway drunk and had lost most of her usual good manners—and because she was in pain—but it hurt anyway.

"Darcy would still be Dad's daughter," I said, my voice tight. "Audrey would still have slept with Dad, and he would still have married you. The only thing I did, was find out about it. It didn't change anything that happened before."

"We wouldn't have known!" Mother informed me.

"It's better to know than not know. And if you weren't drunk and angry," and hurt, "you'd agree with me."

I didn't wait for her to answer—just in case she came up with something even more cutting. I just turned on my heel and walked out, grabbing the bag on the way. When I closed the front door behind me, I heard the clinking of glass against glass from the parlor.

I called Dix from the car. The office was in the opposite direction of the one I was going, or I would have stopped by again before leaving town. But at the moment, I just wanted to get out of Dodge as quickly as the speed limit would allow me.

"I'm headed home," I told him.

"To Nashville?" Dix said. "Why?"

"Mother informed me it was her house and her brandy, and if I didn't like it, I could get out. So I did."

There was a beat. "She's drinking?"

"She's not just drinking," I said, sparing Yvonne McCoy a thought as I zoomed past the shuttered Beulah's Meat'n Three. Hopefully the meeting with Catherine would go well this afternoon. "She's stinking drunk, and ugly with it. She said some very regrettable things to me."

"Mother?"

"I know she's normally only very politely rude—even if she can be extremely rude when she's polite—but this was flat out ugly. She's polished off most of a bottle of brandy. At least there wasn't much left when I walked out. I don't know how much she started with."

"She must be very upset," Dix said.

No kidding. "That doesn't mean she has to be stupid. A hangover on top of everything else isn't going to help."

"Did you tell her that?" My brother's voice was amused.

"I tried," I said. "She wasn't going to take it from me. She said it was all my fault. If I'd only left well enough alone, this wouldn't have happened."

Dix sighed. "I'll get Catherine and go over there."

"Don't take Darcy," I told him.

A second passed, and then— "No. That wouldn't be a good idea."

Probably not. Not yet, anyway.

He added, "You can stay with me, you know. You don't have to leave town. We have an extra bed. So does Catherine."

So, probably, did Darcy. My other sister.

Although it was likely too soon to stay over with her. If this was strange and awkward for us, it must be equally so for her.

We'd gained a sister. She'd gained two sisters, a brother, two brothers-in-law, a half-dozen nephews and nieces, a mother, a dead father, and a stepmother who acted like the Wicked Witch of the West. Plus Aunt Regina and Uncle Sid and a long line of relatives, dead and alive, on the Martin side of the family. And probably a few people on Audrey's side, too.

And while we had each other, Darcy had no one.

"It's all right," I said. "I've been away from Rafe for a few days anyway. I'd like to see him." Dreadlocks, gold teeth, and all. "And there's something we have to talk about."

Dix didn't ask me what. He probably assumed it was this same situation we were all dealing with.

"I'm sorry to leave you to deal with it all, though," I added. "I'll drive back down in a couple of days. I just really need to see Rafe right now."

"It's fine," my brother told me. "I'll call you tonight. Let you know how things are going."

I told him I appreciated it. And then I put the phone down and my foot on the gas pedal and booked it up the interstate toward home.

It was still early, just going on lunchtime, when I drove into Nashville. Rafe would be at work, whatever that meant these days. Normally, he'd be working out of the TBI building close to our house, but right now, who knew? So I called him again.

"Listen," I said when he picked up. "I need to talk to you about something."

"You already did, darlin'. Just an hour ago. Remember?"

"This is something else. Something personal."

"And that wasn't?" I heard voices in the background, and then he was back. "Sorry, darlin'."

"Where are you?"

"Antioch," Rafe said.

"Why?"

"One of the neighbors saw a car go by just after the duplex blew up the other night. Black Dodge Magnum with tinted windows."

Whatever that looked like. "OK."

"Looks like it might belong to one of the guys whose life we saved on Friday."

"You're kidding," I said. "Someone in the other gang? You made sure he wasn't shot, and he repaid you by throwing a bomb through your window?"

"Looks that way. We're sitting here around the corner from his place, waiting for the car to show up. We gotta SWAT team on standby once he gets here, so we can go knock on the door and take him down."

And my husband was ready to put on riot-gear of his own, no doubt, to be in on the takedown.

"It doesn't sound like this is a good time for us to have that conversation," I said.

"Afraid not, darlin'. Unless it's life and death, this takes precedence."

Of course it did. And it wasn't. Life or death, I mean. I wanted to get it over with, now that I'd made up my mind to do it, but not when he was busy doing something else. Especially something like this.

"It can wait. Will you be home tonight?"

"At the house? Depends on what happens between now and then. I imagine so."

"I just drove into Nashville," I told him. "Mother kicked me out."

"What?"

"She didn't take the news about Darcy very well. When I left her, she was looking at the bottom of a bottle of brandy."

"Your mother?"

"The one and only," I said. "She told me it was her house and her brandy, and if I didn't like it, I could leave. So I left. I'll be sleeping in our bed tonight."

A smile colored his voice. "Then I'll definitely be there."

"And we'll talk?"

"After we do something else," Rafe said. "Listen, darlin'. Don't go there yet."

"The house? Why?"

"We pulled Clayton and José off guard duty. They're on their way here. The place is empty, and I don't want you there alone."

I felt a chill creep down my spine, and not from the air conditioning. "You think this guy might go there?"

"I think he mighta been there already," Rafe said. "The gun Lamar had—"

"Who's Lamar?"

"The kid who got blown up the other night. His gun didn't melt. And the bullets don't match the bullets that killed the other two. So we're thinking Lamar didn't kill'em after all. That this guy we're after now—"

"From the rival gang."

"Right. He killed all of'em."

Oh. Yes, that made a difference. And a lot more sense. And he already knew where the house was, since—it seemed—he had killed Lamar's comrade inside it.

"I'll find something else to do until you call and tell me you've got him," I said. "Maybe I'll go to the office or something." Where it was nice and safe and I was surrounded by other people. "Grab a salad from somewhere and eat lunch at my desk."

"Thanks, darlin'."

"No problem," I told him sincerely. I had no desire to come face to face with this guy. None at all. He'd killed three people—that we knew of—over the past three days. I'd much rather survive and make love to my husband tonight. After we'd talked about Carmen and her baby.

Or maybe before. He might not be in the mood after.

"Just call me when you have him."

He promised he would, and I assured him, again, that I wouldn't go near the house on Potsdam until he was with me. And then we hung up. He went back to his surveillance, and I kept going in the direction of the real estate office.

Twenty

I was almost there when the phone rang again. And I got very excited at first, because I thought it might be Rafe calling back to tell me the guy had come home already, and had walked straight into the loving arms of the MNPD SWAT team.

But the phone wasn't playing *Hot Stuff,* just the generic ring tone I use for the people who don't call me enough to get their own special song.

I glanced at the display. *Dixon Calvert Martin,* it said. Someone who should have his own ring tone. Maybe I'd dig up the theme song from *Legally Blonde.*

I pushed the button. "Hi."

"Drunk as a skunk," my brother intoned.

"Excuse me?"

"Mother. She's drunk as a skunk, and maudlin with it."

"I don't think skunks get drunk." And maudlin had to be better than combative.

"Our mother does," Dix said. "Catherine and I just poured her into bed. I had to carry her up the stairs. I just hope she didn't drink so much she makes herself ill."

"Better get her a bucket."

"We did," Dix said. "But that wasn't what I meant. She downed most of that bottle of brandy, and on an empty stomach. I'm sure she'll be violently sick. But I hope she didn't drink enough to get alcohol poisoning or anything like that. I'd hate to have to take her to the hospital to have her stomach pumped."

Yikes. "Hopefully it won't come to that," I said, and took the exit for Shelby Avenue. Off the interstate at last, and onto the friendly streets of home. "You don't really think she will, do you?"

"I'm not sure," Dix said. "I've never seen her like this."

None of us had. "Today was a lot for her to deal with. Not only that the man she was married to for more than twenty-five years had a child with someone else. But that that someone else was her best friend. Who never told her about it, in the more than thirty years they were friends."

Dix grunted. I assumed it was assent.

"I don't really understand this part," I added. "I mean, Audrey said she was in love with Dad, right? Before he met Mother? I don't understand why she'd want to become friends with Mother after that. Wouldn't you think that would be salt in the wound? Not just to see him happy with someone else, but to be best friends with that person?"

"I don't know," Dix admitted. "Maybe... In a strange way, maybe she felt like she got closer to him. Like, in a way, when Mother talked about her marriage—and I'm sure she did—maybe Audrey felt a little like she was married to him, too?"

"That's a little creepy, if you ask me."

I'd been dealing with just that possibility last year, when Rafe had been eating at Fidelio's with Carmen. I'd been in love with him, and he'd been going around with her. If he'd ended up marrying her—and at the time, I'd thought they had a real relationship, so that was a possibility in my mind—there would have been no part of me that would have wanted to get any closer to the two of them than I had to. Listening to her talking about their relationship—the relationship I wanted—would have been agony.

"I don't think we should judge," Dix said.

"I know we shouldn't. I'm just saying that I don't think I

could have done it. Or would have wanted to."

Dix grunted again.

"So is someone going to stay with her?"

"I called Aunt Regina," Dix said. "Catherine has an appointment at one. And I've got work, too."

"And besides, Aunt Regina needs to know what's going on. Darcy is her niece."

Something struck me, and I added, "Do you think she knew? Aunt Regina? She was Dad's sister. She might have known that he was sleeping with Audrey."

I had spoken to her about this just yesterday. She hadn't told me anything then, if she did know something.

Although she might have figured it out at that point. Maybe she'd known that Dad and Audrey had an affair, but she hadn't known that Audrey got pregnant. Not until I told her about Darcy. And then she might have put two and two together, and contacted the sheriff after I left, and told him what she suspected. Maybe she'd asked him whether he knew any more than she did, and between them, they figured out the truth.

It wouldn't surprise me. Nothing much about my Aunt Regina surprises me. She was the one who told me, last Christmas, about Great-great-great-grandma Carrie and the groom. She'd been sitting on that information since she was a girl, but she'd never mentioned it to Mother. Or to any of the rest of us, until I came out about my feelings for Rafe and my fear that Mother was going to give him hell for being mixed race. Aunt Regina had told me about Carrie and her son William to give me some ammunition.

"I don't know," Dix said. "I can ask her."

"It doesn't matter. I just wondered, that's all. So she's going to stay with Mother. Hopefully this whole thing won't be fodder for the society column. I guess we're society as far as Sweetwater is concerned."

"I don't think Aunt Regina would air the Martin dirty

laundry on the society page of the *Reporter*," Dix said.

"She put Rafe's and my wedding on the society page of the *Reporter*."

"Your husband isn't dirty laundry," my brother informed me, and put me squarely in my place.

"Right. Sorry."

"No problem. I just wanted to let you know what was going on here. Are you almost home?"

"Almost to the office." I told him what Rafe had told me. "He wants me to stay around other people until they catch this guy. So I'm going to grab some lunch and get some work done. And hopefully by quitting time, the guy will be behind bars and I can sleep in my own bed tonight."

Next to my husband. After I told him that he might be about to be a daddy. Again.

"Good luck," Dix said. "I'll call you tonight and give you an update. Be careful."

I promised I would, and hung up. And turned down Eleventh Street toward the office.

A sports bar and restaurant called the FinBar is right down the street from LB&A. I parked in the lot and ducked inside—quickly, so no nutcase with a gun could get a bead on me before I was through the doors and safe. And since I was there, I decided I might as well just eat there instead of getting something to go. So I hauled my extra bulk up onto a bar stool—one where I could see the door—and ordered a salad and an iced tea. I wasn't really concerned that Rafe's gang banger had somehow picked me up along my route, and followed me here, and was planning to come in and shoot the place up—why would he?—but better safe than sorry.

So I sat there and sipped tea and watched the door, when who should walk in but Alexandra Puckett.

I wrinkled my brows. It was Monday, wasn't it? And it

wasn't a holiday. There aren't any of those in August. So shouldn't she be in school, in the middle of the day like this?

"Alexandra?"

She turned in the direction of my voice, and flushed when she saw me. "Savannah."

"Come sit with me." I gestured to the empty stool next to me.

"I'm just ordering some takeout," Alexandra said. She moved toward me, but not eagerly.

The bartender gave her a friendly smile. "I can take care of that for you. Just have a seat and tell me what you'd like."

Alexandra lifted her butt onto the seat next to me. "I guess I'll take two hamburgers with fries to go."

The bartender told her he'd put it in. "Would you like a drink while you wait? It's hot out there."

Alexandra shrugged. "Sure. A Diet Coke, I guess."

A few seconds later, the Diet Coke materialized in front of her. The bartender went off to put in the hamburger order and hopefully bring me my salad.

"I know you're eating for two," I told Alexandra, "but two hamburgers and fries might be excessive." Especially at this stage of the game, when she didn't even know if she was going to keep the baby.

"Oh." She flushed. "They aren't both for me."

I hadn't thought they were. "I didn't realize today was a holiday. Are you and Austin home?"

Alexandra shook her head, the color in her cheeks deepening. "Austin's at school. He spent the night at a friend's house, and they took him in. Dad's on a business trip until tomorrow."

"So because your dad's away and your brother had a ride, you decided you didn't have to go to school?"

"No," Alexandra said, flushing.

"Did you go see the doctor?" Was that why she was here in the middle of the day?

"Not yet," Alexandra said, and I guess it would have been

something of a miracle to get an appointment this quickly. So much had happened over the past few days that everything seemed like it had happened longer ago than it really had. It was just two days since Alexandra and I—and Darcy—had had lunch together at the barbeque place.

"You'll never guess what happened," I said. "Remember Darcy and how we were trying to find her birth mother?"

She nodded, and took a sip of her Diet Coke.

"Turns out she's my sister."

Alexandra's eyes grew huge. "How's that possible?"

"You know about the birds and the bees, right? Darcy's mother slept with my father before he met my mother. She got pregnant—Darcy's mother, I mean, although my mother eventually got pregnant too, or I wouldn't be here. And she didn't tell my father about it. So he married my mother, and they had Catherine and Dix and me. And Audrey had Darcy and gave her up for adoption. And now I have an extra sister."

"Wow," Alexandra said, her eyes wide.

"I know. It's weird. But kind of cool, too. But definitely a lot to get used to."

The bartender brought my salad, and I lifted my fork. "You don't mind, do you? I'm starving."

Alexandra shook her head. "Go ahead."

I went ahead. "So tell me what's going on with you," I instructed between bites. "Why aren't you in school? Does your dad know? Are you feeling sick?" Or maybe she was feeling weird about it. About being pregnant and in high school. "The worst thing you can do is not finish high school, you know. If you're going to have a baby, you need an education. Babies aren't cheap."

"It's not that," Alexandra said. "And I don't know if I'm having a baby."

"I don't suppose you've heard from Jamal?" No one else had,

so it wasn't likely he'd thought to contact Alexandra in the midst of all that was going on. But I figured it couldn't hurt to ask.

"No," Alexandra said. And looked very guilty.

My spider senses tingled. "Are you sure?" With her dad away on business, and Austin at a friend's house for the night, it would have been a golden opportunity to spend some time with her guy. Even if her guy was up to his ears in an undercover operation this weekend. "Who's the second hamburger for?"

It wasn't her father, not if he was away on a business trip until tomorrow. And it wasn't Austin, if he was in school.

"Nobody," Alexandra said.

"Sure."

She sighed. "Don't tell my dad, OK?"

"Tell him what? That you cut school today and asked Jamal to come over so you could tell him that you're pregnant?"

Alexandra hung her head. It was all the answer I needed.

"Oh, my God!" I told her, driving my fork into the lettuce and leaving it there, upright and quivering. "Rafe's been going crazy, trying to find Jamal. How long has he been with you?"

Since yesterday, as it happened. Steven Puckett had left in the early afternoon on Sunday for a two-day business trip to Omaha. He had meetings starting this morning, so he'd had to leave yesterday and stay in a hotel to be there bright and early today. And as soon as Alexandra had dropped him off at the airport, and taken Austin to his friend's house, I'm sure she had been on the phone with Jamal.

"You have to tell him to call Rafe," I said, as the bartender approached with Alexandra's to-go bag. "I'm serious. Right now he's AWOL, and everyone's worried. He can't do that without warning. If he isn't careful, he's going to lose his job."

Alexandra looked worried too, as she pulled out her wallet to pay for the burgers.

"I'll take my check, too," I told the bartender. He produced my bill after running Alexandra's card, and then he took mine and went to do the same with it while Alexandra signed hers. "Tell him, OK? He really does need to call Rafe. Or Wendell, or somebody. I know you had something important to tell him, and if he plays it right, this could be a mitigating circumstance, but he can't disappear in the middle of an operation like this."

Alexandra promised she'd tell him. "Listen, I've got to go. The food's going to get cold."

"Just don't forget."

Alexandra said she wouldn't, and then she took her burgers and walked out. I waited for my credit card to come back to me, and then I signed the slip and left, too. I was out the door in time to see the tail end of Alexandra's Miata turn out of the parking lot.

I knew where she was going, of course—or at least I knew where she had told me she was going: her father's house on Winding Way. But I watched until she disappeared around the corner in the direction of Main Street anyway. And then I got into my own car and followed.

It wasn't that I didn't trust her to do what she'd said she would. More that I just thought she might forget to tell Jamal to call Rafe. Or that she wouldn't impress upon him just how important it was that he did. And the last thing either of them needed right now, was for Jamal to lose his job.

Besides, I wasn't doing anything else. I might as well go up there and tell him myself. Rafe didn't want me to be alone, but I wouldn't be alone. I'd be even safer there than at the office, since no one would expect me to be there, and so no one would be able to track me down.

And once I'd told Jamal how important it was for him to call Rafe, and maybe had a few words to say about Alexandra and the baby and his not making sure to keep his pecker in his pants around under-aged girls, I'd go back to the office and spend the rest of the afternoon there.

Unless Rafe and the others had caught the bad guy by then. And they might have.

Hell... heck, I should probably just call him and tell him where I was going, and that I'd found Jamal for him. Maybe it would score me a couple of brownie points. And he wouldn't be able to yell at me for changing plans and going somewhere without telling him.

Keeping Alexandra's car in sight, seven or eight cars up ahead of me on Gallatin Road, I dug my phone out of my purse and hit the speed dial button for the most recent call. By the time the light changed and we were moving again, the phone was ringing on the other end. And ringing.

Finally the machine kicked in.

"Hi," I told it. "It's me. I'm sorry to bother you again. I guess maybe the guy got home and you're too busy apprehending him to take my call, huh? That's great! Anyway, I wanted to tell you about a change of plans. I was sitting at the FinBar having a salad when Alexandra Puckett walked in for takeout. It turns out Jamal's with her. She must have contacted him to tell him about the baby, I guess. He's been there since yesterday. I don't know why he hasn't been answering your calls, but I guess maybe he's ashamed because he knocked up a seventeen-year-old girl he met at your wedding, and he didn't want to have to tell you about it."

That made sense, at least to me.

"So I'm on my way to Alexandra's house, to try to talk him into calling you. I'm not sure I can trust her to do it. And then I'll go to the office afterward. Just call me when the guy is contained, and I'll meet you at home. I love you. Bye."

I disconnected and peered up the street. The Miata was still up ahead.

We passed the grocery store, and a few minutes later, the Inglewood fire station and on the next block, the Inglewood library. Alexandra's turn signal flicked on at the last moment, and she zipped around the corner and disappeared down Winding Way. Twenty seconds later, I made the same turn and followed.

Halfway down the block I saw her car pulling into the driveway of their oversized 1940s Tudor. Across the street sat Maybelle Driscoll's little stone cottage, with a low-slung black car in the driveway.

Once upon a time, I had been caught by Officers Spicer and Truman, breaking into Maybelle's house. Or if not breaking, at least trespassing where I didn't belong.

Maybelle was in prison in Mississippi now, thanks to me and that break-in—and Alexandra asking my help in getting her father out of Maybelle's clutches before it was too late.

Her house should be empty. And she'd never be caught dead in a black car with tinted windows and black wheel wells. It looked like a ghettofied hearse.

Maybe it was Jamal's personal vehicle, and he'd parked it across the street instead of in Alexandra's driveway so the neighbors wouldn't talk.

It looked brand new, though. And like it would cost more than a TBI rookie could afford.

I had seen one of those cars recently. Where was it...?

When Darcy and I had been waiting at the light on Potsdam Street and Dresden on Saturday afternoon, on our way back to the house to see the SWAT team in action, we'd waited for a car like this to turn off Potsdam onto Dresden in the opposite direction.

And what kind of car was it Rafe had said the witnesses had seen driving away after the firebombing of the duplex? A black Dodge Magnum, wasn't it?

Was that a Dodge Magnum parked across the street from the Tudor?

I wanted to stop and look, but Alexandra was already in the

process of retrieving the to-go bag from the passenger side of her car. If I took the time to pull into the driveway across the street to check the make and model of the car parked there, she'd be inside by the time I caught up. And then it might be too late.

I pulled into the driveway behind her and jumped out, as quickly as the stomach allowed. It tends to get wedged between the seat and the steering wheel these days, so everything takes a little longer.

"Wait!"

Alexandra sighed, but stopped. "What are you doing here?"

"I wanted to talk to Jamal," I said. "Just for a minute."

She headed up the flagstone path to the front door, and I followed. "Is that his car across the street? In Maybelle's driveway?"

Alexandra's steps slowed, and she turned to glance across the street. "No. I picked him up. He didn't want his car sitting here, in case any of the neighbors noticed, and told Dad."

"So whose car is it? Is something going on at Maybelle's house?"

"I don't know," Alexandra said, shifting the bag with the hamburgers to the other hand to fish for her keys in her bag." It wasn't there when I left. Looks like it belongs to one of the Sopranos." She grinned.

Or another gangster type. "Is that what a Dodge Magnum looks like?"

Alexandra shrugged. "How would I know? Do I look like I care about cars?" She pulled the keys out of her bag and turned to the door.

"Wait a second," I said.

"Why?" But she waited.

"I'm not sure I like this." Correction: I was quite sure I didn't like it. "Jamal must have heard us drive up. Why isn't he opening the door for you, so you don't have to juggle both the burgers and the keys?"

"He's asleep?" Alexandra suggested, jingling the keys. I winced, and she added, "What's wrong, Savannah?"

"I have a feeling," I said. "A bad feeling. And it might be my imagination. But I don't think so." I told her about the black car I'd seen driving away from my house around the time gang banger number 2 had been put out of his misery, and the car that had been seen driving away from the duplex after the firebomb. "Rafe said it was a Dodge Magnum. A black Dodge Magnum. If that's a Dodge Magnum over there, it could be the same car."

"What's it doing here?" Alexandra asked, eyeing it.

"Well, if it is the same car, I assume the guy in it is looking for Jamal." And at this point we had no idea whether he was inside the car—the windows were too dark to see anything—or whether he was in Maybelle's house, keeping an eye on us from across the street, or whether he was already inside Alexandra's house.

"Why would he want Jamal?" Alexandra asked.

"Because he's eliminated all three of the guys from the rival gang who weren't arrested on Friday. And Jamal's still walking around."

"But Jamal didn't do anything!"

I shushed her. For all we knew, the guy was standing just inside the door listening to us. "Put down the burgers for a second and get away from the door."

Alexandra rolled her eyes, but she did as I asked.

"Come on."

I herded her away from the door, toward the corner of the house. There were no windows there, and if we whispered, maybe he wouldn't be able to hear us.

If he was inside, that was, and wasn't taking aim at us from the house across the street.

Did these types have long range rifles, or just pistols? Could a pistol hit us at that distance?

Maybe we'd better get behind the house, just in case. A bullet couldn't go through brick; I did know that much.

I led the way, hugging the side of the house, until we were safely tucked away behind the chimney, half hidden by a couple of holly bushes, in a spot where I felt pretty certain that no one inside the house could hear us talk, and nobody could shoot us, at least not from across the street. The leaves were prickly where they touched my bare arms and legs, but being safe felt good.

"Here's what we'll do," I said, keeping my voice just above a whisper.

Alexandra nodded.

"I've only been here a couple of times, but there's a patio on the back of the house, right? One where we can see in?"

"There are French doors from the family room," Alexandra confirmed, "and a single door from the kitchen. There are windows in both."

Good. We'd easily be able to see in. My days of climbing trees and walls are long behind me, and in my current condition, I'm not sure I could, anyway. What if I fell?

And since Alexandra was in the same condition I was—even if her baby was a bit more padded than mine—I didn't want to risk her health on climbing, either. If she decided not to keep the baby, that was her business, but I wasn't going to make her risk losing it before she'd made up her mind.

"The first thing we need to do, is see whether the guy is inside."

"Shouldn't we call the cops?"

We could. But if the car in Maybelle's driveway belonged to some innocent relative going through Maybelle's filing cabinet looking for information on her mortgage lien, nobody would thank us for wasting taxpayer money. I have no problem calling in reinforcements when I need them, but I do want to be sure it's not a false alarm before I do.

"If we see him, we will. But let's make sure first."

We made our way carefully out from behind the holly bushes and crept along the wall to the corner of the house. There we surveyed the backyard for any sign of activity—there was none, apart from a squirrel hopping across the grass with something in his mouth—before we ducked around the corner.

The patio was up ahead: a beautiful half-circle of stone pavers inside a hip-height brick wall. Heavy planters sat at intervals, brimming over with late-summer flowers.

"Your dad probably uses a landscaper," I muttered.

Alexandra shrugged. I took that to be a yes.

Not that I have any room to talk. My mother does the same thing. It's just us plebeians who have to mow our own lawns and water our own flowers.

I hoisted myself up and over the wall. Alexandra legged it after me, and we hugged the wall again, up on the patio this time.

The double doors to the family room were ahead. We crept forward. Once we arrived safely, we carefully extended our noses past the edge of the glass and peered in.

I remembered the room. Once upon a time—just about a year ago—I had sat in that room while Alexandra confessed to her father that instead of spending the night at her friend Lynne's house, she'd gone to a party at her boyfriend's place. Her very unsuitable boyfriend, whom Brenda had tried to buy off.

I wondered whether Steven would be any more taken with Jamal. Had he even known about Maurice Washington until that night? Knowing Brenda, she probably wouldn't have told him. She'd been the kind of woman who just had to control everything and everyone around her, and handle everything herself.

Although Jamal did have the benefit of gainful employment, even if he had quite a lot of other strikes against him.

As long as we could keep him employed, that was.

"I see him," Alexandra breathed.

I pulled my wayward thoughts back. "Jamal?"

She nodded.

"Alone?" I couldn't see him. Not yet. "Where is he?"

"Dining room table," Alexandra said softly. "Through the door."

Ah, yes. There was a door on the other side of the family room, and through it, we could see a sliver of the dining room. And a sliver of Jamal. He was sitting on a chair, half hidden behind the wall. I could see his profile, his nose and mouth and forehead, but most of his face wasn't in view. Most of his body was gone, too, save for his hands and arms. They were conspicuously folded on the table, as if someone had told him to keep his hands in sight.

Or maybe I was just imagining that. But he wasn't doing anything. Not reading a book or manipulating his phone or even fiddling with something. Just sitting, with his hands folded.

Most people don't behave that way naturally.

"At least he isn't dead," I said.

Alexandra drew in a quick breath, and I added, "Sorry."

She shook her head.

"Where can we go to see more of the dining room? Can we see another part of it from over there?" I glanced at the kitchen door, up ahead by another fifteen feet or so.

She nodded. We moved forward. Passing in front of the glass double doors was a little scary, but I figured if we couldn't see anyone else, he couldn't see us, either. And nobody tried to shoot at us, so it was all good.

A few seconds later we reached the kitchen door, and repeated the process with the noses.

The kitchen was big and fancy, filled with dark wood cabinets and marble counters. Very ostentatious. Very Brenda.

Very empty. There was a butler's door between the kitchen and the dining room—the kind that swings but doesn't latch—

and it had been pinned against the wall with what looked like a cast-iron dachshund. I guess someone had gotten tired of it swinging a million times a day.

A man was sitting at the dining table with his back to us. And he was a big man, so it was hard to see past him. Jamal was tall, so we could see the top of his head above the crown of the other guy, but that was pretty much it.

The guy was black, I could see that much. Short and squat, with a shaved head, wearing an oversized sports jersey. And I could see the gun in his hand. It was pointed at Jamal.

I could see something else, too. My own face, reflected in the mirror above the sideboard behind Jamal.

Twenty-One

"Shit!"

I ducked and pushed Alexandra away.

"What?"

"Mirror! Move!"

She shot a startled glance through the window, and then she moved. We scrambled across the patio again, basically flinging ourselves over the low wall, and ducked behind the corner of the house. And there we stood, trying to catch our breath and pricking our ears to hear if the patio doors opened.

Nothing happened.

"Now can we call the cops?" Alexandra asked after a minute.

We'd better. I reached for my phone, only to realize I'd left it—along with my entire purse—on the passenger seat of my car. "Damn. I mean... darn."

"I have mine," Alexandra said. She reached for her back pocket, and that's when we heard a click behind us.

My heart stopped for a second, before it kicked into double-time.

We both turned around, slowly, raising our hands. There's something automatic about it, when someone has a gun. And I was pretty sure that click I'd heard was the safety coming off a pistol.

It was. The guy from the dining room was standing behind us—or in front of us now—with his weapon pointed squarely our way.

So much for thinking he hadn't noticed our faces in the mirror. Obviously he had, but instead of coming out through the patio doors, he'd gone through the front instead. A pincer movement, or whatever Rafe would call it.

Alexandra squeaked and ducked behind me. I held my ground and looked him straight in the eye. His were small and beady black, deep-set in a face as round as the moon. "What did you do to Jamal?"

I got the immediate feeling my lack of fear frustrated him. That he expected me to cower and cringe at the sight of the gun. And it wasn't like I particularly enjoyed having it pointed at me. But to be honest, I'd had a lot of guns pointed my way, and I'd only been shot once. Chances were I'd make it through this with my life, too. He had no reason to shoot me. It was Jamal he was after.

"Is he OK?" Alexandra added, her voice shaking. "Did you kill him?"

I glanced over my shoulder. "He didn't."

We would have heard it, had this guy shot him while we'd stood here. There was no silencer on the gun. I don't know much, but I do know that. He couldn't have shot Jamal within the last minute, right inside the house, without us hearing.

It clearly made him happy that she was upset by the thought, though. My attitude didn't please him near as much.

"Homeboy and I ain't done talking," he said. "When we done, maybe I kill him."

"And maybe you won't," I said. "You've killed a few people already this weekend. Are you sure you want to increase the body count? It won't help your chances any when they catch you."

"They gotta catch me first." He grinned.

He had two gold teeth in the front of his mouth. And unlike Rafe's, I'm sure these weren't designed to come off.

One of the gold plates had a design and looked like it was set with a diamond, although I guess it was more likely to be a cubic zirconia. Surely nobody would risk putting a diamond in a place like that?

It probably just looked extra faceted and shiny because it was wet.

He gave me a belligerent look. "What you looking at, bitch?"

"The stone on your tooth," I said, making the choice to ignore the insult. "Diamond?"

He grinned. "Ladies dig the diamond."

Sure they do. "Aren't you afraid it's going to fall off one night when you're brushing, and you'll lose it down the drain?"

He looked blank.

"Never mind," I said. Maybe he didn't brush. "So what did you do with Jamal? You didn't shoot him. We would have heard the shot. And I didn't see a handy coil of rope on the dining room table, so you probably didn't tie him up..."

He growled, and sounded like a rabid dog. "You always talk so much, bitch?"

"I'm afraid I do," I said, since I know that sometimes, if I keep talking long enough, I get rescued from situations like this. And even if that doesn't happen, I give myself time to come up with something useful I can do to extricate myself from trouble.

If he really had done something to incapacitate Jamal, we were likely to be on our own in this case.

Unfortunately, I'd left my handbag with my handy-dandy lipstick-canister pepper spray and serrated knife in my car.

"Why don't we go inside and talk this through?" Maybe there, I'd come across something I could use for a weapon. There was nothing out here. The flower urns on the patio were too heavy, and there was nothing else on offer. No lose bricks in the chimney or anything like that. Steven kept the place in good repair. "The longer we stand here, the more likely someone will drive by and see us."

He contemplated me in silence for a second, with eyes that were flat and black and totally devoid of emotion. For that moment or two, he really did look like he'd shoot me as soon as look at me, and leave me here, just so he wouldn't have to deal with me anymore. I felt a chill creep down my spine.

But he must have realized that that would attract attention, and my suggestion made more sense, because he gestured with the gun. "Yeah. Good idea. Move, bitch."

I moved. Alexandra scrambled after me, and fumbled for my hand. "What are we going to do?"

"What he says," I told her, wrapping my fingers around hers. "You just worry about keeping yourself alive."

She sniffled but didn't say anything else.

We rounded the corner and headed for the front door.

No sooner had we stepped across the threshold than Mr. Gang Banger slammed it behind us and locked it. "Brought you your girlfriend," he announced loudly, followed by a word I'm too delicate to repeat.

There was no answer, and Mr. Gang Banger clearly didn't like that. He pushed us ahead of him toward the dining room. Alexandra sniffed and stumbled. I looked around for something I might use as a weapon.

There wasn't much on offer. A big vase it would be satisfying to break over the bastard's head, but it was on the other side of the room. He'd shoot me before I could get to it.

There were tools beside the fireplace, among them what looked like a nice, heavy iron poker. And that I could get to—it was just a few feet away—but it would take too long to get it out of the stand. And again, he'd shoot me.

And then we were through the living room and into the dining room, where Jamal was slumped over the table.

Alexandra shrieked. She dropped my hand and ran for him.

The gang banger cursed and brought the gun up.

I didn't wait, just threw myself at it. From the side, so there was no chance he'd shoot me. I was more worried about Alexandra and Jamal.

The shot went wide and took out the glass in one of the windows. The entire pane collapsed in a deafening crash. The pistol fell to the floor and slid. Alexandra screamed, and Jamal swore.

Alexandra stopped screaming and stared at him.

The gang banger dove for the gun. I went in the other direction, for the fireplace poker.

It was heavier than I had expected it to be. Real iron. No effete modern replicas for Steven Puckett. It was the kind of poker you could have used to roast a whole pig, at least if the pig was fairly small.

We came up at the same time, the gang banger brandishing his gun and me clutching the poker.

He grinned. The diamond glinted.

My eyes narrowed.

And then Alexandra rose from the table like the vengeance of God and cracked him over the head with the centerpiece.

I dodged, just in case the gun went off.

It didn't. Instead, it clattered to the floor. The gang banger himself fell like a redwood, with a thud that shook the house. The centerpiece—a misshapen but solid ceramic bowl, maybe something Alexandra or Austin had made in art class when they were younger—fell on top of him and then off onto the floor, all without breaking. The contents— half a dozen ripe peaches—rolled across the floor in all directions.

I raised the fireplace poker, just in case he needed another whack to stay down. But he didn't move.

"Ohmigod!" Alexandra squeaked, turning it into a single word. "Ohmigod! Is he dead? Did I kill him?"

"Find out, please." My voice was a little strained. The poker was heavy, and keeping it lifted taxed the muscles in my arms.

But at the same time I wasn't about to put it down until I knew for sure it wouldn't be needed.

Alexandra went down on one knee next to the fallen bad guy and reached out. I tensed, ready to bring the poker down on the back of his head if he tried to grab her.

He didn't. A second later, Alexandra breathed a sigh of relief. "I didn't kill him."

Good to know. "Is he conscious?"

"He doesn't seem to be," Alexandra said.

"Go find something to tie him up with, please. I'm afraid if I hit him with this, I really will kill him. It's heavy."

She opened her mouth, took one look at my face, and went to do as I said.

"What about me?" Jamal asked. Or at least I'm pretty sure that's what he said. He had a piece of duct tape across his mouth, so he couldn't say much at all, or nothing very intelligible.

I glanced at him. "We'll cut you lose once she comes back." We hadn't noticed it when we looked through the window, but the reason he hadn't moved from the chair was that his ankles were also duct taped to the legs.

I raised my voice. "Alexandra? Bring a pair of scissors, please. And look for the duct tape. There has to be some somewhere."

"Got it." Alexandra was already on her way back, spinning a roll of duct tape around her finger.

"Cut Jamal lose first." I waited until she had, and then added, "Let him tie the guy up. He'll do a better job than you."

Alexandra nodded, seemingly happy to relinquish the responsibility. Jamal was obviously itching to rip off the piece of duct tape covering his mouth, but he obliged me by kneeling beside the bad guy first.

I kept the poker raised until the bad guy's hands were taped behind his back. By the time I was able to lower it back into the stand, the muscles in my arms were shaking.

The rest of me was shaking a little, too. Adrenaline, I guess. Jamal got awkwardly to his feet and started picking at the duct tape on his face, grimacing and moaning. When Alexandra moved to help him, he twitched her off. She looked hurt, but took herself off in the direction of the bathroom to look for rubbing alcohol, which was supposed to help dissolve the glue on the tape.

Just when I thought it was safe to relax, there was the squeal of brakes outside, and a second later the slam of a door and the pounding of feet up the walkway.

Jamal glanced out the front window and winced. He made a sort of aborted move toward the kitchen.

"Don't," I said. "You're in enough trouble already. And you got the bad guy. That has to count for something. And besides, you look pathetic. That probably counts, too."

He grunted something from behind the tape, but I don't know what it was. Out front, someone tried the doorknob, and when the door didn't open, I knew what was about to happen.

"No!" I shrieked and threw myself at it. It was a beautiful, original-to-the-house, solid wood door with a round top, very unique, that Rafe would kick in in a couple of seconds if I didn't stop him. And once the lock splintered, there'd be no way to fix it. "Don't! I'm coming!"

He didn't. But when I threw the bolts back and flung the door open, he scowled at me. "Where's your phone?"

"In my car," I said. "Did you try to call?"

He didn't bother to answer, since the answer was obvious. Now I felt bad for having worried him.

He gave me a searching look. "You OK?"

"Fine. He didn't hurt anybody. Except maybe Jamal."

I glanced over my shoulder at the young man, who was still picking at the duct tape, and wincing every time a section of it came off.

"Here," Rafe said and moved past me. "I'll do it." He reached out and grabbed a corner of the tape before Jamal could stop him, and yanked the whole thing off. It took some of Jamal's skin with it. Jamal shrieked like a little girl, and clapped both hands to his face as tears flooded his eyes. A litany of four-letter words followed.

Alexandra came running, and stopped in the doorway to stare at Jamal with wide eyes.

Rafe gave him a minute to recover. When the curses slowed, he asked, "You OK?"

Jamal nodded, still wincing a bit. "He was having too much fun telling me that he was gonna kill me, and why, to actually do much to me."

"So when you were slumped over the table..." I said.

"I was providing you with a distraction," Jamal told me.

Ah.

Alexandra sniffed. "I thought you were dead."

Jamal glanced at her. "Sorry." And then he seemed to realize that something more was called for, so he put out a tentative arm. When Alexandra stepped into it and turned her face into his chest and began sobbing, he patted her back awkwardly.

"Gonna have to learn to do better than that," Rafe told him, but I wasn't sure whether he was referring to the way Jamal was—or wasn't—comforting Alexandra, or the whole fiasco.

His attention moved to the body on the floor. "This the guy?"

We all nodded. Or Jamal and I did. Alexandra was still crying.

"He dead?"

"We don't think so," I said. "He was still breathing when Jamal taped his hands."

"What happened?"

I let Jamal tell it. What it boiled down to, was that the guy had showed up after Alexandra left to get the hamburgers, and he had kept Jamal quiet and cooperative by threatening to shoot her when she walked through the door again. Then he'd seen us in the mirror behind Jamal's head, and realized we were outside. He'd slapped a piece of duct tape over Jamal's mouth so he couldn't yell and alert us, and then he had left Jamal sitting at the dining room table, and had gone outside. He had rounded us up and brought us inside, and then, as Jamal put it, all hell had broken loose.

"I pretended I was dead, 'cause I thought it might give somebody a chance to do something. Alexandra screamed, and your wife went for the gun."

Rafe arched a brow at me, but didn't say anything.

"It wasn't pointed at me," I told him. "I wouldn't be that stupid."

"Sure." He turned back to Jamal. "Then what?"

"He dropped the gun. It went skidding across the floor. He went after it. Your wife went for the fireplace poker. And when his back was turned, Alexandra brained him with the... thing. The bowl. It was on the dining room table."

Alexandra sniffed and raised her head. Jamal had a big, wet spot on his shirt. "I made that bowl in fifth grade."

"Nice work," Rafe told her, either about the solidity of the bowl or cracking someone's head with it. Or both. Or possibly about soaking Jamal's shirt with her tears.

Alexandra straightened. Jamal's arm fell away, and she stood on her own. "What's wrong with your teeth? And your hair?"

I couldn't help it. I giggled. Rafe gave me a look before turning back to her. "Undercover work ain't always pretty. This time I got to pretend to be this guy's cousin."

He nodded to Jamal.

Alexandra gave him a long look. Then she gave Jamal one. Jamal squirmed. And then he braced, obviously waiting for some kind of verdict.

It didn't come.

"I'm going to the bathroom," Alexandra said. "My face is wet."

She didn't wait for anyone to say anything, just walked off. Rafe grinned appreciatively. "Hit him with the bowl, huh?"

"She did. Hard enough to make a sound." I glanced down at the prone body, still out cold. "His skull might be broken. I'm not sure. I didn't check. I was still holding the poker. But I definitely heard a crack when she hit him. And it doesn't look like anything happened to the bowl."

"No hair to soften the blow," Rafe agreed, squatting next to the trussed-up gang banger to run his fingertips over the back of the guy's head. "He's getting a nice goose egg right here, anyway. I don't feel anything moving, though, so he's prob'ly all right. But he's gonna have a hell of a headache when he wakes up."

"Good," I said. "He deserves it. He scared us."

Rafe straightened. "That his car across the way?"

I told him we assumed so. "That's what I noticed first. That's Maybelle's house, and she's in prison. Nobody's supposed to be parked over there. That's why we didn't just unlock the door and walk in."

Although who knows; things might have turned out the same either way. Unless he'd been serious about shooting Alexandra when she walked through the door.

"That's the kind of car you told me had thrown the firebomb into the duplex," I added, "isn't it?"

He nodded, and turned to Jamal. "We got some talking to do. When you're part of a team, you can't go off on your own like this and don't tell nobody where you are."

Jamal hung his head. "Are you gonna fire me?"

"It ain't up to me to fire you," Rafe told him. "I didn't hire you. Wendell did. And let me tell you, he ain't real happy. Between now and when he gets here, you better come up with a real good story to show him why he'd be stupid to let you go."

Jamal winced and lowered his voice. "She's pregnant."

Rafe nodded.

"She's seventeen!"

"Not real smart."

Like he had any room to talk. Elspeth had been that age when he'd knocked her up. I looked at him, and he looked back at me, and I knew he knew what I was thinking. He made a face and turned back to Jamal. "We'll figure it out."

"You must think I'm an idiot," Jamal muttered.

Rafe snorted. "I was eighteen when David was born. And in prison. You ain't the first idiot, and you ain't gonna be the last. But you got options. More than I did back then."

Unquestionably.

The sound of more engines and the slamming of more car doors outside heralded the arrival of the rest of the rescue team.

"You must have flown to get here this far ahead of everyone else," I said to Rafe.

"I was motivated." He pulled me in close. Jamal looked away, politely, and then, after a few seconds of awkwardly shifting his feet, he went to greet the newcomers.

"Don't leave your effing phone in your effing car so I can't get hold of you again," Rafe said into my hair.

"It wasn't really a conscious decision," I told him. And I was a little breathless, since he was holding me kind of tight, and also because, after a year, he still affects me that way. "I saw the car across the street, and I had to stop Alexandra before she walked into a potentially bad situation. It wasn't so much that I chose to leave the phone in the car. It was more that I was in too much of a hurry to remember it."

"Either way. Just keep it in your pocket after this."

The scene became chaotic after that. Wendell arrived, and so did José and Clayton. All three descended on Jamal to make sure he was OK. Once they knew he was, they all started berating him for not getting in touch.

Meanwhile, Officers Spicer and Truman showed up, and a minute later, so did Tamara Grimaldi, to collect her murderer. After much discussion, it was decided that he should probably be seen by a paramedic first, so someone put in a call for one. A couple of minutes later, an ambulance from the fire station two blocks away rolled down the street, sirens blaring and lights flashing. Now we had TBI, police, and fire all parked in the driveway and up and down the street.

And in the middle of it, a cab pulled up and deposited Steven Puckett.

He looked around at the crowd gathered in his front yard. "What on earth...?"

"Alexandra," I said, since she was out of the bathroom by then. "Your dad's home."

She turned pale.

"Look at it this way. He'll be so relieved that you're OK that the fact that you're pregnant probably won't bother him that much."

"You don't know my dad," Alexandra said, but she ran to throw herself in his arms anyway.

They disappeared inside the house, and left the cleanup to everyone else. At some point I'd had enough—it had been a big day with a lot of excitement, starting with Audrey's revelation this morning, which felt like a lifetime ago—so I told Rafe I was going home. He gave me a distracted nod.

"It's safe, right?"

"What...? Oh. Yeah. This was the guy we were looking for. Nothing else is gonna go wrong now."

I wasn't so sure. I still had Carmen to tell him about. But there'd be time for that later.

"I'll see you when you're done cleaning it all up, then."

He nodded.

"I love you."

"Love you too, darlin'. Drive carefully."

Right. I got in the Volvo, maneuvered my way carefully around all the squad cars, ambulances, and TBI vehicles, and skirted a TV truck on its way down the street as I headed for home.

Twenty-Two

Nobody jumped out at me when I got back to the house on Potsdam. Sorry if that sounds anti-climactic, but truthfully, it was nice.

I was careful, of course. I went through the house from top to bottom, just to make sure I was alone, and I didn't relax until I knew I was. But the house was empty and quiet. It was just me, with the doors locked and nobody gunning for me.

The body was gone, and so was the kitchen table. It had either been taken away by the cops, as evidence, or Rafe had decided to get rid of it and had José and Clayton haul it out. I was a little sad to see it go—our unborn child had been conceived on that table—but after seeing someone's blood and brains spattered all over the surface, I didn't think I'd ever be able to eat there again, so it was just as well.

The first thing I did was dump all my dirty clothes from the past couple of days into the washer. Then I poured a bunch of bath salts into the old clawfoot tub and had myself a leisurely bubble bath. After that, barefoot and in clean clothes, I moved the laundry from the washer to the dryer, before deciding that I needed to cook dinner.

We eat out a lot. It's easy, and during the months of morning- (and afternoon-, and evening-) sickness, when the smell of food turned my stomach, it had probably saved my life, or at least my sanity. But tonight I didn't want to go anywhere. I wanted privacy for the conversation we had to have.

So I defrosted chicken and chopped vegetables and set the table with nice dishes and stemmed glasses—even though I couldn't drink wine and Rafe much preferred beer. A table with stemmed glasses just looks more festive than a table without.

While I was in the middle of it, the phone rang.

I glanced at the time. Six-fifteen.

It might be Rafe telling me he was going to be late.

I glanced at the display. It wasn't.

"Dix." I tucked the phone under my cheek and kept working. "Hi."

"Hi, yourself," my brother said. "I just wanted to give you an update."

"Go ahead." A lot had happened here too, but it probably wasn't something he was interested in. I hadn't talked much about Rafe's case while I was down in Sweetwater. And it couldn't compare to this morning's revelations. Not for our family.

"Mother survived the afternoon," Dix informed me, "but she looks like death. I've never seen her so pale. Not even after Dad died."

In a weird sense, she probably felt like he'd died again. Or maybe like Audrey had. A thirty-three year old friendship, down the drain.

"I'm sure it'll take time for her to get used to it," I said. "But I'm glad she didn't end up in the hospital having her stomach pumped."

My brother grunted agreement. "She's still very upset—"

"Naturally."

"But she isn't drinking anymore. And I don't think she will again. Not for a while. She's feeling pretty miserable."

And not just because she was hung over. "Did she say anything about me?"

"No," Dix said. "Why? Is there something you haven't told me?"

Rather a lot, but nothing to do with this. "I just wondered whether she felt bad for kicking me out of the house."

"If she does, she hasn't mentioned it. But then she has other things to worry about."

Yes, indeed.

"How are you?" he added.

"Fine," I said. "The undercover sting is over. Rafe is coming home soon. I'm making dinner. Everyone we care about is alive and well. Everyone else is in prison or dead."

"That's good," Dix said. After a second he added, "I guess."

"It's good. Everything's back to normal." Or as normal as my life ever is, with someone like Rafe in it. "I can't wait to see my husband again. Without the long hair and those awful teeth."

Although that probably wouldn't be tonight. It would take time to get those things taken care of, and I doubted he'd had any to spare this afternoon.

"Have you spoken to Darcy?" I added.

"She worked until the end of the day and went home. Business as usual, pretty much. It's going to take her a while to process it all." He sighed. "I guess I'll have to give her a raise."

I smiled. "She's a Martin, too, it seems."

"Christ," my brother said, not a sentiment I hear from him often. We've all been brought up not to take the Lord's name in vain. It doesn't mean we always do—or don't—but Dix doesn't swear a lot. It probably comes from having children.

I lowered my voice. I don't know why, since there was no one around to hear me, but it seemed appropriate. "You're OK with this, right?"

"With what? Darcy? I'm going to have to be, aren't I? She's Dad's daughter whether we like it or not."

Yes, but... "That wasn't what I asked. I know she's Dad's daughter whether we like it or not. But how do you feel about it? Do you like it? Or not?"

"I like Darcy," Dix said. "I wouldn't have hired her otherwise. And I wouldn't have kept her on for two and a half years. But having her as a sister is a little different from having her as a receptionist."

Yes, it was. "I think it's going to take all of us some time to get used to this. Especially Darcy. This can't be easy for her, either. And at least we have each other, you know? She has nobody."

Dix murmured something.

"And it isn't her fault that Dad slept with Audrey and knocked her up. Or that he met and married Mother. Or that Audrey never told him the truth. None of it is Darcy's fault."

"I know that!" Dix said, in a modified shout. And added, a bit more calmly, "You think I don't know that? I'm not stupid, Savannah!"

"I know you're not."

"It's just..." I waited while he very audibly got himself and his breathing together. "You're right. It's just going to take time. Right now I'm mad at all of them. Dad for having a baby out of wedlock. Audrey for never telling him—or us. Mom, for being so emotional about it. Even Darcy, for being born. And I know it isn't her fault!"

"It isn't anybody's fault," I said. "It just happened. Nobody planned it or meant to hurt anybody else. They all just did the best they could at the time. And now we have to learn to live with it. Because it is what it is."

Outside the house, I heard the familiar rumble of the Harley-Davidson, and the crunch of gravel as Rafe made his way up the driveway to the front porch. A moment later, the engine shut off.

"Listen," I told Dix, "Rafe is here. I have to go. We have things to talk about."

"Believe me, I know."

He didn't, but until I'd told Rafe about Carmen, I wasn't going to tell anyone else. So I just let my brother believe I hadn't already called my husband to tell him about our newfound sister. "I'll drive down this weekend and see how things are going."

"Sure," Dix said, as Rafe's footsteps came up onto the porch.

"You may have to put us up for the night, if Mother won't allow me in her house anymore."

"That's not a problem," Dix said, as I heard the sound of the key going into the lock, "but give her some time. By this weekend, she might have calmed down."

And she might not. "I'll call you tomorrow, OK? Just to see if there's any news."

"Do that," Dix said, as Rafe's footsteps came into the foyer and the front door closed behind him. I heard the jingling of the security chain and the slide of the deadbolt before he came down the hallway toward the kitchen. "Have a good evening, Sis."

I told him to do the same, and put the phone down just as Rafe walked into the kitchen.

I had been prepared to see dreadlocks, so when I saw that they were gone, I grinned. He grinned back, and I saw that the gold teeth were missing, too.

"Sorry I'm late," he told me. "It took a little while to get it all gone."

"It's not a problem," I said. "I'm just happy to see you. Instead of Ry'mone."

"And here I thought you were starting to think Ry'mone was hot." He backed me against the nearest cabinet and leaned in.

"Ry'mone *was* hot." I tilted my head to give him better access to my neck. "But only because he was you. And I like you better this way."

I slid my hands up his arms to his shoulders, and from there up to his head. The scratchy fluff of his buzz cut felt familiar under my palms.

"I like me better this way, too," Rafe said, and sniffed.

"Smells good."

"Chicken fajitas."

"Smells more like flowers."

"That's me." Or my body lotion.

"I know," Rafe said. "Even when I'm hungry, I can tell the difference between you and chicken fajitas."

"Are you hungry now?"

"For you. Not chicken fajitas."

"How about I turn off the chicken fajitas," I suited action to words, "and we can go upstairs and feed you?"

"Works for me." He didn't wait for me to walk on my own, just picked me up and strode out of the room with me.

"One of these days," I told him breathlessly, "you're going to throw your back out doing that."

"When I'm sixty. You're safe for the next thirty years."

He headed up the stairs with no hitch in his stride. Twenty seconds later I was on the bed. Twenty seconds after that, so was he, naked as the day he was born. I opened my arms.

And that was all any of us said, at least for a while.

But that's how it came to be that we were in bed, stark naked, when I told him the news.

"Listen. There's something I have to tell you."

"Yeah? Who was that you were on the phone with when I walked in?"

"My brother," I said. Might as well get this out of the way first. And give me a couple more minutes before I had to lay the big news on him. "He called to update me about Mother."

It might make a nice segue into the Carmen conversation too, come to think of it. There were similarities.

"What's going on?"

"Nothing. I mean, nothing you haven't already heard. She was slugging brandy when I left this morning. Dix and Catherine drove over and put her to bed. Now she's awake again, with what sounds like the mother of all hangovers—which seems appropriate. We're all struggling a bit with this."

He nodded.

"Darcy too, I'm sure. She was looking for her birth mother, and instead she found a whole family. A family she knew, but didn't know was hers. And a family that has to deal with the fact that our father slept with someone other than our mother and had a baby."

"It ain't like he cheated," Rafe said. "You said it was before he met your mama, right?"

"It was. A couple of months before. The baby..." I had to stop doing that, "Darcy was born while he and Mother were engaged, but before they got married. He never even knew about her."

"Whaddaya think he woulda done if he'd known?"

I blinked. It hadn't even crossed my mind to wonder. "I'm not sure. He was in love with Mother. And he and Audrey were never serious about each other. So I can't see him dumping Mother and marrying Audrey instead."

And Audrey obviously hadn't wanted that, either, because she hadn't told him about Darcy or made her pregnancy an issue.

If she had, would he have thrown Mother over for her? To do the right thing, even if he didn't love her?

I shook my head to dislodge the thought. Not something I wanted to dwell on. Especially now. "We have to talk about something."

"I thought we were talking about something," Rafe said, stretching comfortably.

It was distracting, and it took me a second to gather my thoughts again. He chuckled as he watched me struggle.

"Stop that," I told him, and tried to sound like I meant it. "This is important."

"Then spit it out." He settled down with his hands behind his head. That was distracting, too. All those nice muscles bunching under his skin. My mouth went a little dry, and I swallowed.

He grinned.

"I mean it," I said. "If you don't stop, I'm going to have to make you get out of bed and put clothes on. I don't want to talk about this any more than you do, but we have to."

His face sobered. "Then talk. Let's get it out of the way so I can make love to my wife again."

"I'm not sure you're going to want to after this."

He arched a brow, and I added, "You remember Carmen Arroyo, don't you? The woman who ran that nightclub in South Nashville for Hector Gonzales last year?"

"Not likely I'd forget, is it?"

Not really. And I had to trust that he didn't mean that in any way but the obvious. "She was arrested back in December. Along with Hector and all the rest of them."

He nodded.

"I saw her the other day, when Darcy and I went to the Tennessee Women's Prison to talk to Denise Seaver. She's there, too. Carmen."

Rafe's eyes narrowed. "And?"

I took a breath. The words threatened to lodge in my throat, and were hard to get out. "She's pregnant. More pregnant than I am. Doctor Seaver said she's due in a couple of weeks. Around the first of September, I guess."

I waited, but he didn't say anything. So I continued. "That would mean she got pregnant sometime around the first of December last year."

He didn't say anything this time, either. Maybe he was going over the math in his head. Or wondering whether it was likely she'd been sleeping with someone else at the same time she was sleeping with him.

I gulped another lungful of air and threw caution to the wind. "What are the chances it's yours?" Or maybe a better question would have been, what are the chances it's not?

He shook his head. "I wanna say slim to none. Not sure I can."

"I know you slept with her..."

"Yes, darlin'." He looked at me. "And I did take precautions."

"I'm sure you did." He didn't always. I knew that. He hadn't with me. And he obviously hadn't with Elspeth, who had caught him when he was drunk and in pain and not quite thinking straight one night in high school.

She'd had some culpability in what happened to her, just as I'd had some in what happened to me, the night I fell into bed with him with no thought for the consequences. It hadn't been only his fault. I should have remembered to use protection, too.

But with Carmen I was sure he had taken precautions. She was part of his job. A suspect he was keeping an eye on, from inside Hector Gonzales's South American Theft Gang, during the couple of months he was pretending to be Jorge Pena. He wouldn't have slept with her without protection. Not under those circumstances.

"Condoms..." I had to stop and clear my throat. "They say they're effective ninety-eight percent of the time."

He nodded.

"That leaves two percent."

"Right."

We lay there side by side a moment, just breathing.

"It might not be yours," I said. "I mean... you didn't have a relationship with her. Right? You weren't, like, dating or anything...?"

Except for that one time I had seen them at Fidelio's Ristorante together; he in a suit and she in a drop-dead gorgeous red dress...

"She might have been sleeping with someone else, too," I said, and sounded a bit desperate, even in my own ears. "Right?"

He nodded. "Sure. Prob'ly did."

"So the baby could be someone else's."

"Could be."

Another moment of silence passed.

"You're going to have to find out, though. Aren't you?"

"I prob'ly should. Don't you think?"

"Yes," I said with a sigh. "That's why I'm telling you. So you can find out."

He slid a hand down my side and rested it on top of my stomach. "I love you, darlin'."

"I know," I said. "I'm not jealous of her." Much. "I know you just did what you had to do when you slept with her. Even though you probably enjoyed it..."

He didn't say anything, just grinned.

"But you married me. And she's in prison. And she'll be there a long time yet. But still... if she's having your baby, she'll always be a part of your life. Our lives."

Just as Elspeth would have been, if things had worked out differently. Just as David was, with his adoptive parents.

"It can't be helped, darlin'." His voice was calm. "Chances are it's got nothing to do with us. But I gotta know."

Of course he did.

"I can pull some strings," he added. "Or see about having Tammy pull some strings. See if there's any paperwork on file with the doc out there that names the father."

That would be a start. However... "There are no guarantees she named the right father, is there? I mean, how would she know? If she slept with more than one of you at the same time—"

He arched a brow and I amended, "—around the same time, it's not like she can know that it's his baby and not yours. Or yours and not his. It would probably take DNA to figure it out."

Rafe nodded. "Good thing she's locked up and can't refuse, ain't it?"

I guess it was. Or maybe not. Part of me wanted to know the truth, part of me didn't.

What would we do if the baby was his? Ask for custody?

We'd probably get it. Carmen was in prison, so she couldn't keep the baby, and if Rafe could prove paternity, he had every right to raise his own child.

I could find myself with two newborns to take care of. One that was hers, and one that was mine.

I tried to imagine it, but my brain rebelled. I adored David. He was a great kid, and he was Rafe's son, and I loved Rafe. Of course I loved David, too. No question about it.

And I had only to look at Ginny and Sam to know that it was possible to love an adopted child as much as one of your own. They couldn't possibly love David any more than they did.

But if I had to raise Rafe's child with me and Rafe's child with Carmen as siblings, was it possible for me to love them both the same? Or would I always feel that Carmen's baby was an interloper, taking my baby's father away from him or her?

My head started spinning, and my chest tightened. Rafe's hand stroked down my arm. "Breathe," he told me. "We'll figure it out."

I turned panicked eyes on him. "But what if it's yours? What do we do?"

His voice was as calm as mine was jittery. "We figure it out then."

"When's then?"

"When we know," Rafe said.

When we know. "When will that be?"

"As soon as I can figure it out."

"When will that be?"

"Tomorrow," Rafe said.

Tomorrow?

My chest loosened. "I can wait until tomorrow."

"I know you can. And in the meantime..." He pulled me toward him, "let me take your mind off this."

If anyone could do it, he could.

"The chicken fajitas..."

"Can wait, too," Rafe said and kissed me.

# # #

ABOUT THE AUTHOR

New York Times and *USA Today* bestselling author Jenna Bennett (Jennie Bentley) writes the Do It Yourself home renovation mysteries for Berkley Prime Crime and the Savannah Martin real estate mysteries for her own gratification. She also writes a variety of romance for a change of pace. Originally from Norway, she has spent more than twenty five years in the US, and still hasn't been able to kick her native accent.

For more information, please visit Jenna's website:
www.JennaBennett.com

63361253R00177

Made in the USA
Charleston, SC
03 November 2016